Praise for

INTERESTING FACTS ABOUT SPACE

"Enid is an eccentric, lovable, wonderfully sex-positive heroine, and we were right there with her even when her story went from feeling like a heartwarming rom-com to a potential spy thriller. This is a funny, tender, and relatable read that also includes lots of fascinating facts about the universe!"

—Apple Books

"Engrossing, funny, and full of depth."

—*Publishers Weekly*

"Quirky, funny, and heartfelt."

—*Booklist*

"A complicated, layered exploration of how bullying, fear, and a desperate desire to fit in have lasting effects."

—*Kirkus*

"*Interesting Facts about Space* glows with macabre humor, neuroses, and charming wit, making for yet another softhearted queer novel by Austin."

—JILL GUTOWITZ, author of *Girls Can Kiss Now*

"A terrifically beguiling mixture of the comical, the surreal, and the moving. Emily Austin, the queen of darkly quirky, endearingly flawed heroines, has created a wonderful character in Enid, a woman who's found her own idiosyncratic way of navigating a world of weird people and events (which may or may not be colored by her imagination). Emily's writing has a clarity and directness that illuminates the novel from start to finish. Full of wit and wisdom, *Interesting Facts about Space* is a testament to the power of confronting the messy truth of life, however tempting it is to retreat into the soothing sanctuary of impersonal facts. A joy to read."

—SARAH HAYWOOD, author of *The Cactus*

"If you've read Emily Austin's debut, *Everyone in This Room Will Someday Be Dead*, you'll love this charming, heartfelt follow-up. If you haven't read her debut, I'm jealous: everything Austin writes is swoonworthy, full of lovely humans struggling to find meaning, love, and belonging in a world that's too often cold. Enid is a marvel."

—ANDREW DAVID MacDONALD, author of *When We Were Vikings*

"Wow, just wow. Emily Austin gets better and better! *Interesting Facts about Space* is a delightful, big-hearted book that made me laugh and think about all the ways in which we convince ourselves we're too weird for this world—and yet it's the most human thing anyone can do. An absolute charmer of a novel!"

—MAI NGUYEN, author of *Sunshine Nails*

"Emily Austin is the patron saint of Sad Girls with Too Many Feelings, and masterful at finding and revealing the universal story in an achingly specific situation."

—NORA McINERNY, author of *Bad Vibes Only*

"Emily Austin has done it again! I love how her quirky dark humor reveals both the absurdity and relatability of the human condition. Enid is undoubtedly a charmingly eccentric Emily Austin™ protagonist: her greatest fear is bald men, her love language is sharing interesting facts about space, her coping mechanism is listening to true crime podcasts, and her secret is that she thinks she has a parasite that makes her a bad person. Fellow parasite-host readers will be both entertained and consoled by where the story goes."

—CELIA LASKEY, author of *So Happy for You*

"Dark humor has so much to teach us about the beauty and absurdity of the human condition, and the risk this book's charming heroine takes to open her fragile and flawed self to love contains a life lesson for us all."

—COURTNEY MAUM, author of
The Year of the Horses

"A vibrantly paranoid mystery and an unexpected love story. Emily Austin creates beguilingly eccentric characters, especially true crime addict and outer space encyclopedia Enid, who's both oddly confident and yearning to disappear. *Interesting Facts about Space* is highly original, engrossing, and hauntingly entertaining."

—PAUL RUDNICK, author of
Farrell Covington and the Limits of Style

"Tensely plotted and full of heart, Emily Austin's second novel follows another endearing heroine I'd follow to outer space and beyond."

—ANNA DORN, author of *Exalted*

Also by Emily Austin

Fiction

Everyone in This Room Will Someday Be Dead

Poetry

Gay Girl Prayers

INTERESTING FACTS ABOUT SPACE

Emily Austin

ATRIA PAPERBACK

New York   London   Toronto   Sydney   New Delhi

ATRIA
PAPERBACK

An Imprint of Simon & Schuster, LLC
1230 Avenue of the Americas
New York, NY 10020

First Atria Paperback edition October 2024

ATRIA PAPERBACK and colophon are trademarks of Simon & Schuster, LLC

Simon & Schuster: Celebrating 100 Years of Publishing in 2024

For information about special discounts for bulk purchases, please contact Simon & Schuster Special Sales at 1-866-506-1949 or business@simonandschuster.com.

The Simon & Schuster Speakers Bureau can bring authors to your live event. For more information or to book an event, contact the Simon & Schuster Speakers Bureau at 1-866-248-3049 or visit our website at www.simonspeakers.com.

Interior design by Lexy East

Manufactured in the United States of America

1   3   5   7   9   10   8   6   4   2

Library of Congress Cataloging-in-Publication Data

Names: Austin, Emily R., author.
Title: Interesting facts about space / by Emily Austin.
Description: New York : Atria Books, [2024]
Identifiers: LCCN 2023010221 (print) | LCCN 2023010222 (ebook) |
ISBN 9781668014233 (hardcover) | ISBN 9781668014240 (paperback) |
ISBN 9781668014257 (ebook)
Subjects: LCGFT: Psychological fiction. | Lesbian fiction. | Novels.
Classification: LCC PR9199.4.A92595 I58 2024 (print) |
LCC PR9199.4.A92595 (ebook) | DDC 813/.6--dc23/eng/20230428
LC record available at https://lccn.loc.gov/2023010221
LC ebook record available at https://lccn.loc.gov/2023010222

ISBN 978-1-6680-1423-3
ISBN 978-1-6680-1424-0 (pbk)
ISBN 978-1-6680-1425-7 (ebook)

For my mom

INTERESTING FACTS ABOUT SPACE

CHAPTER ONE

"*The teenaged girl was brutally axed to death by her grandmother.*"

A cashier is scanning my groceries. I have headphones in. My favorite true crime podcast is playing. I read the cashier's lips. She asks, "How are you today?" while the podcast host simultaneously says, "*They found the girl's body in the old lady's basement.*"

"I'm good, thanks, how are you?"

I put the divider between my groceries and the groceries belonging to the man behind me. I would hate to accidentally purchase his Vienna sausages, or worse—for him to get away with my tampons.

The podcast host explains that the teenager's body was found decomposing in a Rubbermaid bin in her grandmother's fruit cellar. Despite the rotting corpse, the grandmother continued to use the fruit cellar. Along with murder, the woman's hobbies included canning. The body was found next to stacks of fruit preserves and pickled beets.

"Do you need bags?" the cashier asks.

"No, thank you, I brought my own." I gesture to my tote bag.

The podcast host jokes, wondering if the grandmother ever considered pickling the dead body. I snort at the grotesque concept while the cashier kindly scans my boxed cake mix and Midol. Sometimes you have to joke about things like pickling murdered teenagers. It's a coping mechanism. It takes the darkness out at the knees.

✳

"Excuse me!" A man rams into my shoulder. The unexpected impact propels my belongings from my hands. My phone, keys, credit card, and the entrails of my wallet sail before me. The angry man storms onward. He does not pause to look back.

A Good Samaritan kneels to help recover my belongings.

"Thank you," I say.

"No problem. Why did that man shove you?"

"I'm not sure."

She stands up. "He must have anger management issues."

I nod. "He probably has a parasite."

"What?"

"Nothing. Thank you again."

✳

I was born deaf in one ear. Sometimes, I'm glad I was. I can easily tune irksome people out. I sleep better. I'm less disturbed by irritating sounds. It took me longer to learn to speak than most people, though. I didn't hear as clearly as other babies. I don't always respond when addressed on my bad side. When strangers say "Excuse me" while trying to pass me, I'm often oblivious to it. I know that because every so often the situation escalates. People shout "*Excuse me!*" as if I'm rude for not hearing them the first time.

✳

When I learned to speak, my first word was "mom." My mom told me that, though, and it's possible that she has reworked the record. I would not be shocked to learn that my first words were less stirring. Perhaps I said something meaningless, like "grass," or something embarrassing, like "butts." I would not put it past my mother to spare me the truth, if that were the case. That said, I am sure that I did say "mom" somewhere near the beginning.

✳

My tampon box is peeking over my bag like a pervert peeking over a windowsill. As I exit the store, I try to strategically position my arm to conceal the box and prevent strangers from knowing which stage of the ovarian cycle I am at.

I turn the volume of my podcast up.

"*The contents of the teenager's stomach revealed that she had eaten peaches two hours before her death. Her autopsy also showed that she . . .*" There is a pause for emphasis. "*. . . was two months pregnant.*"

Sharp pain radiates from my lower back. I fish into my tote

bag for the Midol I just bought. While searching, the automatic door behind me opens. A blast of air-conditioning cools my back. I glance at the customer exiting. It's a man carrying a forty pack of toilet paper above his head like it's a trophy. He has sweat stains in his armpits and the noticeable outline of a condom in his pocket.

I discreetly swallow a dry pill while I listen to the podcast host say, "*It was soon discovered that the girl was dating an older man named Jerry Nit. Jerry, a bald man in his early forties—*"

I rip my headphones out and immediately google "space news."

Flashes on the sun could help us predict solar flares. Solar flares can impact Earth. They can disrupt radio communications and create electrical blackouts.

✳

"Am I speaking to Enid?" a woman in my phone asks.

I can't tell if it's scorching out, if I'm having period-induced hot flashes, or if I've taken a wrong turn and accidentally descended into hell. My back aches. I'm lugging home groceries. My shirt is pasted to my wet body like papier-mâché. I skipped the previous episode of my podcast and am now listening to the next. This new episode is about a cannibal. The host was just detailing how the man seasoned his human flesh (thyme and rosemary), when the story was interrupted by my phone ringing.

"Yes?" I struggle to hold my phone up to my good ear. My tote bag presses into my shoulder. Sweat stings my eyes.

"Are you fucking Joan?" The woman's voice cracks.

I stop walking. A cyclist in full-body purple spandex swerves around me. He rings his bell as he pedals furiously ahead.

"Are you dating Joan?" I ask.

I had no idea Joan had a girlfriend.

"No," she says.

I exhale, relieved.

"I'm her wife."

✳

The strap of my tote bag slips from my shoulder and slides down my arm. I fumble to grab it, but my box of tampons topples out. After performing a double backflip, the box lands upside down on the mauve rug lining the hallway of my apartment as if it's just landed the splits.

Before I can recover the box, a door in the hallway opens. Light from inside the apartment shines a yellow block on the rug. I hear keys jingle and a man sigh. Someone new just moved into that unit. I prepare myself to greet him. I position my face, ready to smile at the sight of him. I watch his shadow overtake the block on the rug before the light switch is flipped, the glow vanishes, and a tall man, with keys dangling from his teeth, enters the threshold.

The man is bald.

I smell smoke. Am I choking? The top of his head is gleaming beneath the hallway light. His scalp is so shiny it looks like it's about to catch fire.

More groceries fall from my bag. Tostitos. Icing sugar.

Our eyes connect. Bosc pears roll, lopsided like tipped bowling pins, across the carpet. The man glances at the avalanche of groceries tumbling around me. I stare at him, frozen, like the face of a mountain in a landslide.

I smell something burning.

"Do you need help?" he asks.

I feel my stomach drop.

"No," I say.

"No," I repeat until he leaves.

✳

Red food coloring bleeds into the yellow cake batter. I stir until the batter turns into a muted, pale pink. I am baking a gender reveal cake despite understanding that the practice is profoundly offensive. It involves dying the insides of a cake pink or blue, so that a pregnant person can slice into it and discover the sex of their offspring. I am doing it because one of my half sisters is pregnant, and she asked me to. It was offered as a sort of olive branch. I considered explaining why I would prefer not to, as well as why I would recommend against celebrating an infant's genitals entirely, but my sisters and I barely know each other, and sadly, I have discovered a new character flaw to add to my already long list of defects: I would sacrifice my values to oblige my estranged sisters.

I want them to like me. I feel like a stray dog, rejected by our sire, trying to be accepted in his new litter of puppies. I don't want them to think I'm some fleabag mutt, or a coyote masquerading as a house dog. I'm a purebred golden retriever, just like them. I want them to think I'm a clean, bug-free, normal dog. I want to prove that our dad was wrong. I am a good girl.

There is something animalistic about it. I feel a bizarre biological drive to connect to them because they're my sisters.

Maybe there's some evolutionary benefit to that. Maybe someday I might need their kidneys or some bone marrow. The primal part of my brain wants me to have a relationship with them because we're blood. I'm supposed to be in their pack.

I think they might feel that biological drive too. That must be why they keep inviting me to events. On a subconscious level, they want my bone marrow.

I keep abandoning my baking to ensure my door is locked and to look out my peephole. I put both hands on either side of the hole before peeking out. There are red cake-battered handprints on my door. Each time I spot them, they startle me. I think, *Are those my bloodied handprints? Am I a ghost? Did my neighbor kill me earlier? Am I trapped in here, reliving my attempted escape for eternity?* Then I remember that I am baking a cake and rush back to the oven to watch it rise.

✳

My mom taught me to watch the oven. When she cooks, she stays beside the food. She has a stool she sits on in her kitchen. It is important, she says, to keep an eye on a hot oven. She also says, for her, it's like watching a show. She likes to witness cookies rise, butter melt, and the edges of vegetables blacken. She turns the oven light on, looks through the window in the door, and watches food turn brown and hiss.

✳

I tried to use an oven timer shortly after I moved out for school. I didn't hear it go off. I thought I would hear it. I always heard

the timer at my mom's house. I think she may have bought a
special timer with my hearing in mind. It had a lower sound
than most timers do. I can't always hear high-pitched noises.
It's because of something called head shadow; when you have
single-sided deafness, high-frequency sounds don't bend the way
they're supposed to. I was cooking a frozen pizza. The fire alarm
went off. At first, I thought, *Oh, is that the oven timer?* I skipped
off to my smoky kitchen, amid the screech of my alarm, where I
discovered the tragic remains of a pizza so severely burnt it could
have been mistaken for an enormous double chocolate cookie.

*

This morning, I polished a glass platter to ice the cake on. I set
it out on my counter before going to the grocery store. While
putting my groceries away, I noticed it looked like it had been
moved slightly. It seemed to have shifted since the morning, an
inch or two to the right.

I am examining it now. I hold it up above my face, in front
of the pendant light hanging from my kitchen ceiling. It is a
clear platter with little carvings of grapes and vines on it. It looks
dirty again, somehow. It looks almost as if someone has touched
it. There are little marks, maybe fingerprints, all over it. This is
unsettling because I live alone, and, like I said, I just polished it
this morning.

I take my phone out of my back pocket and open my email.
Maybe my landlord came by and touched it. I have only lived
in this apartment for a year, but my landlord has managed to
come by at least fourteen times already. He has never provided
sufficient legal notice.

I see that I do have an email from him.

Dear resident,

This is a reminder that absolutely no pets are allowed on the premises. This includes small pets, such as goldfish, hamsters, or birds.

Regards,
Peter

I roll my eyes. I do not have a pet; however, I have an inkling that Peter believes I lied to him about that. He sends me frequent anti-pet reminders like this one. I always respond along the lines of, "*I have no pets, Peter,*" but nothing I say prompts him to relent.

Maybe he was in my apartment today, snooping around for an illegal bird, touching my glass platter.

✳

"Please, hurry, come in." I hold my apartment door open for Polly, the woman whose wife I've been seeing. I want her to come inside quickly so I can avoid seeing my bald neighbor again.

"Can I get you a glass of water?" I look over her shoulder while trying to hustle her inside.

Earlier, over the phone, she asked me if we could speak in person. I said, "Yes, of course," and told her my address. As I baked the cake celebrating baby genitals, I reflected on whether that was a prudent choice. Meeting your date's wife is sort of like online dating; it is better to meet in public. I do a lot of online dating though, and I rarely ever meet in public. That safety protocol is more applicable to straight women. One of the perks of being a lesbian is that it is less critical for me to vet whether my date will kill me. I tend to fear I am the person in the equation who dates should be wary of. I have been giving my address out to strange women, willy-nilly. I did not stop to consider whether I should suggest a coffee shop, park bench, or police station parking lot to Polly.

Her face is flushed. She has beads of sweat resting on her forehead and upper lip.

She ignores me. Her eyes dart around my apartment. She walks inside gingerly, like a newly adopted cat. She looks at the blush-colored, un-iced cake on my counter, and at the dirty dishes piled in my sink.

I usually tidy up before having company. I wash my dishes, bleach the bathroom, make my bed, and sometimes even spray perfume, time permitting. I often go as far as to leave out books that I think reflect well on me, or to pause a premeditated show on my TV. I welcome my guest inside, acting as if I was just casually reading or watching, and not as if it has all been staged.

In this case, I thought it might be more polite not to do any of that. Thoughtfully, I chose to wear a dirty shirt, and to keep my house askew. I left the red handprints on my door, and the dishes I made in the sink. I did not apply deodorant or comb my hair. In an effort to soften the blow of her wife's infidelity, I am offering her solace in the fact that at least I am a disgusting slob.

I lock the dead bolt and look out the peephole.

When I turn around, I see her tilt her head, confused.

I realize it might have been strange of me to lock her inside my filthy apartment, and to look out the peephole after. This is how murderers behave after luring victims inside.

In an attempt to seem less like a murderer, I say, "It's nice to meet you."

She furrows her brow and does not say it back.

I recognize in the silence that it probably is not very nice to meet the person your wife has been cheating on you with.

"I'm sorry," I decide to add.

She closes her eyes.

"I didn't know Joan was married—"

"How long has this been going on?" she interrupts.

"I'm not sure," I say. "Let me check."

I open my phone. I scroll up in my text conversations with Joan to unearth when we started talking. Polly and I stand quietly while I scroll.

I finally reach the top of our texts and announce, "One month."

I look into her face to see if that is good news or bad news. A month is quite short, I think. It's not like it has been going on for years. A month is nothing, really. It's a blip.

She puts her face in her hands. Her shoulders quake.

Maybe it was her birthday this month. Maybe it was their wedding anniversary.

"Are you sure I can't get you some water?" I ask.

She doesn't reply. She cries silently into her palms.

"I feel terrible about this," I say, my throat tightening.

I feel something twitch in my stomach.

"It's not your fault," she says, uncovering her face. "We've been unhappy for a while." Tracks of mascara are sledding down her cheeks. "We've had a difficult year. Joan's dad died four months ago. There's a crack in the foundation of our house that we can't afford to fix. I think I might have MS—"

I don't know what to say.

She exhales loudly, then looks me dead in the eyes.

I do not look away. She and I stare into each other's pupils for longer than is comfortable. Her irises are the same color as Mars, rusty brown and bloodshot. Her eyelashes are clumped with wet mascara.

This moment feels very intimate. Neither of us are speaking. I look at her mascara tracks and think of the slope streaks that form on Mars when it is warm, and there are landslides. We have blinked more than once and are still staring. Blinking.

Should I say something?

She is breathing heavily, as if she can't catch her breath.

What should I say?

Should I tell her about recurring slope lineae on Mars?

Her chest is pounding up and down. I watch tears build and roll over her eyelashes before trickling down her cheeks in a way that reminds me of being a kid in the back seat of my mom's van, watching rain roll down the window.

"I don't really like Joan," I say. "If that's any consolation. I've been dating other people."

"Really?" she says, her voice cracking.

"Yes. I just went on a date with someone else last night. I have like ten dating apps on my phone. Look." I open my phone to show her.

She looks, grunts, then exhales loudly. Her sad tears convert into cries of laughter. She starts cackling. She holds on to my shoulder for balance while she throws her head back, roaring.

I am not sure what to do.

I laugh too, not because I find it funny, but because the break in tension is such a relief that laughter emerges from me like steam from a hot kettle.

✳

Polly and I are lying on my kitchen floor drinking cans of gross, floral-tasting craft beer. A woman I had over last week abandoned them in my fridge. I'm tipping my can to my lips and mulling about gravity. Right now, there is an invisible force compelling this liquid to fall into my mouth. It's pulling planets toward the sun, and the moon into Earth's orbit. It's what's keeping Polly and me on this tile right now. It causes ocean tides. It's not just mass it affects, either. It pulls light.

"My first girlfriend cheated on me," she says. "I broke up with her right away. I remember standing in her doorway, shouting that I didn't deserve that. I felt so enraged. I was devastated by it, and it fucked me up, but that sort of fueled me to break off all contact with her, and to stand up for myself. I felt so mad."

She sighs.

"I don't think I have the energy for this. I'm thirty-seven. I already felt emotionally drained before this. I don't think I have the capacity to feel impassioned. And breaking up with Joan isn't just emotionally exhausting, we have car payments—do you know what I mean? We own a house together. And I hate moving. How exactly am I going to meet someone new? Half the time I'm too tired to grocery shop. I can't take on finding a new girlfriend. Do I have to live alone now? I don't think I can live alone. I'd be so lonely. It feels like my options are to bottle up that this happened, and stay in this sad relationship, or to leave and be sad alone. I have this sickening, hollow feeling in my stomach."

She is looking at the ceiling.

"I told Joan every fleeting thought I had," she continues. "She knew every little part of my life. I told her if I tripped walking to work. I told her what I ate when she wasn't around. She had a full relationship behind my back. I feel like I never knew her. She knew which yogurt brand to buy me, do you know what I mean? It's as if my entire world has been built on a fault line."

I watch her like a voyeur, as if I am observing her doing something private through her curtains. I feel how I would watching her undress or use the bathroom. I feel like I'm not supposed to see this.

"Have you ever been cheated on?" She rolls over.

"N-no," I answer, swallowing a swig of my disgusting beer. "But I have, uh, never really dated someone exclusively."

I look away from her to avoid witnessing her reaction. I am twenty-six years old, and I have never been in an exclusive relationship. I do not often disclose that kind of personal information to people, let alone total strangers, but Polly has been spewing her guts, so I feel like I owe her something.

I swallow again. "My dad cheated on my mom, though. I was their only kid. He started a whole new family. He ended up having two other daughters. That's probably the closest experience I've had to this. Do you think that might feel kind of similar?"

"I don't know," she says. "It depends. How do you feel about that?"

I open my mouth. I don't know what to say. I pause for a moment, holding my jaw open, like a door, waiting for unexpected words to emerge.

None materialize.

"Do you not know how you feel?" she asks.

I glance at her. "I guess mostly I feel bad for my mom."

✳

Polly is doing my makeup. I stopped wearing makeup several years ago, but she asked if she could put some on me. I felt like

I had to say yes on account of having sex with her partner and ruining her life.

I think she might be drunk. She has only had two beers, but she seems unbalanced and flushed. She keeps suppressing hiccups.

My eyes are closed. I can feel makeup brushes sweep across my eyelids and Polly's slight fingers touch my jaw. The makeup she is using smells like chalk and roses.

"You have nice skin," she says as she rubs something liquid into my cheeks.

"Thank you," I say. "I used to have acne. I took pills for it."

"You'd never know," she says. "My skin is terrible. I've got wrinkles."

"You're older than me," I say, endeavoring to console her by flagging that it makes sense that she has some wrinkles. As soon as the words escape, I wish I could take them back. They came out wrong.

"I mean," I try to backpedal. "Just—I'm sure when I'm your age, I'll have worse wrinkles than you do. I'm sure when you were twenty-six you had better skin than me. That's all I meant."

I'm floundering.

"You have nice skin," I assert.

I think of telling her my favorite planet is Mercury. It has the most craters. I decide not to. Maybe it would sound rude.

I say, "I-I noticed you had nice skin when you came in. You have very nice skin, really. You have nice hair, too. You're really pretty, honestly—"

I feel her mouth touch mine. My eyes were closed, so I was not prepared. I do not flinch, but I am startled. I open my eyes and watch her kiss me, confused.

✳

I lather soap on Polly's back in the shower. I think she's crying, but it is hard to tell under the running water. She suggested we shower together. I assumed it would be a sort of sexual, revenge-fueled shower, but instead she is sitting, hugging her knees, and I am washing her back like the loving nurse of a tired, geriatric patient.

I shampoo and condition my hair, and then Polly's. I rinse her curls and wring the water out. I consider shaving my legs but am concerned the precedent set might require I also shave hers, which is more than I feel qualified, or willing, to do. Instead, I stand behind her, like a Peeping Tom watching a vulnerable, naked stranger for so long that my skin begins pruning. I think of a podcast episode I listened to recently that mentioned dead human flesh turning to mush after being left prolonged in a shower.

When we finally emerge from my steamy bathroom, I hand two towels to Polly. Only three of my towels are clean. The rest are dirty in my hamper. I normally use two; one for my hair and one for my body. I decided to be a good host, and mistress, and to sacrifice my hair towel to her. I wrap the remaining towel around my torso and let my wet hair drip down my back.

I feel a draft as we exit the bathroom. I wipe water off my brow with my forearm, and glance around my apartment. I notice that my bedroom window is open. The curtains are swaying.

"Did you open that?" I ask, clutching my towel tighter to my body. I know I didn't open it.

She wraps her hair in her towel and says, "No, I haven't even been in there."

I stare at the curtains wafting toward and away from the window, like lungs breathing in and out.

Who opened that?

CHAPTER TWO

I punch my curtains. I brace myself to hit an intruder behind the fabric, standing flush to the wall. I find no one. I slam the window shut. A corner of my towel snags where the pane meets the sill. I yank until the window unclutches my terry cloth. I get down on my knees and inspect beneath my bed. I prepare myself mentally to confront a face staring back at me, but instead discover nothing but a half-empty Gatorade bottle, a graphic T-shirt I thought I lost, gross masses of dust and hair, and a condom.

What the fuck? Why is there a condom? I reach for it.

Never mind. It was a discarded sucker. I didn't see the stick.

Polly is searching with me. She says, "Do you really think someone came in here?"

"Maybe not, but why take the chance?"

I tear the wrapper off the old sucker and put it in my mouth. It's lemon.

Polly has my closet door open. She is rooting around inside, searching for a trespasser among my button-downs and sweaters.

"Do you knit?" she asks.

"No, my mom does." I glare around my apartment, expecting to spot a lampshade placed over a man standing stiff and still, trying to be inconspicuous.

"Did she make you all these sweaters? Wow. There's a little solar system knitted into this one! I love these. Did she make you all of—"

I shush her.

We stand silently while I keep my pointer finger in the "shh" position before my lips. I cup my other hand around my good ear, listening intently for rustling or breathing. I hear nothing but my refrigerator hum.

After about eighty seconds of silence, Polly whispers, "I should go."

※

Cold drops from my wet hair are soaking the shoulders of my T-shirt. I shudder. The air outside is brisk. It's the end of August, and the sun is setting. The sky is orange and there are no stars visible yet—just Venus and the moon.

Polly and I are saying goodbye on the sidewalk. She's hugging me. I did not realize until we had already been hugging for a while that my arms were hanging limp at my sides. I hold her quickly for the end of the embrace. As we release each other, she locks eyes with me. I look at the streetlights reflected in her irises, rather than truly at her, while she says, "Thank you," in a tone so sincere it almost makes me flinch.

As she drives away, I sit down on the concrete step at the front of my building. I put my headphones in. I always put both headphones in, despite my deaf ear. Headphones serve more than one purpose. I don't just wear them to listen to my murder podcast. I also wear them to prevent people from talking to me. Having one headphone in signals that I am open to small talk, or to having my shoulder tapped on. I am not, so I put in both.

I click play on the next episode. I feel all my muscles un-clench. Nothing puts me at ease more than hearing someone calmly discuss homicide. They don't scream, cry, or retch while they detail the worst horrors humans are capable of. Instead, they say, "*Ralph decapitated his wife, and this episode is sponsored by GOOD LUNCH, a weekly delivery box of preportioned ingre-dients for your tasty lunches.*" It makes me feel safe, like there's no reason to panic. Sure, women get their heads chopped off by men who vowed to love them forever, but we can still plan to eat Atlantic salmon on basmati rice next week.

This episode is the first in a series about Ted Bundy. I'm already well acquainted with Ted, but I don't mind hearing the same story over and over. In fact, I prefer it. I like knowing what happens. I feel more control over it. As the host reintroduces me to Ted, I copy a block of writing I keep saved in my Notes app and text it to Joan.

Hey, this has nothing to do with you, but I need a little space, so I am no longer dating. Sorry if this is weird, or coming out of the blue, I just wanted to let you know. Again, nothing to do with you. I really like you, and I would love to stay friends if you would.

Almost immediately, she replies,

k.

I read her text twice before standing up and putting my phone in my back pocket. I trudge to the front door of my building, swing it open, and gasp.

I unexpectedly unveiled a woman and her child standing in the doorframe. The woman is reaching for the doorknob that I got to first. After gathering myself, I hold the door open for them. I smile as they exit, flustered.

I hate being startled. I prefer controlled forms of fear. I like my podcasts, horror movies, and ghost stories that I can pause and rewind. I handle fear sort of like a warhorse. I could charge bravely into a planned battle, take in the sights of bombs and corpses, but I would still be spooked by an unanticipated barn rat.

✳

"There's a great red spot on Jupiter," I tell my mom. We're on the phone. About five minutes ago, I got a push notification reminding me that tomorrow is my half sister's party. I tend to call my mom when I'm reminded of my sisters. I feel guilty interacting with them. I consider their existence a great red spot on my mom's life.

"It's an enormous storm," I explain. "It's a vortex big enough to engulf Earth. It's been raging for centuries. There are records of it being seen over three hundred and fifty years ago. On Earth, hurricanes slow down when they reach solid land, but there is no solid surface on Jupiter."

"There isn't? What's Jupiter made of?"

"Mostly hydrogen and helium. It's a cloud."

"So is the spot permanent?"

"That's hard to say. It shrinks and grows. Sometimes it changes color. It gets intensely red. It might go away someday, but yes. It could last as long as the planet."

"Fascinating," she says. "Space is so interesting, isn't it?"

"Yeah," I say while I tap ignore on another reminder about the party tomorrow. "Did you know light travels 186,000 miles a second?"

"Does it really?"

"Yes. The moon is 238,855 miles away, so it takes 1.3 seconds for light to travel from it to us. That means when we look at the moon, we don't really see it as it is. We see it as it was 1.3 seconds ago."

"Boy, that's neat, isn't it?" she says.

"Because of how far away the sun is, we see it eight minutes ago. Depending on the orbit, we see Mars as it was three minutes ago, or twenty when it's further away. Saturn is an hour. Our nearest star is four years. The Andromeda galaxy is 2.5 million years."

"Wow," she says. "That is hard to wrap your head around, isn't it?"

"It is possible that some life force light-years away is watching us now but seeing us in the past. Or they could see us now in the future, millions of years from now, depending on where they are, and their technology."

"Shall we wave?"

"They shouldn't be able to see us wave," I say. "Because we're inside. Are you inside?"

"Yes, I'm inside, and oh, that's a relief. So, it's safe to say that no one could be watching us when we are inside our homes?"

I look at my window.

"Enid?"

"Yes?"

"What else do you know about space?"

I clear my throat. "Well, space is how we could see back in time. If we could travel faster than light, and if Earth gave off enough of it, and we had some innovative telescope, that is how we could see our past. We could look back and see the dinosaurs. We could watch the meteor hit."

"That's incredible, wow. Though I think I would rather watch the time when you were a little girl. I'd prefer not to see the dinosaurs die."

✳

The comforting lull of my murder podcast is rocking me to sleep. I am lying on my side, clutching my knees to my chest, heeding the familiar tale of Ted Bundy. I feel myself drift in and out of sleep. I dream of my mom reading me a bedtime story.

In a green, green room there was a telephone. And a red balloon. And a picture of Ted Bundy with his unibrow. There were three little bears, sitting on chairs, and at least twenty victims. And a little toy house, and a young mouse, and a comb and a brush and corpse made of mush. And a bald man whispering "hush." Goodnight moon, goodnight tomb.

✳

I have frequent nightmares. It's been an ongoing issue since I was a kid. Once, I dreamed the sun exploded. I saw it fill the sky, turn red, and boil the oceans. I held a Barbie in my hands and watched her face melt. I woke up in tears, beside myself. Rather than shout *"Mom!"* or run to her room, I yanked my blankets over my head and thrust my face into my pillows so she wouldn't hear me cry.

＊

"When the sun explodes," I tell my mom over the phone in the morning, "it'll take eight minutes for Earth to know. Because of what I said last night about space and time."

I called her again. I woke up to another reminder in my phone about my half sister's party.

"When can we expect that to happen?" she asks.

"In about five to seven billion years."

My coffee maker is percolating.

"Have you had your coffee yet?" I ask.

"No, I think I'm out of beans."

"Do you have groceries?"

"No, you caught me at a bad time."

I don't reply. I watch coffee drops gradually fill the pot in front of me.

"What will happen to Earth when the sun dies?" she asks.

The coffee machine hisses.

"It's hard to say. It'll consume Venus and Mercury. Earth will probably become a lifeless rock. I wouldn't worry about it, though. Humanity will die out before that happens. The typical life span of a large mammal species is a few million years."

"Is it? Yikes. How many years have humans existed?"

"Three hundred thousand, I think."

She exhales. "Phew! So, we still have quite a while to go, then?"

I pour cream into my cup and say, "Mhm," even though I doubt humans will live a million years. I watch the cream swirl in my coffee and form a shape that looks like the Pinwheel Galaxy.

※

I smear buttercream over the cake I baked. I had it in my freezer. I read that makes it easier to ice; however, crumbs are churning into the icing, forming lumps that remind me of cystic acne. As I run my knife over the cake, my podcast host explains that Ted Bundy would pretend that he had a broken arm to lure unsuspecting women into his car. He would ask them for their help, they would oblige, and then he would rape and murder them. The host describes Ted as attractive. That is often the narrative pushed about him. I have learned, however, that it is not true. I've heard that his victims often thought that he was creepy-looking. They helped him anyways, because of the broken arm schtick, and because women are trained to be polite to men even when men are ugly and make them feel uncomfortable.

Some pictures of Ted are moderately handsome, I guess. In some photos he looks strange. It's hard for me to tell if he was ugly. I can tell that I wouldn't be attracted to him, but that is true of every man except for a few very specific celebrities, and some fictional male characters who were written by women.

I do not know why we assume attractive people are less likely to be killers, anyways. In my experience, good-looking people are more likely to be depraved.

I strain to push green letter icing out of a tube. I write BOY OR GIRL? on the face of my hideous cake. When I finish, I stare down at the monstrosity as if I have just successfully bred a human with a pig.

*

In dark moments of self-loathing, I watch the YouTube videos I filmed when I was a kid. I can't delete them. I don't remember the password to the account. I filmed thousands of videos from the ages of ten to seventeen.

As an older teen, I tended to film makeup tutorials or shopping hauls. Sometimes, I produced artsy videos. I filmed trees swaying in the wind in sepia tone, water rolling down a creek in black and white, and a match striking.

I don't remember filming any of the artsy videos. I have no recollection of filming anything as a teenager.

As a child, I recorded myself talking. I was not a gifted speaker by any stretch. I touched my face too much, I stammered, and I struggled to form words. Nonetheless, I filmed myself ineptly discussing the cartoons I liked and the books I read. I filmed shaky tours of my yellow bedroom. I treated YouTube like it was my diary or my friend.

A video is playing on my TV while I struggle to assemble an outfit. I have the closed captions on. I have tried on every pair of pants I own. I am now standing, pantless, in front of my TV, watching my child-self ramble about *SpongeBob SquarePants*.

I have held newborns before and thought, while looking into their dark, cloudy eyes, *They must be struggling to adjust to their human coil.* There is this sense I get while cradling babies that their life force is imprisoned in their ineffectual baby bodies, and that a large part of being an infant involves grappling with your physical existence until you have the dexterity to shake a rattle.

I watch my fleshy child face. I think I was delayed. I think I took longer to grapple with my human coil than most people.

I moved awkwardly, as if I were incapable of having a mouth without touching it or fingers without chewing on them. My voice shakes, and I mumble. I watch myself obsess over *Sponge-Bob SquarePants* as if I am seeing myself learn to walk.

I pick up the remote and scroll through the videos on my channel. There are dozens of me discussing my middle school. I was bullied, and I go on frequent tirades about it. I have videos titled:

"Confronting My Bullies. That's Right, Chelsea, This One Is for You."

"When I Grow Up and Am Famous, I Am Going to Tell Every Interviewer that Theodora Called Me a Dyke."

"Ten Reasons Why Dimitri's Wrong About Me Being a Loser."

"Ten Reasons Why Dimitri's Actually a Loser."

Sometimes I report the videos, hoping some benevolent YouTube employee will find it in their heart to remove them, but mostly I just watch them as a sort of self-harm. It feels like watching prehistoric footage of Earth. It is this strange history of life that feels almost fake despite the dinosaur bone proof.

"*Today we are going to go for a more natural look,*" I tell my audience.

I then open a predominately purple makeup palette.

"*You can use bright colors and still look natural,*" I assure my undoubtedly uneasy viewers as I apply dark shadow directly beneath my brow bone.

"*You just have to blend.*"

The auto-generated closed captions misinterpret what I said. The text beneath me says, "This just has to end."

It is bizarre to see myself as a teenager. I can't remember being that age. I didn't like being a teenager. I don't think back to that time. I find no enjoyment in doing so, and when you don't hark back on memories, they fade. Besides these videos, that stage in my development is almost blank. I can't remember anything. I wish I hadn't filmed these. I wish I had no way of remembering myself then. I wish watching myself as a teenager required that I fly light-years away from Earth.

I continue to stand in my underwear, watching mindlessly, pausing every so often to listen to my quiet apartment. I get an inkling, every third video or so, that I should assess my surroundings. I feel like someone is watching me.

∗

I set the cake down on Gina's marble countertop. The moment my fingers release the glass platter, I feel the same sort of reprieve killers must after successfully burying a body.

To celebrate ridding myself of the transphobic baked good, I fix myself a mimosa. There is orange juice, champagne, and strawberries on the counter. There are also little crustless cucumber sandwiches and a charcuterie board with honeycomb, blueberries, and various cheeses on it.

I pop two strawberries into my glass flute and hold a sandwich in my mouth to avoid having to get a plate. The plates are stacked behind two women I don't know. They are chatting, and I feel uncomfortable interrupting them to ask them to move.

"Enid!" I hear Gina's voice shout.

Gina was married to my dad.

She hurries over to me. I feel her acrylic nails dig into my shoulders as she embraces me.

"How are you, honey?" She takes my hands away from my body to look at me.

I try to reply but I am mute with the sandwich in my mouth, and I feel anxious to have my limbs returned to my torso.

She smiles. "Thank you so much for coming. We are so excited that you're here!"

Gina hates me.

✳

I found naked pictures of Gina on my family's desktop computer when I was little. They were tucked in a folder titled "Taxes." I must have been interested in accounting. Instead of perusing receipts, I saw Gina in all her glory.

There is something disturbing about seeing a strange, naked woman unexpectedly when you are a little girl. I don't know that I would have been less disturbed by photos of dead bodies. It was a traumatic incident in my life, and sadly, I'm not embellishing. I regularly wish I were traumatized by something more interesting than Gina's butt.

✳

"Ted Bundy wasn't actually hot," I tell the throng of women sitting with me on Gina's beige sectional. "That is just the narrative pushed to make the story interesting. Look at him." I open an ugly photo of him on my phone. I show it to everyone. "This guy looks like he'd bludgeon and rape a woman with a metal rod from her bedframe, doesn't he?"

There is a palpable silence after I finish speaking. It is so silent that I wonder, at first, if it's because of my half-deafness. As I rub my bad ear, I realize that the silence has nothing to do with my hearing. The reason it is quiet is because these women are dumb with offense. I glance around the couch at their speechless, affronted faces.

My half sister Edna is sitting next to me. She looks especially appalled.

I am not sure there is anything I can do to negate mentioning raping a woman with her bedframe. Maybe it is important for me to assert I find it horrible too?

"It's horrible what he did," I say quietly.

They stir. Some compassionate bystander tries to throw me a life raft.

She says, "You know a lot about murderers, eh?"

I bite the insides of my cheeks. Should I say yes, or would that make this worse?

I don't usually let myself talk this much around Gina, my sisters, and the people in their orbit. I tend to be quiet. I wear the mask of a well-mannered distant relative; a young lady who crosses her legs at the ankle and laughs at banal jokes. That is a new character for me, however. I have not mastered her yet. I *have* grasped the characters:

Enigmatic temporary love interest.

Reliable employee.

My mother's aidful daughter.

Unobjectionable patron at a store or restaurant.

In the past I learned to play *shy teenaged girl, tidy roommate*, and *diligent student*, through some trial and error, but those roles are behind me now, thank God.

"Do you just look up murderers and read about them, or what? How do you know all that detail?"

I look into my cup. Some strawberry seeds have dislodged from the fruit and are floating like drowned fruit flies. "I listen to true crime podcasts mostly, but yeah. I used to watch a lot of *Dateline* when I was a kid."

"Oh, that explains it," Gina hollers from across the room.

"You shouldn't have been watching that kind of thing, honey! My girls just watched cartoons when they were little!"

✳

I watched *Dateline* with my mom. I associate it with eight p.m. on school nights. I think of getting out of the bath, having wet hair, putting on clean pajamas, and greeting my mom on our couch. She would lift the corner of the orange knit blanket on her lap for me to sit under. I always stayed in the bath too long. The water was cool by the time I emerged. I felt chilly until I sat under the blanket with her, in the nest of her trapped body heat. We had a lamp with a yellow stained-glass shade that made the light in our living room warm. We sat together in that light learning about serial killers while my mom clicked her knitting needles.

The orange blanket had a grassy smell, even after it was washed. We used it a lot. I remember falling asleep on it in our backyard. My mom and I would lie on it in the summer. She would sunbathe and read romance novels. I would lie beside her, cupping ants and ladybugs in my palms, feeling the heat of the sun on my skin. We sat under it in the winter on the sidewalk when we watched the parade. I remember getting sticky candy cane residue on it and have memories of pulling it up to my chin in the cold. We brought it camping. We lay under it at night while we made shadow puppets on the wall of our tent with a flashlight.

My dad left when I was about six. My memories of him are foggy. I can't tell if they're real, or if I made them up. I think I watched him paint a yucca tree once. Though, that might have been a dream. I have a memory of him and me coloring in the same coloring book, but it's hazy. It might have been someone else.

When I was a kid, I played pretend games. I played that I was a lion, an orphan, a ghost; that I was raised by wolves, that I was a boy, or that I had a dad. I would roam around the house, acting out the game. I would crawl and roar like a lion or speak out loud to my make-believe dad.

As I got older, the imagination games morphed into daydreams. I invented interactions between me and my dad, as well as with other people. I did it so often that it's now hard for me to distinguish between real memories and memories of scenarios I made up. Everything has melded together.

I think I saw him once at the beach. My mom and I were lying on our blanket. I had just erected a sandcastle. She had excavated the moat. We smelled like sunscreen and salt water. We had sunglasses and zinc on our noses, and we were wearing wide-brimmed wicker hats.

He was with Gina and the girls. Gina was wearing a red-and-white-striped bathing suit. She stood near the shore with her hands on her hips to supervise her daughters' swim. My dad sat under the shade of their beach umbrella, reading a paperback. My mom pointed him out to me. She told me who he was, but we didn't say hello. I don't know if he saw us. After they packed up and left, I wandered to the sand they occupied. I looked at their footprints and umbrella hole as if inspecting where an asteroid hit.

I'm not sure if that memory is real. I may have made it up. It might be that we went to the beach, but I fell asleep and dreamed up the rest. Or maybe it did happen. It's hard for me to tell.

＊

Gina's medicine cabinet is stocked full of vitamins. I have examined each bottle, hoping to uncover pills that suggest Gina has been hiding a secret violent hemorrhoid disorder. Unfortunately, I have only found Tylenol, multivitamins, and antacids. Her Tylenol is not even extra strength. The most sensational medication she owns is a motion sickness ear patch sitting behind some calcium chews. She must get carsick, or something.

I shut the cabinet and turn on the tap. I think of my mom's medicine cabinet. She has a miniature pharmacy behind her mirror. She takes Xanax, Lexapro, anti-inflammatory medicine for depression-triggered arthritis, vitamin D, vitamin B12, occasional oxycodone for her chronic back pain, daily thyroid medicine, and a potpourri of other drugs that I am perpetually afraid will react with her daily pills if she pops them.

I lather a bar of pink soap in my hands. The water is hot. I keep my hands under the tap despite the temperature. Steam rises from the basin and dews my face.

After my hands are sufficiently scorched, I turn the tap off. I run one of my red hands over the mirror to wipe away the condensation and look at myself.

I practice my smile.

I look like my mom. Strangers have approached me before to ask if I am her daughter. I am taller than she is, and have someone else's hands, but I am often told that I am the spitting image of her. She is chicer than I am. She wears bright colors and complicated shoes. I don't pluck my eyebrows or wear makeup, but she always wears lipstick, unless she's sad, and her brows are always groomed. Despite our styling differences, sometimes, when I look through old photo albums, I mistake pictures of her for me.

I dry my hands on a white towel.

There is a framed photo of their family affixed to the wall above the towel rack. My dad and Gina are standing behind the girls with their hands on their shoulders. Both girls have pink and purple pinwheels in their hands. The sky is blue behind them. All four of them are smiling.

I think of myself as a kid while I dry my hands. I think of my mom standing alone behind me.

I take my phone out of my back pocket. I tap until I find my mom's name. When I think of her, rather than call her or text her a message that says something like, *Hey, I'm thinking of you*, I tell her interesting facts about space.

I text her,
Hey mom, did you know sunsets on Mars are blue?

*

My half sisters both resemble Gina. They are all short, thin women, with small frames, and little facial features. Today Kira is wearing a knee-length, cream dress. She has accessorized with little pearl earrings, and taupe-painted nails. Edna, my other half sister, is wearing a long floral maternity dress. Her nails are pink and almond-shaped. They have little jewels stuck on them.

I don't look like them. I am tall, I have short hair, sharp facial features, and a sleeve of tattoos featuring anthropomorphic rats wearing Victorian dresses. I have a long-sleeved shirt on today. It covers my tattoos, but the rats' presence is sensed. One of their long tails creeps out of my sleeve, up my wrist. I'm not usually insecure about my appearance. I am not usually critical of other people's looks either, but I find myself looking judgmentally at Gina and my sisters. I look at their clothing, their hair, and their fingernails. They look like women who have packaged themselves fully to oblige the male gaze. They look like people who would be baffled when a woman with long hair gets a pixie cut. When I am around them, I find myself trying to cover my arms.

Kira is a nurse and Edna is a teacher. A lot of the people at this party are their coworkers, or people that they went to university with. The conversations happening around the house are all related to classrooms, students, hospitals, and patients. I don't know how to participate.

"What do you do for work, Enid?" a white-haired, older woman near me asks. I noticed her eyes on my wrist, glimpsing the tip of one of my rat's pink tails.

At face value, her question seems polite. She wonders what I do. That is a normal thing to ask someone. A lot of people identify with their jobs. A person's career is often a defining part of their life. She might just be trying to involve me in conversation. I have a feeling, though, that her question is not really rooted in a desire to know me. What she wonders is if a girl with short hair, rat tattoos, and too much intel about murderers can find employment.

"I work for the Space Agency," I reply.

"Oh wow," she says, unable to veil her surprise that I am not unemployed, a drug dealer, or working in organized crime. "What do you do there?"

"I am an information architect," I say. When I tell people I work for the Space Agency, they usually assume I'm an astronaut or an engineer. My job has much less to do with astrophysics than it does with organizing information. I got my master's degree in information science. I keep track of interesting facts to tell my mom, but I'm not an astrophysicist.

This woman does not care about any of that, though. She

is asking me to be polite, and to hide that the true objective of her original question was to find out if I am employed at all. I suspect that if I were to go into any detail about my job, her eyes would glaze over, or she would start talking to someone else while I was midsentence.

Instead of dealing with that, I ask, "What do you do?"

"Me? Oh, I am a retired teacher. It's been almost five years since I retired, actually. I can't believe it. I am loving it, though. I spend a lot of time at my cottage. I miss all my coworkers, of course, and a lot of the students, but not all of them!" She laughs. "I have already been on two cruises. I went to the Bahamas with my sister last winter. It was amazing. I can't wait to go back—"

I nod and smile while she tells me about Bahamian cuisine and the volunteer work that she has been doing with the school board. I find it difficult to hear her, but I nod along.

Behind me, I can hear Edna, Kira, and their friends chatting. Their voices sound clearer than this woman's does to me. They are talking about baby names. The teachers and pediatric nurses sitting with them are cautioning Edna on which names to avoid.

The woman talking to me interjects, "Do not name the kid Ainsley! I had two separate kids in my classes named Ainsley and both were hell on earth."

"Avoid Mallory, too," a woman adds.

"If it's a boy, we might name him after Dad," Edna says.

Everyone coos.

"If it's a girl, we're thinking Amelia Di."

I open my mouth but quickly shut it. I fight an impulse to warn Edna that "Amelia Di" sounds a lot like "Amelia Dyer," who was a famous Victorian serial killer. I have, however, exceeded my serial killer conversation quota for this baby genital reveal party—so I will keep this information to myself.

"Your dad would just love it if you named the baby Elmer!" Gina's voice carries across the room like noxious gas.

✳

"It's a girl!" the crowd cheers.

Women leap from their chairs. Gina has tears in her eyes.

They're shrieking. "A girl! A girl! A girl!"

Edna is jumping up and down with the knife that she used to cut the cake. I try not to wince while watching her round, pregnant belly bounce near the silver blade. I picture her puncturing her gut and her belly popping like a pierced balloon. I think of confetti.

Edna's husband looks disappointed. He is smiling with his mouth, but not his eyes. He must have wanted a boy.

"A girl!" Gina and Kira are shrieking.

"A sweet little princess! A girl!"

I cheer along with them despite already knowing the sex, and not feeling particularly exuberant. Cameras flash. A voice shouts, "Say cheese!" The crowd, including me, huddle together. I smile with teeth while someone unfamiliar puts their arm over me. A camera is pointed in our faces, and we are shot repeatedly with flash.

"One more!"

My cheeks hurt. I hate that someone is touching me.

"Did you get one on my phone?"

When I peruse old photo albums, I like seeing pictures of my mom and me. Most of the photos are of me alone because she was always the photographer. There are only a few of us together.

One is at Halloween. We were dressed in bedsheets with holes cut in the eyes. If I did not remember that Halloween so well, I might not know that it's a photo of us. I remember it though. I had no one to trick-or-treat with so she came with me as a ghost.

There is another one of me wearing oversized gardening gloves, holding a garter snake as if I were restraining a viper. In the background, I can see my mom laughing. She is holding her stomach, in tears. I love those photos. I like seeing evidence of my mom and me happy.

"Did you get a good one?"

I doubt it's possible to have a baby and not imagine what you want for it. If I were to ever fall pregnant, I would wonder what the sex of the baby is. Celebrations that center expectations around gender depress me, though. I don't think I am what someone would envision if they cut into a cake and saw pink. If I saw photos of my mom, teary-eyed at the thought of me being a girl, I would feel even more guilty for being born the way I am.

I hope there's an alternate universe where my mom is married to some kindhearted man who loves her. I hope she has a sewing room, and multiple well-adjusted kids. I think that would have happened if I weren't born. It might have happened if I was a different type of kid. She had to spend all her time with me. I didn't have friends. I was antisocial. I was always home with her. Something was wrong with me.

"Bows, dresses, and fairy tales," Gina says, breathless. "Aren't we ladies blessed?"

❋

The first time I ever spoke to Kira and Edna was two years ago, at our dad's funeral. It was strange I attended. I didn't go to say goodbye, or to get closure. I went because my half sisters asked me to. I felt bound to oblige them, for some reason.

On the morning of the funeral, I looked in the mirror while combing my hair, and laughed at how absurd it was that I was attending an event with Gina, Edna, Kira, and my dad—however dead. I wasn't sad or upset, I was energized by the oddity of it. I felt like I was going to the live taping of a reality TV show that I had been invested in for years.

My sisters were standing in the receiving line next to his casket. I shook their hands and said, "I'm so sorry."

"Thank you," they replied, pale and puffy-eyed. I then shuffled forward with the crowd to find my place amid the strangers.

I rehearsed what to say to them. My first draft was, *I'm so sorry for your loss.* I omitted *for your loss* because I didn't want to emphasize it being *their* loss, and not mine. That was the case, but I worried focusing on that might be like saying, *I'm so sorry for your loss that is not mine because our deceased dad abandoned me.*

I didn't want to center myself. Their dad was dead. I wanted to focus on them.

I also planned not to say, *It's nice to meet you* at any point, because I wasn't sure if we had met before. When I was a kid, I used to imagine meeting them. It was one of the scenarios I played out. I pictured us bumping into each other at the mall. I imagined a stranger remarking that we looked alike. We all agreed, exchanged names, and I said, *Oh, I think we might be half sisters.*

I stopped imagining that as I got older. Years passed, and by the funeral, I couldn't remember if it really happened or not. I have a lot of false memories like that. I often recall things that didn't happen, and worse—I have discovered memories I thought I dreamed, really had occurred. I once saw a ghost, for example. I thought I dreamed it, but my mom remembers too. I screamed; the ghost absconded from my bedroom, and then my mom arrived. I was shaken. I also have this sense that I have almost drowned before, and that I have been in a fire. I don't know if I really have or not.

If I could choose, I would rather not know that I once saw a ghost. I wish I could wonder if I dreamed that. Knowing that I truly saw a ghost, or at least that I truly believed I saw a ghost, is an unpleasant reality. It either means that ghosts exist, or more likely, and more worrisome—it means that I am capable of hallucinating.

I find it rarely serves me to clarify my memories. It just stirs up needless horrors. I would rather forge on, leaving every stone unturned.

The moment I saw my sisters at the funeral it was apparent that my memory of meeting them prior was contrived. Facing that forced me to also face the sad reality that I used to fantasize about meeting them. I felt humbled in their presence, knowing they were like celebrities to me, while also feeling remorse for my pitiful child-self, and grief at the reminder that my sisters and I were total strangers. All of that came crashing down on me, like a ceiling collapsing in a fire, while I shook their hands next to our father's corpse, masked my distress, and uttered that I was *so* sorry.

My dad died of a heart attack. My mom found out somehow. She got me the information for the funeral. I didn't think I should go, but she said that she spoke to Gina and the girls, and the girls asked me to come. I had never heard of my mom speaking to them before, but I guess she reached out to offer condolences. I asked her to come with me, but she said she couldn't.

Gina gave the eulogy. She opened with, "Elmer was a devoted husband and father." I stifled a laugh while picturing myself standing up to object like it were a wedding, not a funeral, and like I were the mistress of the bride, and not the abandoned daughter of a deadbeat dead man.

Gina then told a story about a homemade picture book my dad wrote and bound for his two girls. It was about a turtle who ate tulips. He illustrated it himself with watercolors.

As I sat listening to Gina choke up about a turtle eating tulips, I felt a startling sadness crack its way into my ribs. Despite thinking I didn't feel passionately about my dad, his death, or our relationship, my eyes stung, and a lump formed in my throat. Every detail of the story sucker punched me. The crowd was chuckling. They thought the story was so cute—so emblematic of Elmer.

There was an old man sitting next to me. I didn't know him, but he put his feeble arm around me to console me as Gina told her terrible story. He must have assumed I was just moved. He said "there, there, honey" while I sobbed into his black cardigan like I had just witnessed a kitten get shot.

✳

My sisters and I barely know each other. After the funeral, we exchanged numbers. Now we occasionally text. They invite me to their events. They send me messages around the holidays. I have reminders set in my phone for when it is their birthdays. I send cards. When Edna told me she was pregnant, I got her a wooden solar system mobile and a copy of *Goodnight Moon*. When she invited me to the gender reveal party, I asked her if I could do anything to help. She said no, but I asked again. I said, "I would be happy to do anything, really." She said if I wanted to, I could make the cake. Despite being a lesbian who has a complicated relationship with my own gender, and who is acutely aware that gender reveal parties reinforce a harmful binary, I said, "I would be honored to make the cake."

In person, we speak on a surface level. They have never discussed my relationship with our dad, his absence in my life, his relationship with my mom, or much beyond them saying, "We wish we knew you when we were growing up."

✳

"Thank you so much for coming, and for making that beautiful cake."

Edna is saying goodbye to me on the front porch. I have my keys in my hands. My fist is gripping them so tightly I can feel my inner fingers bruising.

"Thank you for having me."

"It's always so nice to see you," she says.

She speaks with a sincerity that I have to fight an impulse not to cringe at. I clench my molars and grip my toes in my shoes.

I wonder why some people are like her, and why some people are like me. She's able to make offhand soppy comments without cringing because she is mentally healthy, well-adjusted, and normal. I can't tell people things like, *It's always so nice to see you*, let alone say something like, *I love you*, without feeling my insides curdle. I have to tell them about sunsets on Mars or bake them offensive cakes. I bet she tells Gina she loves her. I bet she doesn't know anything about stars.

Sometimes I think I have a parasite. I feel like there is a

creature crawling inside me, trying to migrate to my brain. I picture him like Plankton from *SpongeBob SquarePants*; a malevolent little mastermind who is trying to use my body like a Trojan horse. I worry that I am a shell for something bad. That deep down, in the spot where most people keep their souls, I keep a weird little bug. I picture him there, leaning on the apple core of my soul, crunching on what remains of what's good of me.

I struggle to stomach sincerity, or to express any authentic emotion, because everything feels insincere when you suspect that deep down, in the chasm of yourself, the most sentient part of you is a little ill-intentioned monster. I feel like a husk, like I am being gradually taken over, and that all my feelings and thoughts are tampered with. I am nervous when I interact with people like Edna. I don't want to expose her to Plankton. I think there have been times in the past where he took me over completely.

I've been cruel to people before. There have been times when my mom disappointed me, for example, and I said spiteful things I regret. I told her she was a bad parent. I said I wished she never had me. I also harbored resentment for people as a kid. I used to think a lot about getting back at kids who bullied me, for example.

I don't like thinking about it. Sometimes, when I'm grocery shopping, or out minding my own business, a little voice in my head reminds me that I've made my mom cry before. I wince at fleeting recollections of myself being terrible. I have this deep sense that I've done awful things—that I've really hurt someone—but I'm not sure if I actually have. When the bug in my head starts whispering about how rotten I am, I distract myself. I turn on a podcast.

I wish I imagined things less. I don't know what's real and what isn't. I do think I am capable of doing something bad. Whether I have actually done anything unforgivable is hazy to me, but I have definitely wanted to. I think I am capable of it. I'm worried that at any moment, I am liable to be taken over by my parasite, and that I will hurt someone.

I doubt it even occurs to Edna to wonder if people have parasites. I bet her soul is a big red apple with no bites taken out of it.

She smiles at me.

"Let's do this again soon," I say with a wave before immediately regretting my phrasing. Do *what* again? Have a gender reveal party?

CHAPTER THREE

I burst into my mom's house as if I have arrived to defuse a bomb. I always feel an urgency to rush inside. I stumble out of my car, bolt across the lawn, and throw the door open. I explode inside before something else can. I scream, "Mom!"

"Mom!"

When I was a kid, I would run to my bed after flushing the toilet. I told myself that some toilet monster was awakened when I flushed, and that he would snatch me if I didn't move. I imagined him chasing me as I flew to my mattress, my pants rarely ever fully pulled up. I thought of his knobbly, green monster fingers reaching for me as I dove into my mattress. I believed the second I was under the covers he would return to the pipes.

It is a similar feeling I have now when I pull up outside this house. Something inside me warns that a timer starts when I spot the front door. If I do not rush, something bad will happen. A monster will wake up.

My mom usually screams when I come in. It startles her. She says, "Why do you do that? You come in here like a bat out of hell!"

I can't tell her why I do it, so I gaslight her. I say, "What do you mean?"

She huffs until her fear gives way to her contentment that I am here. She then laughs and says things like, "Who raised you?"

✳

Half of the lightbulbs in my mom's house are burned out. The whole place is dirty. She has filled the barrel of her washing machine so high it would break if she tried to run the load. Sheets are knotted around the agitator. A musty red towel is lying over the lip of the machine. It looks as if the washer is sticking its tongue out at me. Her kitchen counters are sticky. Her sink is teeming with crusted plates, pots, and tea bags. The bread in her cupboards is fuzzy, and the whole house smells like turned soup.

It is not always like this. She goes through a sort of cycle. When she is happy, she applies lipstick and does her dishes. When she is depressed, her milk rots and her lips are bare. When I lived here, I took care of things when she did not wear lipstick. Now that I don't live here, I have to come and check.

When she is depressed, she doesn't admit it. She never discusses how she feels or asks for help. It is apparent by the state of her home and her body, but she always speaks as if everything is the same. I was molded by her behavior, so when I feel compelled to confront her about it, rather than say, "You are depressed," I say, "Your house is dirty." I say, "You're not wearing lipstick."

She usually replies, "You just caught me at a bad time."

So I say, "Okay, then I'll come back tomorrow." And I return every day until her lips turn red.

"You should try oat milk," I shout while pouring chunky two percent in the toilet. I imagine the monster who chased me guzzling it and feeling grateful, given what is normally served to toilet monsters. "It has a longer expiration," I add.

I'm not sure if she answers. I think I heard a muffled reply, but I can't make it out.

When I flush, I resist the urge to bolt to my old bed. Instead, I walk to the kitchen.

"I've been learning about dark matter," I say while filling the kitchen sink with Dawn and water.

"Oh?" she says. "What's that?"

I start scrubbing her dishes. "It's actually easier to say what it isn't."

"What isn't it, then?"

I try to scrub caked-on food off a fork. I apply a large squirt of dish soap directly to the utensil. I say, "It's made of particles that don't emit, absorb, or reflect light. So, it's material that can't be seen. When you can't see something, one way to understand what it is, is by assessing how it affects the things that you can see. So, for example, places with a high concentration of dark matter bend light."

"That's interesting."

The food on the fork finally dislodges. I look at the rest of the dishes, all equally encrusted, and sigh. "Your house is dirty."

She avoids my eyes.

"You caught me at a bad time."

✳

Our washing machine broke when I was eleven. It wouldn't stop spinning. It wobbled around the laundry room like it had come to life. We were afraid to touch it. It was making a loud banging sound. I thought it might blow up. My mom called the fire department. They arrived with two big trucks and an ambulance. They had their sirens on. I was embarrassed by the commotion, but they told us it was good we called. They turned the machine off for us.

After the machine stopped, they removed our laundry. I was mortified by this because it was full of my pajamas. For an inexplicable eleven-year-old girl reason, I thought my pajamas were humiliating. They were pink. Somehow, my mom sensed that I felt embarrassed, and made a point of telling all the first responders that the pajamas they had recovered from the machine belonged to her.

She said, "Thank you all for saving *my* pajamas."

✳

"Omar's older sister is really his mom." Vin plops his lunch box down on the break room table.

"Excuse me?" I look up from my wobbling cereal. The table has uneven legs. "I think I misheard you. Say that again into my good ear."

He stands on my good side and enunciates, "Omar's older sister is his mom."

Omar is Vin's boyfriend.

I put my hand over my mouth. "What are you talking about?" My cheeks are full of Lucky Charms.

He sits down. "Remember how I got him one of those

at-home DNA tests for his birthday? Well, it turns out his family hid that his sister had him when she was fifteen. He has no idea who his dad is. His parents are actually his grandparents."

"Holy shit."

He leans back. "Yeah. So, we spent the whole weekend crying."

"Why were you crying?"

"You know I'm an empath."

Vin works in IT. He and I started working here at the same time about four years ago. Now we are not just work friends. I know his siblings' occupations and his mother's maiden name. Sometimes, when other people are around, he looks at me while they're talking, and I know what the look means. Often it means, *Get a load of this idiot.* Occasionally it means, *I'm in love.*

He seems to understand what my looks mean, too. Usually mine mean, *Help.*

"How was your weekend?" he asks while he unpacks his lunch.

"Well, I didn't spend it crying," I lie.

He snorts. "Fuck you."

I haven't met Omar yet. They have only been dating for a couple of months. Vin usually introduces me to his boyfriends at around four months. His family is not supportive and don't want to meet them. Because of that, there is a gravity to my meeting them. I feel a responsibility to represent Vin the way his family should, and often pick up on his boyfriends' trying to impress me the way they should a sister.

I have never introduced Vin to anyone I have dated. I once ran into him when I was at the mall with a girl, and he immediately added her on social media. She and I only went out twice, so I asked him to unfriend her. That upset him. We didn't speak for a week.

He offers me a slice of cucumber from his lunch. Before biting into it, I hear weak whistling. Vin and I pause like deer hearing predatory feet crunch against the forest floor. Our co-worker Maveric is heading toward the break room. He always whistles while he walks. He is a loud, type A person who dominates conversations, interrupts people, and talks too much about sports. He often asks both Vin and me, two people who have expressed no interest in athletics, if we "caught the game last night."

He enters the room and Vin shoots me a look that means, *I hate him.*

"Hey guys," Maveric says. "Oops, sorry, I mean—hey guy and girl!"

Everyone I work with is a man. Almost every day, I survive my coworkers overcorrecting themselves when they address rooms of employees as fellas, only to realize they failed to notice me. They then apologize and adamantly acknowledge my gender until every person in the room looks at me. Most meetings I attend devote one agenda item to formally acknowledging that I am a woman.

"You two catch the game last night?" he asks as his kettle hisses.

Vin and I exchange a look.

*

My wrists hurt from typing. I have my headphones in. An episode of my podcast is playing. I have just learned that people in small towns don't lock their doors until they find out the local turkey farmer tortures people in his shed.

The sound from the podcast is being distributed oddly into

my headphones. I noticed there were unusually long pauses and discovered after examining my headphones that there are parts of the story going into my deaf ear.

I sip my tea, then spit it back into my thermos. It's cold. It has been sitting on my desk since lunch. It is almost four now. I forgot to drink it. I have been busy sitting here, hunched, testing a search tool I built for a major project. We are sending a rover to the moon. It's supposed to survive one moon night, which is fourteen Earth days. It will be extremely cold and dark. The tool is supposed to aggregate all related project information, so everyone involved can find everything in one place; however, something is wrong with it. It's not working.

Whenever I query the word "shadow," for example, the tool inexplicitly returns nothing. It presents a condescending error message, which reads: *Sorry, something went wrong!* The exclamation mark reads especially rude. It might as well say, *Fuck you!*

There is a lot of information that should be returned with the word "shadow." I defined search synonyms, so when someone searches a word like "shadow," it should bring back all results associated with darkness. Darkness is a major component of this project.

I try again.

I try "dim."

"Blackness."

"Unlit."

Each attempt prompts the *Fuck you!*

✳

After committing more than one hour of my life to cleaning my apartment, my phone dings. I skin off my rubber gloves and

look at my screen. I read a text from the girl I was cleaning for.
It says,

I have to cancel. I'm sorry. I have to work late.

She was coming over to watch a movie. We had planned to
order pho.

I reply,

No problem.

She apologizes again.

I write,

Forget about it, really. No worries.

Beyond just washing my dishes and sweeping, I went as far
as to dust the trim. I scrubbed the crumbs from the seal in the
door of my fridge. I also frantically showered, shaved, and ap-
plied my more costly sprays and lotions.

I usually observe a similar ritual anytime I expect company.
It is how I get into the role. I put perfumes over the true smell
of my skin and whittle off all the controllable reasons why someone might dislike me. I think that if there were no one else alive
I wouldn't clean my house. I would pile garbage everywhere.
I would collect wrappers, acorns, and rocks, and hoard them
around me like a dirty little ferret. If I existed alone, I doubt I
would wash my hair. I would shave my head. I would perch on
a hill of my own trash, naked.

It happens often that people I match with on dating apps
cancel at the last minute. It comes with the territory. I think part
of why I make these plans is to experience it. I think on some
level I am less interested in dating than I am in being repeatedly
rejected so that I can stew in that comfortable bad feeling. There
is something soothing about being rejected. It really anchors
you in your body. It feels like a bath.

✳

The light above me is flickering. I am waiting at a counter for food. I ordered pho and spring rolls. I plan to bring it back to my spotless apartment where I will consume it nude in my bed.

The restaurant is loud. Plates are clinking against each other. Patrons are chewing, swallowing, talking. There is music playing. Someone is laughing.

Brains filter out noises that are not useful, but that is hard for mine to do without two ears that hear. In environments like this, I struggle to hear people when they talk to me. The hostess is trying to tell me something. I can't hear her, and I can't read her lips. I don't know what she's saying. She gestures at an area.

"Do you want me to wait over there?" I ask.

She nods.

I look at the space she is directing me. It is away from the front counter, in the dining room. While I walk, I notice that the woman who canceled on me is sitting in a booth nearby. I zero in on her. Her hands are holding a man's hands from across the table.

I am outraged. Not that she lied to excuse herself for another date, but that she got pho. At least have the decency to get Mexican food, or something. Get a German doner.

I pull my hood up, hoping she doesn't notice me. I glance at her and her date's hands. I watch her run her thumb along the man's knuckles, down his fingers, over a ring. Is that a wedding ring? It is a gold band on his fourth finger, on his left hand. I look at her hand. She's wearing one too. Are they married?

I lower my hood. Now I want her to see me. I stand straight like a statue. Like someone with good posture.

When the hostess brings me my order, I project my voice. "Thank you very much."

The woman and her husband look at me. "Oh," I say, my eyes connecting with hers. "Hi."

I am tempted to ask, *Is this where you work?* but I am not confrontational enough. I wish I were braver.

I think saying "Hi" was enough, anyways. She is squirming. I open my little white paper bag of spring rolls while she stammers. I bite into one. It burns my mouth, but I chew it as if it's tepid. Flakes of fried rice paper fall at my feet like ash.

"H-hi," she says. "No. Uh. This is my husband. Eugene. Eugene, this is my-my friend."

She's forgotten my name.

I open my mouth. Steam from the scalding spring roll flows from my lips while I say, "My name is Enid."

✳

I walk home angry. Why do I keep being nonconsensually tied up in other people's extramarital affairs? I don't want to be anyone's mistress. I don't want to ruin someone's marriage. Do I have to start asking people if they're monogamously married? I don't want exclusivity, but I'm not interested in being the figurehead of anyone else's failed relationship. I hate the idea of being at the core of someone's heartbreak. I don't want to be anywhere near other people's hearts.

My skin feels hot. Something angry inside me wants me to march back into the restaurant. I want to slam the door open and storm over to her table. My parasite wants me to yell at her. I picture myself shoving my pointer finger into the groove of her shoulder. I imagine myself shouting. I picture her in tears.

I turn the volume of my podcast up. I need to drown out my thoughts. When I'm spiraling, it helps to listen to my murder stories. I think they might be an outlet for my parasite. Rather than actually unleash any anger, and risk ruining Eugene's dinner, I feed the evil bug in my heart depraved stories. I distract myself and soothe him in a little bath of horrors until my anger simmers and my molars unclench.

※

A YouTube video of my child-self wearing a yellow dress is playing. The video is mind-numbing. Child-me yammers on and on about Gary the snail from *SpongeBob*. The closed captions are making me hyperaware of how often I said "Um" and "Like." Gary was my favorite character. I am ineloquently retelling my favorite Gary scenes. I keep backtracking, saying, "Um. Wait, I forgot something!" and then retelling the story I was almost finished telling, with a trivial detail added.

I am watching the video much less for the Gary content than I am to observe my dress. My mom made it. I remember. She used fabric she got from a thrift store. It had the type of skirt that flew up when you spun.

The first time I wore it, I spun in it all day. My skirt soared around me like the rings of Saturn. My mom was lying in the grass on our blanket. She wore white, heart-shaped sunglasses and her hair in pink curlers. She had a romance novel open on her chest.

"Will I ever have a baby brother or sister?" I asked as I spun. Our backyard blurred around me.

"You have sisters, remember?" she said.

"No, but a real one," I clarified.

I stopped spinning, but the world kept moving.

"Those girls are real," she assured me.

"Ones who live with us." I tried not to fall over. "Ones I can talk to and play with."

"I'll get you a baby doll."

"No, I want a sister." I fell to the grass. I felt like the world went sideways.

"You can have a mother and a doll. That's it."

"That's not enough."

"It's plenty."

I lay on the lawn while the sky circled me, gripping the grass like I would fall into space if I let go.

✳

Checking my mail usually involves opening my mail cubby and tossing grocery store flyers and McDonald's coupons into the recycling bin in the mail room. It's essentially a garbage handling task. Today, however, I have discovered a pale pink envelope in my mailbox. It has a sunflower sticker on it. Edna's name is written in the return address.

I tear it open. It's a thank-you card. It has a picture of flowers in a vase on the front. The flowers are lilacs, I think. Inside, Edna has written the following:

> *Dear Enid,*
> *Thank you so much for celebrating our new family member with me.*
> *Having you there meant the world to me.*
> *Love,*
> *Edna*

✳

"Earth is zipping through the cosmos. We do not just orbit the sun. The sun is moving. Our galaxy is moving. The universe is expanding. We are soaring through space," I tell my mom. I called her after opening the card from Edna. "And we are spinning at the same time. We spin a thousand miles a minute."

"Why don't we feel like we're moving?" she asks.

"Because it's constant. If it stopped, we would feel it. It would be like being in a car when someone slams on the brakes."

She starts to reply, "That makes a lot of sense . . ."

I glance over my apartment as she chats. I pause, overcome with an abrupt, eerie feeling. I smell a faint, unfamiliar cologne.

I look over my shoulder and gasp.

"What? What happened?" she asks.

"Sorry." I laugh, putting a hand to my chest. "I thought I saw someone standing in my apartment, but it was just my bookcase."

✳

I am adding synonyms to the broken search tool. Rather than continue to troubleshoot the problem, I am feeding the tool words as if it is working. Sometimes, when things are broken, I find they fix themselves if you just pretend that they are fine and give them time.

An episode of my podcast is playing. This episode is about a man who snuck into women's bedrooms at night to watch them sleep. He killed them if they woke up. If they slept through his observation, he said that meant God spared them. His name was Jeff, though, not God.

I jump. Vin just entered my cubicle. I didn't hear him approaching. I was listening to my podcast, and my desk is positioned so that my bad ear faces the opening to my cubicle. I am often startled when people appear beside me.

He is holding two plates of cake.

"It's someone's birthday." He hands me a plate. It has a slice of white sheet cake on it.

I take my headphones out. "Whose?"

"I don't know. The part of the cake with the name on it was eaten," he says. He did not bring us forks and is scooping his piece into his mouth with his fingers.

I follow suit and ask, with fingers and cake in mouth, "Do you think you can sense when someone's watching you?"

"Yeah, I can. The hairs on the back of my neck stand up. Why?"

I shrug.

He looks at me. "Maybe you should get a mirror for your cubicle, so you aren't so startled when people walk up behind you."

I cover my mouth. "No way. Everyone will think I'm hiding something and need to guard that I'm slacking off. They'll think I'm a bad employee, or that I do weird things at my desk."

He snorts. "You're half-deaf. I think it's reasonable to not want to be scared."

＊

I dream that I am Ted Bundy. I have put my arm in a sling. Everyone keeps calling me handsome. When I look in the mirror, though, I see a ghoul.

"Do you find me handsome?" I ask the woman I have tied and bound in my passenger seat.

She nods. She cannot say yes because I have gagged her.

"Now, be serious," I say. "Are you just being nice because I've tied and gagged you?"

She shakes her head.

"You really think I'm handsome?"

✳

My date for this evening is named Kae. They are leaning on a shiny white car outside my apartment. We matched on a dating app, and they invited me to go for a drive. They told me they just got the keys to their new car and that I could be the first to ride shotgun.

I wave. "Kae?"

"Enid?"

I smile. "Nice car."

"You like it?" They lean on the open door next to me. "I drove this shitty used hatchback before it for like ten years. Driving this feels like driving a Ferrari."

I do not know anything about cars so I say, "I like the color."

Most rockets are painted white so that they reflect sunlight. It helps keep the cryogenic fuels inside the rockets cold, especially prior to launch.

Kae shuts my door and skips around to the other side of the car while I stew in the shame of complimenting the plain, boring color white. Should I tell them rockets are usually white? They jump inside, turn on the radio, and hum along to music while pulling out into the road.

"So, tell me more about you," Kae says, turning down the radio.

My approach to dating is to say as little as possible. I find people fill in the gaps with what they want. They imagine I am whoever they decide I am. I used to be too quiet. I learned as I aged that I need to say what needs to be said to keep conversations rolling. I give brief answers and then I ask questions. I say things like, "That's interesting, tell me more about that."

"I work for the Space Agency," I say. "What about you? Where do you work?"

"The Space Agency? Wow, that must be neat."

"Yeah, what about you? Where do you work?"

"I work for the garden center off Elm."

"Oh, that's interesting, tell me more about that."

They drive us through the city while discussing fiddle-leaf fig trees and orchids. They tell me that their living room is like a greenhouse. I say, "Wow, I would love to see that." I look forward as they chat about plant food and share that they recently got a tattoo of an African violet on their ribs.

"Would you like to get some ice cream? There's this new place a few blocks away."

"Sure—"

A car swerves next to us and honks.

"What the fuck?" Kae grips their steering wheel.

The car zooms in front of us and starts erratically braking, like the driver wants us to crash into them.

"What is going on?" Kae brakes to prevent an accident.

"I don't know," I say, repositioning my seat belt on my chest.

I squint at the driver. His face is red. He is screaming and gesturing at us. His eyes are bulging out of their sockets. He's bald—

"This fucking idiot." Kae gives him the finger. "I must have done something I didn't notice that pissed him off. He's road raging. What the fuck, buddy! This is fucking dangerous! This is a brand-new car!"

I smell something burning. The bald man's head is reflecting a glow from the streetlights. I hold the sides of my seat, bracing myself as if I am on a raft at the edge of a waterfall.

The man brakes again. I close my eyes. The image of his burnished head plays across my eyelids. My heart races. Kae furiously lays on their horn. We are both taken aback when their car lets out a feeble *meep*. It sounds like the noise a deflating balloon makes when a little air escapes. After registering the sound, our eyes connect, and we both burst out laughing.

Kae has tears in their eyes. "Was that *my* horn?"

The humor of the *meep* is amplified by the intensity of the bald man's anger, and by the fact that Kae had furiously decided to honk. The passion of the moment has been completely punctured by the wimpy *meep*.

The angry driver is now next to us. His head is still glistening. His window is rolled down, and he is barking at us, but we are ignoring him because we are too consumed with the hilarity of the *meep*.

Kae is cackling, tears rolling down their cheeks. I haven't inhaled properly since it happened. I fan my face with my hands.

The man thinks we are laughing at him. His face is turning redder and redder. It looks as if it is about to pop. Kae honks the horn again, and I almost pee my pants.

After spitting inaudible threats at us out his window while we continue cry-laughing, the incensed driver finally peels off.

✳

Kae and I are hooking up in their car. They were asking me questions about myself, so rather than answer, I put my hand on their knee. We are parked on the outskirts of a forest. Our windows are rolled down and it's cold. I am on top of them in the driver's seat. I can see pine trees through the back window. The gaps between the trees are so dark that the forest looks almost black. I start to wonder what animals live in there. I wonder if there are wolves.

The radio is playing "After Hours" by the Velvet Underground.

I see a shadow in the forest between the trees. Is that a bear? Or is it a person?—

The song reaches the bridge where it says, "Dark party bars, shiny Cadillac cars, and the—"

MEEP.

I shriek. My butt just set off the horn.

Kae laughs. I have a hand to my chest. The noise scared me.

I roll off them into the passenger seat, and we both laugh so loudly it echoes around us through the woods like we are hyenas.

✳

We pull up outside my building. Kae says, "It was nice to meet you. I would love to get to know you better. Would you like to do this again sometime?"

I look out the window before unclicking my seat belt. I notice a man skulking next to the entrance.

I stall.

"Are you good?" Kae asks.

"Yeah," I lie while straining to climb out of the car, still eyeing the man.

"It was really nice to meet you," they say.

"You too," I reply quietly, shutting the door softly behind me.

I look at the figure by the door. My palms are sweaty.

I stand still. I live on the first floor. My window faces the side alley between my building and the one next to it. I wonder if I could get inside through my window.

I march to the side of the building.

My windows are a bit high off the ground, but I am tall.

I stand on the tips of my toes and reach to see if I can slide the windowpane open.

The glass inches with my fingers, indicating the window is unlocked. This is both good and bad news because I could have sworn I locked it.

I find a garbage can and tip it over. Trash spews across the concrete. A water bottle half-full of what I hope is lemonade rolls ahead of the rest of the garbage. An apple core and the corpse of a Happy Meal struggle to race the bottle while I balance on the unstable garbage can like it is a step stool. I almost fall but manage to shift my weight by stretching out my arms. I feel a dent form beneath me. I reach my fingers out as far as I can. I slide the glass pane open. I then muster every ounce of my upper body strength to lift myself over the windowsill. I knock over a small potted cactus and lie with its dirt on my rug.

* * * * *

I hear scratching. I can't always pinpoint where a sound is coming from. Human brains know where sounds originate by which ear receives the sound first. It's called sound localization or directional hearing. Because I can only hear from one ear, I have difficulty figuring out where sounds originate. I think the scratching is coming from the hall.

I am lying under the covers in my bed, trying to sleep, but the noise keeps raising the hairs on the back of my neck. I have crawled out of bed, wrapped in my sheets, and tiptoed to peer out my peephole twice now.

It sounds sort of like someone's clothing brushing against the wall that separates my apartment from the hallway. I approach my door and stand with my hands on either side of the peephole. I have one eye peering out.

I see nothing in the hall besides the usual buzzing fluorescent lights and the door that faces mine. I turn around and mistake a coat on a hook for a person. I scream and punch it off the wall.

I look at it crumpled on the floor.

I don't want to sleep here alone tonight.

※

Blood rinses down my bathroom sink. I flossed too aggressively, and now my gums are bleeding. I have to clean my mouth because a woman from Tinder is coming over. I brushed my teeth and am now gargling with the brown version of Listerine, which is the most revolting and therefore, I suspect, effective.

The woman coming over is allegedly named Susan. I say allegedly because I don't trust her. "Susan" only had photos of her body in her profile. This is painfully suspicious. Under normal circumstances, I would not recommend meeting someone whose dating profile contains only body shots, but she was the first person to agree to sleep over.

I feel a little energized by the strangeness of hooking up with a person whose face I have never seen. She could be anyone. She might be beautiful. She might be hideous. She might have face tattoos, or a scar. Maybe she has an eye patch, who knows? She might be a celebrity.

I hope she isn't someone I know.

I open her profile and squint at her photos. She has dark skin, defined biceps, and thin wrists. Have I seen any of this before?

Hopefully she isn't a murderer. She looks quite small, so I think I could take her if so. Unless of course she comes with a weapon.

I have a metal baseball bat that I keep nearby in case someone attacks me. This is a safety tip I learned from one of my podcasts. I put a sock over the end of the bat, so that if my prospective attacker tries to grab the bat as I swing, they will not be able to grip it.

I hope she isn't a man using fake photos, pretending to be a woman. Predatory straight men are often on the women in-terested in women side of Tinder. Who knows what their end game is? I wouldn't put it past one of them to try to catfish me with a no-face profile though. I should probably reverse image search her photos—

I hear a knock at my door. It's too late.

I rush to look out the peephole to assess whether it is safe to let her in. I see that she does in fact match her pictures, and she is not someone I know. She is older than I would have guessed. She has strands of white in her hair, dark eyes, and a bump in her nose. She is very pretty.

I open the door and begin to say, "Hello," but she starts making out with me. She is shorter than I am but manages de-spite it to lift me up. I try not to deflate the moment by voicing concern for my safety. She is strong, but I am bigger than she is, and it is hard to repress the worry that she might drop me.

She carries me, stumbling to slam the door behind her, while I latch to her like a cat gripping a tree branch in a windstorm. She begins opening doors, presumably trying to find my bedroom. I can't direct her because I am mute with her mouth on mine. She opens a closet and the bathroom until finally resolving to drop us on the couch.

I land on the cushion, almost bouncing off, while she takes her shirt off.

I wonder what her story is.

※

While we have sex, I ask her if Susan is her real name, but she does not reply. I can't tell if she is ignoring me, or if she is just bad at multitasking.

After a few minutes pass, I say "Susan?" to see if she will react—sort of like trying out names on a lost dog.

She does not react.

I consider trying other names. I look at her and squint. What names suit her?

"Luna?" I try.

"Who?" She stops and squints back at me.

"No one," I say.

"Are you calling me by someone else's name?"

"No. I was just—never mind. It doesn't matter."

"My name isn't Luna," she says pointedly.

She is offended.

"Sorry. What is your name, then?"

"It was on my profile. It's Susan."

"Well, yeah, I saw that, but I was just wondering if you lied."

"Why would I lie?"

"Because you only had body photos on your profile."

She squints harder. "So what?"

"So that's weird," I explain. "That's not normal."

"My name *is* Susan. I just didn't have any good photos of my face."

✳

After we finish, she has a shower. She pops her head out of the bathroom to ask if she can use my shampoo. I say, "Yes, of course, help yourself to anything."

I cleaned my apartment quickly before she came over. I scrubbed the shower, refilled the soap dispenser, and Windexed all the mirrors. I intentionally left one mug out on my coffee table so it wouldn't look too staged.

While the water runs, I look around my apartment to see if I missed tidying anything. I look at her pants, balled up on the floor. I stand up and check her pockets for a wallet. I rummage through it for ID. I find she has a coupon for a spa and a photo of a baby. Is that her baby? After rifling more, I find her driver's license.

Her name really is Susan. She didn't lie. For some reason, that disappoints me. I wanted her to be lying.

When she comes out of the shower, I help her blow-dry her hair. I put a little product in it to style it. After she is dressed, I have her sit at my table. I point a lamp and my phone camera at her. I spend about forty minutes directing her to pose. I tell her to think of something funny. "Look candid," I say. I take about sixty pictures of her until finally capturing a flattering yet honest shot of her smiling.

I show her the photo. She says, "Thank you. I love it."

While lying next to her in bed, I smile when I peek over

her shoulder. I can see her updating her dating profile with the picture.

✳

I dream that Susan lied and that she was a predatory man who came to murder me. As she attacked me, I shouted, "Susan!" in the same way that I might shout a rabid dog's name if I knew it. As if knowing his name was Susan might calm him down.

"Susan!"

"Heel, Susan!"

"This isn't you!"

✳

In the morning, while Sue buttons her pants and slips into her shoes, I say, "I would walk you out, but I'm afraid of my neighbor."

She laughs as she ties her laces. She thinks I'm joking.

"It was lovely meeting you," she says before leaving.

"You too." I smile before shutting the door and locking the dead bolt behind her.

✳

A man in an orange vest spots me climbing out my window. Rather than mind his own business, he watches me struggle to lower myself to the concrete. He sips his coffee and bites his bagel while I topple, fall, and land on my butt.

I believe that had I not had a spectator, I would not have fallen. Being watched always makes me trip. I can cook on my own, but I always burn myself when someone else is in the kitchen.

Despite that, I smile at the man when I pass him. I pretend as if I don't blame him for my falling. As if I don't think it is rude to watch people privately climb out their own bedroom windows.

He laughs. "Is your door broken?"

I catalog his face in my mind where I track my grievances.

My father.

Gina.

Kids who were mean to me in elementary school.

All bald men.

Everyone named Josh.

Anyone I loaned a pen to who didn't return it.

People who don't like cats.

A lady who spoke to me for an hour and didn't tell me there was something in my teeth.

Men on the "women interested in women" side of dating apps.

My landlord and all landlords.

Married people who try to date me.

People who get on public transportation before waiting for other people to get off first.

This man in an orange vest.

I dust myself off. "I'm just trying to avoid a neighbor, actually."

He laughs. "That's crazy."

✳

My coworker Maveric knocks on my cubicle wall. I have my headphones in, but I feel my desk pulse under his knock, and I sense him standing behind me.

"Sorry to interrupt," he says as I take my headphones off. "Were you listening to love songs?"

What a strange comment. What does he mean by that?

I was listening to the gruesome murder of a hitchhiker. She was thrown from a bridge into a frozen lake, where her body was preserved for over a year before she was found by a fisherman.

"They want you to join a meeting on the tenth floor," he says. "They sent me to come get you. Are you free?"

*

"There's a bug," I tell the men in the boardroom. Each is wearing a suit in a different shade of blue. They are members of the executive management team. They asked me to come for an update on the search tool.

The room murmurs with proposed solutions.

I am not usually invited to meetings with these men. I prefer it that way. Being in this room requires I participate in small talk with people I have nothing in common with. They always ask me if I golf. My hobbies include listening to murder stories, having casual lesbian sex, and telling my mom interesting facts about space. I am not well-equipped to discuss skiing, sailing, and whatever other depraved hobbies occupy the time of opulent middle-aged white men.

Despite feeling uncomfortable here, I try to appear relaxed. I feel like I am on a stage. I feel pressure to perform, as if I am an actress wearing the mask of my own face, playing the role of a professional, put-together young lady.

I stretch nonchalantly, yawn, and maintain good but casual posture. I enunciate when I speak. While the room chatters, I take my jacket off and hang it on the back of my chair, despite feeling chilly. I do that because I think it makes me look professionally prepared but socially informal, which puts these men at ease. They think I must be comfortable. They don't know it's calculated.

When I was in middle school, I remember standing in front of my English class, forced to give a book report. I had cue cards that trembled in my hands as if I were presenting on windy bluffs and not in a still, silent classroom. I remember looking at my shaking cards, seeing the letters as if they were abstract art, and whispering, "I can't read."

My classmates laughed and I was humiliated. I have a YouTube video debriefing the matter, thank God. It would be a shame to not immortalize that traumatizing memory. In the video, I am adamant that I can in fact read. I find absolutely no humor in the matter. I hold up a book for the camera, titled *Spooky Stories*, and read sternly from it for my audience.

"*Chapter one*," I say firmly, holding up the page for the camera to demonstrate those were the words printed on the page.

I have addressed that sort of behavior. I do not think people see me the same way they did when I was younger. I have learned how to mimic manners I wish came to me naturally. I have to remind myself how people use their hands. A theater prompter lives in my head and shouts cues at me incessantly.

Don't touch your face.

Smile.

Say "Thank you."

Laugh.

Take your jacket off. Hang it on the chair.

Smile.

Smile.

Not too wide. No teeth.

One of the executives turns to me. "There's a new guy who might be able to help you with your search problem. He just started last week. I was on his interview panel. He's good. Real clever. He reminds me of you, actually. I can connect you."

I say, "Thank you. That would be great. What's his name?"

His lips move but the room is loud so I can't hear him.

"I'm sorry, can you please repeat that?" I ask.

He repeats himself, but I still don't hear him.

Rather than ask again, I say, "Thank you. I'll make a note of that."

✳

My mom and I are lying on the hood of my car. Our heads are resting on my windshield, leaning against the corpses of squashed fish flies and mosquitoes. We are parked on the outskirts of the city where there is less light pollution. The air here smells like churned dirt. We come here whenever there are worthwhile sky events. I keep track of when there are rare moon phases, and other events worth driving into a hayfield for.

The summer is almost over, and it is getting cool at night. My mom brought our orange knit blanket for us to sit under. My body is warm beneath the blanket, but the air on my face feels sharp. Tonight, there is supposed to be a meteor shower. We should spot ten to fifteen every hour. I have been monitoring the weather, worried it would be too cloudy, but the sky is clear. The moon, planets, and stars all look bright and stark.

"Did I ever tell you about the time I almost died in a hayfield?" she asks.

She has, but I say no because I like to listen to her tell stories.

"I was a teenager, and I was out with a boy. His name was Christopher Kent. There wasn't much to do in those days for kids our age. It would have been too expensive for us to go to dinner, and the closest movie theater was over an hour away. He was a farm kid, and he had no extra money. Now, I've never been too extravagant a date. You know me. I was happy to agree to go for a simple walk with him. It was almost fall, it was around this time of year actually, and it got darker sooner than we expected. We were out in the hayfield, just walking, when the sun started to set. I had, of course, dressed for the date. I had little kitten heels on and a skirt. Bless my heart. The heels, of course, got stuck in the dirt and it was getting darker and darker and darker. Christopher was starting to talk a lot about coyotes."

"Oh no," I say.

"Oh yes," she says. "That boy told me to walk barefoot because he wanted us to move faster. He said we had to rush because we were essentially prey for coyotes out there. And I remember thinking, *Why is this farm boy so afraid of coyotes?* I know sometimes coyotes kill people, but it's rare. They really aren't that big. You'd need a pack of them to attack you, and they're not that brave. They're usually afraid of people. Now, of course, as soon as I started to explain all of that to him, what did we see?"

"A coyote?"

"A pack of coyotes. And poor, cowardly Christopher—who I now appreciate was just a fifteen-year-old boy, but still—took off. He bolted! He abandoned me in that field with my kitten heels dug in the dirt!"

"What a charmer," I say.

"What a charmer, indeed. So, what did I do? I took my shoes off, like Christopher had suggested, and I smacked the heels together as loudly as I could to scare off the dogs. Dirt flew off my shoes into my hair, all over my clothes. And, of course, off the coyotes went, in the same direction as Christopher. At this point it was completely dark out. It was as dark as it is now."

It is very dark out now.

"I started to convince myself I had sicced those dogs on that poor fearful boy. By the time I got back to the farmhouse, I was grieving. I was certain I had killed him. Just as I was imagining having to break that dreadful news to his parents, I found him, crying on his front step. He thought he'd killed me."

She laughs.

I smile. "Did you ever go on another date with him?"

"Oh no, never. He ended up marrying a very strong-looking woman, and I am glad for it."

She pulls our orange blanket up further on her lap.

We look at the sky. She likes when I point out constellations. She has a hard time seeing them unless someone connects the dots for her.

I point. "There's Ursa Major."

"Where?" She squints. She has binoculars and her glasses hanging around her neck. She wears her glasses on a gold beaded chain.

"Right there." I point again.

She positions the binoculars where I directed her. She says, "Wow. What's that one of again?"

"It's of a great she-bear."

"Oh, lovely—wait. Isn't that the Big Dipper?" She lowers the binoculars.

"The Big Dipper is part of Ursa Major."

"Oh, right, of course." She looks up at it again. "Boy, it's got a lot going on, doesn't it? Do you know how many stars Ursa Major is made of?"

My mom is a retired early childhood educator. Sometimes, she asks me questions in the same tone she might use with a toddler. It is as if she's asking, *How do you spell* cat?, *Why is yellow your favorite color?* or *Why is sharing important?*

I don't mind it though. Sometimes she asks very complicated questions in that same tone. She doesn't mean to be patronizing.

"I'm not sure, actually," I say. "It's got fifty galaxies in it, though, I think."

"Galaxies?" she repeats, amazed.

We keep looking upward until she spots the first meteor.

She gasps and points, and I watch her face light up rather than the sky.

✳

It is after midnight. I dropped my mom off and returned to my apartment. I am parked at the front of the building, looking at the entrance and the alley. It is dark in the alley and bright by the front door.

When I was a kid, I would fixate on things that scared me. I thought of the sun exploding. I thought of fires. Murderers. I remember squeezing my eyes closed tightly, and reciting rhymes to prevent the thoughts from arising. I would whisper to myself rapidly, "*Do your ears hang low? Do they wobble to and fro?*"

I take my keys out of the ignition and hold them in my fist like a weapon. I grit my teeth and whisper, "Can you tie them in a knot? Can you tie them in a bow?"

I get out of my car and rush to the front door. I unlock it with the same vigor I would if someone followed me home. I make sure the door is bolted before I speed through the hall to my apartment. I whisper as I run, "Can you throw 'em o'er your shoulder like a continental soldier? Do your ears hang low?"

Once inside the apartment, with the dead bolt locked, I tell myself that I am crazy. I laugh and say aloud, "Boy, you are nuts."

✳

I have my laptop open on my chest. I type "YouTube" into the search bar, and then write my old username. Flowergirl69. I was the flower girl at my mom's friend's wedding. The 69 part is just an unfortunate random number, I think. I don't believe that I knew what reciprocal oral sex was when I was a kid. I'm not sure I really understood until I was twenty-three.

There is a mirror across from me. It's mounted to the top of my dresser. I can see myself now reflected in it, from the shoulders up. I can also see myself as an eleven-year-old girl in my computer, also from the shoulders up. It is as if me then and now are sitting next to each other.

Child-me slouches, chewing on strands of her hair, and yanking her T-shirt away from her torso. I have trained that sort of behavior out of me, like you might train a puppy not to nip, but deep down, under my spitless hair and straight posture, I am still that animal. I want to gnaw on the cuffs of my sweaters and let my hair drape over my eyes like a curtain.

Child-me is rambling about ghosts. I keep repeating myself. Stammering. I can't maintain eye contact. My eyes dart away from the camera while I say the same things over and over. I keep using the word "spectre." Spectre.

I glance at myself in the mirror. I mouth the word, *spectre*, and maintain eye contact with my reflection.

I have worked on myself since being a kid. I now carry myself, for the most part, like I am socially apt and confident. I am, in many ways, socially apt and confident. I started mimicking the behavior of confident people when I was a teenager, and I have worn that mask so long now that my face is melding with it.

There are parts of me I wish I could train out that I can't. You can train a dog not to bite, sit on the furniture, or piss in the house, but you can't train them to become birds. I don't like a lot of unalterable things about myself. Even when I'm not viewing footage of me on YouTube, I always feel sort of tortured as my own spectator. I want to boo, cringe, and splat rotten fruit at my own head until someone closes the curtains. I want to heckle that I wish I were someone different. I hate my voice. I hate the words I choose. I hate my instincts and the way I think. I hate that I am self-absorbed enough to hate myself in detail. I think I am a bad person. I feel self-loathing so deeply I think if I cracked myself open, I would see the physical manifestation of it calcified in my bones like a geode.

I feel sad watching myself as a kid. I was a weird, disoriented tadpole, and now I am this warty toad. Part of why I watch the videos is to see how it happened. I want to pinpoint when my little tadpole body grew big ugly toad legs and ribbited.

I click a new video. In this one, my skin looks inflamed. I had acne. There are scabs clustered on my forehead and chin. My cheeks are red, and my T-zone is so oily it looks reflective.

This is around the time I don't remember. Watching it feels like watching footage of me sleepwalking. It feels like I am watching myself in an alternate universe. I don't remember filming this. I don't remember being this age.

"*Welcome back to my skin journey,*" I tell my audience.

This video has forty-five views.

"*I know I look gross, but I'm working on it. My mom got me this,*" I say, holding up a bottle of green face wash.

It is strange to hear my voice come out of a child. It is my voice. It hasn't changed.

"*It hasn't done shit,*" I add.

I pause the video. I think I hear a noise. I cup my hand around my good ear and listen. Was the sound coming from the hall?

I stand up and walk over to my peephole. I look outside it and see nothing.

I exhale, turn around, and spot a pale bald face in my window.

I shriek and the face disappears.

CHAPTER FOUR

The bus is crowded. I am going to work despite not sleeping last night. I sat up on my couch, gripping my baseball bat. I watched two and a half seasons of *SpongeBob SquarePants* to stay awake. I now feel as if I am walking through the world dead. My eyes will not focus, and I feel skittish. I decided to take the bus out of consideration for the people I ran over in an alternative universe where I decided to drive.

The bus is a hostile environment right now. I feel wary of every person near me. Every time someone makes a sudden movement, I brace myself. A few minutes ago, a baby hurled their sippy cup across the aisle, and I flinched like she had thrown a grenade.

I am concerned that I imagined the bald face in my window.

It felt real, but I doubt my senses. I might have hallucinated. I have a history of that; I had that one incident with a ghost. I really believed I saw a ghost. I was afraid of them. I watched spooky ghost movies and fixated on them. I obsessed over how afraid I was of ghosts until it spiraled to the point that I manifested one in my bedroom.

I have been struggling lately with an irrational fear of bald men. It is possible that I am reliving my ghost problem. Maybe I'm imagining bald faces the way I imagined that ghost because I've been fixating on bald men, and my brain likes torturing me. Maybe this is all some complicated form of psychological self-harm. The meat in my skull wants me to suffer. Maybe I deserve to suffer.

The hairs on the back of my neck are standing up. I glance around me.

It is also possible that a pale bald man was peeping in my window last night.

I turn the volume of my murder podcast up. Maybe the podcast is making me more paranoid, but I appreciate that it drowns out my spiraling thoughts. This episode is about the Happy Face Killer. He identified himself via graffiti in a public washroom. The washroom was located in exactly the setting I suspect all serial killers frequent. A Greyhound bus station.

"*Two people had been wrongly convicted of his crime. This seems to cause a conflicting predicament for egomaniac killers. They think they evaded prison due to their expert killing skills, but simultaneously feel bummed that they didn't get the credit.*"

It is strange to me when killers want credit for their murders, as if it is an accomplishment. Killing someone is not much of a feat. It is simple, logistically, to kill someone. People die pretty easily.

I glance around.

Unless you are killing someone who has an armed guard, like a president or a mob boss, I do not get the sense of achievement. A person who murders someone is really just proving that they can do what everyone else assumes they can without needing proof. Even when I factor out all the moral and practical reasons why killing someone sucks, I believe it is more of an accomplishment to never kill someone.

I flinch when the man next to me adjusts his backpack on his shoulder.

"*In the bathroom, the Happy Face Killer wrote the name of the woman he killed, the date he killed her, and how he killed her. He also said he loved it. He said, 'Yes, I'm sick, but I enjoy myself, too. People took the blame and I'm free.' He then drew his signature smiley face.*"

The podcast goes on to explain that his bathroom graffiti did not generate the stir he desired. He ended up writing letters to media outlets. Finally, after two failed suicide attempts—solidifying what an amateur killer he truly was—he was arrested.

I reach my stop. I weave through the crowd of people to the door. Their bodies brush against mine. I scratch the back of my neck, climb off the bus, and glance behind me at the other passengers getting off, as if they are all suspects in a lineup.

✳

I brought Vin a coffee. I am hovering by his cubicle like a moon while he takes the plastic lid off and blows into it. Steam wafts from it like dry ice.

"Blonde roast?" he asks.

I nod.

I came here to tell him about my peeping Tom, but I am hesitant now. I think I imagined it. I am worried that he will think I am crazy.

I watch him sip his drink.

If I am murdered, I bet Vin will be in the documentary. I wonder what he will say about me. He is nice to me, so I think he would lie. I think he would say flattering things. He might even talk me up. He might say I was a good friend. A good person. He wouldn't even allude to my parasite.

I taste my coffee.

"Would you say I light up a room?" I ask.

He chokes. "What?"

"I noticed from my podcast that women who light up rooms get murdered."

He laughs. "You've got nothing to worry about."

※

My boss, Fergus, knocks on my cubicle wall. "George Fox is here."

I jump. I didn't expect Fergus to appear behind me. I had a website listing local sex offenders open.

"I thought the three of us could try to put our heads together to resolve the bug," he adds. "Do you want to join George and me in my office?"

"Who is George?" I ask, confused.

"He's the man the execs recommended we connect with about the search tool. Remember?"

"Oh. Yeah. Of course. Sorry. I'll be right there," I say, trying to position myself in front of my monitor.

I was looking at the sex offenders to see if any match the face I saw in my window.

He leaves while I gather myself. I exit the sex offender registry, collect my notebook, and grab two pens in case one dies.

I walk into his office, ready to greet George, and scream. George is bald.

"Jesus Christ, what's wrong?" Fergus says.

There isn't a single strand of hair on his head.

"Sorry," I say, breathless. "S-something startled me."

"What?" he asks.

"A spider," I lie.

"Where?" George asks, looking over his shoulder. The top of his head seamlessly flows into the nape of his neck like he is a monstrous earthworm.

"I-it ran."

"Jesus Christ." Fergus laughs. "You scared the shit out of me."

"Sorry."

His laugh tapers. "It's okay. This is George. George, Enid."

Sorry, George, I mouth.

George smiles. I smell something burning. Am I about to have a seizure?

"It's okay," he says. I think. I can't hear him well. "I'm afraid of spiders too."

Good. Now I know his weakness.

"Have a seat," my boss says, gesturing at us to occupy chairs next to each other.

I pull my chair as far away as possible from George before sitting down. I then pretend to listen to them talk about the search tool, while trying to ignore the warning signs of a seizure. Every time George moves, I recoil. I pretend to write things in my notebook, but really, I just write the word "fuck" over and over and over.

*

The ladies' room has a rusty tampon dispenser affixed to the wall. When the machine releases my tampon, I clutch it and retreat to a stall as if I am a racoon coveting a handful of stolen cat kibble.

Today is day twelve of what I once naively believed was my period but now, after careful googling, believe is either the side effect of a cancerous lesion on my uterus, or of a terminal STD. I thought my period stopped a few days ago. I hooked up with both Kae and Susan believing I was in the beginning of my free days. I now feel concerned about what they went through. I don't think there is anything wrong with having sex on your period, but I would not have chosen to do so with a total stranger without so much as warning them first.

My period is normally seven days long. Since googling why it has not stopped, I have learned that apparently most people's periods are two to seven days. If I weren't staring down the barrel of uterus cancer right now, along with dealing with all the other horrors of today, I would be pretty miffed that my life's dice roll landed on seven-day periods when some people are out there rolling lucky twos.

*

"Are you feeling okay?" Vin asks.

His desk is covered in papers.

"No," I say. "I feel faint and brittle. Do I look like a porcelain doll?"

He examines my face. "You are very pale, but you're covered in rat tattoos. I've never seen a doll like that."

I scowl.

"What's wrong?"

I consider telling him. I consider confessing that I saw a bald face in my window, that I have had my period long enough to gestate an opossum, and that I think Fergus saw my computer screen open to local sex offenders.

He asks, "Is your mom wearing lipstick?"

He knows about my mom.

"I don't know." I avoid looking at him. "I'm feeling off. I think I might be seeing things. And I was weird in a meeting earlier. I wrote the word 'fuck' over and over in my notebook rather than take minutes. And I think I might have uterus cancer or like a terminal STD— "

"You think you might have *what?*"

I look at him.

"You're going to the doctor," he says sternly, like a parent.

✳

The paper sheathing covering the exam table beneath me tears under my weight. The clinic is cold. I came here to announce that I am seeing things and desperately need to be committed, but then I chickened out. Instead, I just told the nurse about my period and hoped somehow she could tell the rest.

I have tucked my underwear into the pocket of my jeans, folded my sweater and placed it carefully over my pants. I adjusted the clothing pile twice before finally sitting back down on the examination table. Even though I am about to lie naked, legs open, on this table in front of another human who will be examining my cervix, I still feel compelled to ensure that same human does not see even a hint of my underwear.

The doctor gives a courtesy knock before entering the room. He then shuffles in, says "Hello," and shuts the door behind him. I look up to return his hello, but before I can open my mouth, I smell smoke.

The doctor is bald.

"How are you today, Enid?"

It's fine, I tell myself, panicked. I am having heart palpitations. I have hot flashes, and I can't catch my breath.

Stay calm. You're being ridiculous. He's a doctor, I tell myself. *You're fine.*

My eyes connect with his. I feel like I am staring directly into the sun. I smile too widely to veil how upset I am.

He has a scab on the top of his head.

"How are you?" he repeats.

I wonder how he got that scab. Maybe someone clawed at his head while he attacked them.

"I-I'm deaf in one ear," I spit out, panicked. I say this to explain why I didn't answer his question the first time. I am pretending I didn't hear him.

"Oh, are you? Okay! Sorry! So! I hear you're having some bleeding issues!" he screams.

I continue to smile. This is my disguise. If I grin, he won't suspect anything is off. It will distract him.

"Yes," I choke out.

His bare, misshapen head is close to me. There are prominent bumps in his skull.

"Okay! Well! Let's get you checked out! Please put your feet in the stirrups!"

I wish I didn't accidentally oblige him to yell at me. I comply but feel how I imagine I would while taking directions from a murderer asking me to lie in the trunk of their car. It would take less self-control for me to scream right now than it is taking for me to bite my tongue.

Stop it, you're fine, I tell myself. *You're being nuts. He's just bald. Who cares if he's bald?*

A separate voice in my bones replies gravely: *I do*. I can't help it. I know it's not a very nice fear to have. He can't help that he's bald. It's not his fault. It might be a sensitive topic for him.

I close my eyes while he puts vagina equipment in me. I try to imagine I am somewhere else. I am on a desert island, a paradise where every man has hair. My legs are shaking. He keeps trying to make small talk with me.

"It's pretty sunny out today, isn't it!"

"Mhm," I reply.

"I'm thinking of going to the beach tomorrow!"

"That sounds nice," I manage to whisper, despite the image of this man at the beach being akin to a gory horror scene.

※

Vin texts me.

How are you feeling?

The doctor said I likely have hormone irregularities and has prescribed me birth control. He said that he would like me to come back in two months to see how I am adjusting. I replied, "Thank you, I will," but the truth is that I have no intention of ever returning. The next time I see that man will be at his home, in the fiery pits of hell.

I write back to Vin,

Who is this?

He replies,

Ha ha. Hope you're feeling better.

＊

The pharmacist dispensing my birth control asked to speak to me in the private corner of the pharmacy. There, she says, "If you miss a pill, make sure you use alternative protection."

"I'm actually not taking it as birth control. It's just for my hormones."

"Yes, well, it's still important that you know—"

"No, sorry," I try to explain, "you don't understand—"

"It'll just take me a minute."

"No, but I—"

She sighs. I've annoyed her. "Please, miss, let me finish. It's my job."

I reply "Okay," uncomfortably, then listen to her while she tries to shill me spermicide and explain when to come in for the morning-after pill.

"Got it?" she asks.

"Got it," I say while shoving the pills into my bag, afraid that if I don't leave quickly, she will make me watch her demonstrate how to put a condom on a banana.

I add "rude pharmacist" to my list of grievances.

As I shuffle out of the automatic front door, a woman's voice shouts, "Enid!"

I spin around. I spot Polly walking toward me. I stop walking and wait for her to come to me in the vestibule separating the store from outside.

"What are you doing here?" She moves into the entrance with me.

We are in a pharmacy. Does she want me to tell her my sickness? I guess I was recently sleeping with her wife. Maybe that entitles her to my health records.

"Well, this is going to sound funny," I explain. "But it's for my hormones. I've had my period for like twelve days—"

An old man says, "Excuse me," as he tries to exit the store.

I shift out of his way while I finish answering her. "I was getting birth control."

The old man pauses instead of exiting. He furrows his brow and shoots me a dirty look.

"What's your problem?" Polly confronts him.

I look at her, surprised.

The man starts shouting. He, like me, must not have expected a combative response to his dirty look. Old men often give me dirty looks, and I have never responded by doing anything more than grit my molars and lean into my deafness.

I can't make out what he's saying. I think I hear the word "whores."

Before I can mentally add his name to my list, Polly rolls her eyes. "Mind your own business! She's taking birth control because she's been bleeding for weeks, sir. Have you ever bled from your genitals for weeks?"

He is so shocked he almost falls over. His mouth is ajar. He is trying to scurry away from us, as if Polly has just revealed that she is an old-man killer and she is gunning for him next.

She exhales loudly as he leaves. Through the glass, I watch him stumble, flustered, to his car. She turns to me and says, "Anyways," casually, as if what she just did wasn't startling. "I used to take the pill too. It makes period pain less agonizing. It's nice also if you hook up with some trans women."

"T-thank you," I sputter. "I hadn't thought of that."

I feel stunned by how brazen Polly just behaved.

"I'm divorcing Joan," she announces.

"Oh," I reply, examining her face to gauge how to react.

"I saw what you texted her after I visited you," she adds. "I respect that. Thank you."

I don't know how to reply. Should I say, "You're welcome"?

"Am I too old for you?" she asks.

I try to form words, but she speaks again before I can process the question.

"I would like to take you out for dinner if you'd be interested. Am I too old for you?"

She waits for my response, but I am unable to form one.

"You can say if I am, it's okay."

"No," I say. "You're not."

She grins. "Okay. I'll call you."

※

"Can I help you find something?"

There is a wall of security equipment in front of me. Rather than return home defenseless, to where I saw a bald man in my window, I came here.

"Which lock would you recommend?" I ask the hardware store employee.

"That depends." He puts his thumbs under his suspenders. "What are you looking to lock up?"

"Myself," I say.

He looks at me.

"I want an additional lock for my apartment, for extra security," I clarify.

He makes a *hmm* noise, then says, "Well, you could add a chain lock."

I eye the chain locks.

"I got my daughter this." He gestures to another type of

lock. "It's a portable lock. You can use it at hotels, too. Any-where you're unaccustomed. Do you travel much?"

"Sometimes," I say, looking at the lock.

"Have you ever heard stories about young women being at-tacked by hotel employees with the keys to their rooms?"

Without missing a beat, I say, "Yes, I have." I take a lock off the wall. "Thank you, I'll buy this."

✳

The portable lock is a metal contraption that you slide through the crack in your door by the doorknob. It makes it impossible for anyone to open the door, even people with keys. I have just inserted it into my door and am now jiggling my doorknob to test it. I wish that I could test it from outside. It seems to work, though.

I also bought a security bar for my window. The bar makes it so the window cannot slide open from outside. Now, for an intruder to get inside my apartment while I am inside it, they would have to break the glass in my window or axe down my door. Assuming, of course, they are not a ghost, or a symptom of my insanity.

✳

Edna texted me a childhood picture of Kira.

She wrote,

Don't you think Kira kind of looks like you here?

I zoom in on the photo.

I write,

She's way cuter.

I add,

And I hope you didn't send this text to her. It's an insult.

She replies,

Hahaha. It is not! Send me photos of you as a kid. I bet you two
are twins.

I scroll through my camera roll. The only childhood photo
I can find of me is when I cut my own bangs. My hair is uneven
and choppy. I'm wearing a purple tracksuit, and a pin that says
LITTERING IS TRASH; however, the light is hitting the pin so that
LITTERING IS is obscured. It looks like I'm wearing a name tag
that says TRASH.

Despite that, I send the photo to Edna. It proves my point,
at least.

She replies, with pink swirling heart emojis,

This is the cutest picture I've ever seen.

I breathe air out my nose.

So, you're a liar?

She writes,

Hahaha.

I smile at my phone, happy to be having a good interaction
with Edna. After I set my phone down, I glance out my window.
I look at the alley between my apartment and the building next
to it. The streetlight on the sidewalk casts some light into the
darkness, but there are shadows. There are places where the light
doesn't touch.

I pick up my phone again.

Edna texted me. She wrote,

I wish I knew you when we were kids.

I read the text twice, then I call my mom.

"Hi Mom."

"Hi honey. What's up?"

"Nothing. Did you know 'spaghettification' is a legitimate term in astrophysics?"

"Is it? I didn't know that. What does it mean?"

"It's when objects are stretched when they contend with differences in gravitational forces, like black holes."

"Yikes. Can people be spaghettified?" she asks.

I pull at my window to test it can't be opened.

"Yes," I say.

"Would it hurt?"

"Yes."

✴

"Listening to love songs again?" Maveric asks.

I am sitting in the break room listening to a story about a woman dismembering her husband. She cut off his penis first.

I look at him. "You know me."

Vin overhears as he enters the room behind Maveric. He gives me a look that means, *What?*

I give him one back that means, *Don't ask.*

Vin sits down with me. "How are you feeling?" he asks.

"I'm feeling much better, thank you," I say. My period finally stopped, and I have not seen a bald man in twenty-four hours, though I am afraid to jinx that. I am worried about running into bald George at work. I haven't actioned any of his suggestions to fix the search tool because I didn't listen to them. I'm worried that he is going to appear at my desk, angry that I haven't done anything he recommended.

"How's Omar doing?" I ask.

"Oh, he's still reeling about the whole sister-mom thing. He feels betrayed. I've been trying to comfort him by comparing his family to mine. I've been saying, 'Okay, sure, your mom is really your sister, but at least they accept you!' My family won't even meet him. I've been going to my mom's house, bringing her dinner almost every night because she has not been cooking for herself, and still—if I so much as allude to my homosexuality it is as if I've just spit in her face. And yet I'm the one who helps her. My siblings rarely even call. Imagine thinking my hetero-sexual dirtbag brother is morally superior to me when I'm out here buying the woman her fucking toilet paper."

Vin's mother is mentally ill, and he loves her despite her homophobia.

"But Omar's okay?" I rib.

He breathes air out his nose. "Yes, he's fine, thank you. He would like to meet you."

"Already? Things must be getting serious."

Maveric interrupts from across the room. "Hey, did you two hear that we're starting up an office fantasy football league? It is going to be clutch. You want in?"

Vin and I exchange a look.

I do not know what the word "clutch" means, though I hope it means, "It's going to be something I never bother you about again."

"No, but thank you so much for the offer," Vin says for both of us.

"George is in," Maveric says. "Have you two met him yet? He just started. Seems like a great guy. He's on the tenth floor."

Vin says, "No, I haven't," and I don't reply.

✳

My mom is sitting on a step stool in front of her oven. She has turned the oven light on and is watching a loaf of yellow bread rise. It's dusk. She does not have the kitchen light on. The room is dim besides the glow that comes from the window in her oven.

"The key with bread," she says, "is to watch it."

She says the key to everything is to watch it. *The key to pasta is keeping an eye on it*, or *A watched pot always boils*.

"Bread takes a long time to bake, doesn't it?" I ask cautiously.

She stares into the oven. "It does."

I sit down on the floor next to her. I look through the window in the oven at the growing hill of dough. I stare at the coils on the floor of the appliance. I think of how hot they would be to touch.

"I bought extra security stuff for my apartment," I say, transfixed by the coils. I think of old-fashioned gas ovens, the ones people killed themselves with by putting their heads inside. "I got a portable lock and this security bar for my window."

My mom often talks to me about how to protect myself. She taught me to walk with my keys in my hands. I learned to hold them in a fist—so the spike comes out through my curled pinky finger. She calls it the hammer grip. If you hold your keys between your fingers, you can hurt yourself when you stab an attacker. You stab with more strength and less risk if you hold your keys in a fist. If someone attacks you from behind and restrains you, you can smash your fist backward into their thigh or their balls, if they have them.

She says, "That's my girl. You can never be too safe."

I consider mentioning that I saw a face in my window. I wonder if she would think I imagined it. I open my mouth to tell her but pause.

Her clothes are sitting loosely on her, and her eyes look tired. She has an oversized T-shirt on. She usually wears more eccentric outfits, even when she is just cooking or cleaning the house.

I say, "You're not wearing lipstick."

She says, "Yeah, you caught me at a bad time."

✳

"Do you want the red or the white?" Polly asks.

We are at a restaurant for dinner.

"I like both," I say. "Which would you prefer?"

"Red," she tells me and the waitress hovering above us.

The waitress takes the drink menu from our table.

Polly looks at me. She says, "I want to apologize to you for how I acted when we first met. You must have such a strange impression of me."

She sits in a way that takes up space. Her arm is leaning on the chair beside her. She's thrown her bag and her coat on another chair.

She flags down a waitress. "Could we have some more bread, please?"

"Of course." The waitress takes our basket.

"Do you think I am an insecure defeatist?" She looks at me again.

"Why would I think that?"

She just confidently asked a waitress for something. It takes me five minutes or more of mentally reciting what I will say before I even look at a waitress. I once ate an entire rack of ribs when I had ordered a tomato sandwich.

"Because I cried in your bathtub after drinking two beers."

I exhale out my nose. "I think coming to your wife's mistress's apartment immediately after discovering that she's been cheating on you radiates confidence."

She laughs loudly and sits up in her chair.

I think she must have a bizarre impression of me too. On top of meeting me because I was hooking up with her wife, she came into my house without me cleaning it first. I told her things she doesn't know I usually keep close to my chest, like that I have never really dated someone. Vin doesn't even know that.

"Let's pretend we didn't meet that way," I suggest.

She leans forward. "Okay, where did we meet, then?"

I think for a moment. "At an art gallery?"

"Oh? What was the exhibit?"

"It was impressionist art," I say.

"And who approached who?"

"You radiate confidence, so you approached me."

She smiles. "What was my pickup line?"

"You tell me."

She thinks, then says, "You could make an impression on Monet?"

I mock, "No wonder we're on a date now. How could I refuse that?"

She laughs loudly. She doesn't try to muffle herself even though the restaurant is quiet. I laugh too, but I do it softly. I rein myself in.

The waitress brings us more bread. Polly says, "Perfect, thank you."

I think of her thanking me outside my apartment after I washed her hair. I think of her red eyes and of her body shaking on the floor of my unbleached shower.

She rips a piece of bread in two and dips one half in a ceramic pot of melted butter. She says, "So, Joan's packed all her things. She keeps trying to take things that are mine. She tried to take my little brass sculpture of a beetle. She almost took a painting my grandmother made. She insisted she bought it in an art show until I drew her attention to the signature. She is being ridiculous."

The waitress returns to pour a splash of wine into Polly's glass. I watch as Polly sips it, pauses, then gestures to fill our glasses. The waitress smiles as she pours.

I have never had to sip wine before accepting a full glass. I am trying not to reveal that to Polly, but I am tempted to ask her if I should be upset. Any time I have ordered wine, it has been given to me whether I liked my first sip or not. Have I been taken advantage of?

"Are you okay?" she asks.

"Yes. Uh. Cheers to divorcing Joan." I hold my cup up.

We clink glasses.

She adds, "I am also happy to report that I found out I do not have MS, and that I get to keep the house, crumbling foundation and all."

We clink our glasses again.

"Cheers."

She sips her wine, smiling. "Did you get to know Joan well?"

I shake my head. "No."

"What did you two talk about?"

We did not talk much. I am hesitant to admit that because it suggests that we spent our time together sexually. That is true, but it is also true that I tend not to be too chatty regardless.

"Sports," I lie. I hope there aren't any further questions.

"Sports?" she repeats.

"Yeah, like hockey. Baseball. You know. Sports."

She narrows her eyes. "You hardly spoke, didn't you?"

I sip my wine, and she cackles. I listen to her continue to vent about her divorce when the hairs on the back of my neck raise. I glance around the restaurant. I feel like someone is watching us.

"Don't ever get married, Enid. It's a trap." Polly's voice swims into my awareness while I continue to scan the room for eyes.

"Hello?"

"Enid?"

"Earth to Enid?"

I scratch the back of my neck and apologize. "Sorry, I felt like someone was looking at us. Do you ever feel like that?"

She glances around. "Sometimes."

I scratch my neck again. I then look at her in the eyes and say, "Okay, sorry, go on."

Suddenly, ice water is splashed in my face. I don't know what happened. I put my hands up. People are yelling. "What the fuck!" Polly is shrieking. Silverware clinks. Glass breaks. Someone is dabbing my face with a towel.

I open my eyes. Joan is here. She and Polly are standing, screaming into each other's faces. She must have thrown water in my face.

The waitress is trying to help me. "Would you like to go to the washroom?" she suggests quietly.

I stand up. Polly turns to me. "I am so sorry, Enid."

"You're on a date with my wife?" Joan roars.

Polly scoffs. "You can't just come and make a public scene like this, Joan! This is embarrassing! Neither Enid nor I belong to you! Grow up!"

"You're on a fucking date with this woman!" Joan screams at Polly, putting her index finger into the groove of Polly's shoulder. "This woman ruined our marriage!"

"Don't touch me!" Polly whips her hand off. "*You* ruined our marriage!"

The waitress escorts me to the washroom. She stands at the
door, arms crossed, like a very short, girlish bodyguard while I
bend beneath the hand dryer, attempting to dry my hair.

"I'm sorry about this," I say.

She smiles. "It's okay."

✳

"So, are you really into sports?" Polly asks from my couch. She
found me in the bathroom after she convinced Joan to leave.
She apologized profusely and asked if she could come over.

Once again, my apartment is not clean. I did not expect
her to come here, and I almost said no when she asked. There
is a hamper full of dirty laundry in the center of my unmade
bed, and the mirror in my bathroom has toothpaste splattered
on it.

I did not say no because I worried that she would interpret it as me blaming her for having water thrown in my face.
I wouldn't want her to think I was upset. Also, I can't tell if she
really wants to date me, or if she is just continuing to engage
with me out of curiosity—as part of mourning her relationship.
I think she might just want more insight into who her wife
cheated on her with. I can sacrifice the care I usually take if that
is the case.

I swallow. "No, I lied."

I glance at her. She has dark hair and a soft jawline. She
dresses in a way that implies she prioritizes that she is comfortable. She wears loose, oversized clothing.

"What things are you really into?" she asks.

I search my mind.

"True crime," I offer. I then begin to ramble, telling her

about a murder I recently learned about involving a policeman who threw his wife off a seventeenth-story balcony.

"No wonder you feel like someone is watching you," she says. "You consume too much disturbing content."

I look at her. "How do you know I feel like someone's been watching me?"

"You said so at dinner."

"Oh," I say. "Well, someone *was* watching us. Joan."

She cringes. "Oh yeah, you have a point. I guess you must have good intuition."

"What about you? Tell me about you."

I watch her hands as she answers. She has a gold ring on her thumb. She claps. "Well, I work for city hall, in the Parks Department. I have a master's degree in Parks and Recreation. I always thought I'd be an archaeologist because my dad is an archaeologist, but I love my job now. My mom is a retired piano teacher, and my sister is a speech pathologist. She has a daughter I love named Lucy. Um. I'm really into nature. I love bugs." She says that last part defensively, suggesting her affection for bugs has garnered negative reception in the past.

"Bugs?" I repeat. "That's interesting, tell me more about that."

"I love them," she says assertively. "Creepy crawling little multi-armed monsters. I'm obsessed. Did you know ladybugs can eat more than five thousand aphids in their lifetime?"

"I didn't. How long do they live?"

"Usually a year."

She rambles on about ladybugs, then touches my leg. "What about you? What other things do you like besides murder?"

I try to think quickly.

Fuck. Do I like things?

Finally, after taking way too long to formulate an answer, I spit out, "Cartoons."

I cringe. *Cartoons?*

"What kind of cartoons? Like adult comedy?"

I shake my head. "No, like, *SpongeBob*."

Why did I say that?

She laughs. "*SpongeBob SquarePants?*"

I suck on my front teeth with my tongue. "Is there another *SpongeBob?*"

She hits my knee.

I hit her knee back.

"Can I sleep over here?" she asks.

"Sure," I reply. "Why not?"

※

I sleep on my side, with my head bowed, my back curved, and my limbs bent and drawn to my torso. I sleep how I imagine someone might in the woods, protecting the vulnerable parts of their body from predators.

Polly sleeps with her arms out, as if she has been crucified. Her chest is open, exposed, and very susceptible to predators. I am balled up in the space left between her outstretched arm and leg. I keep watching my front door.

I can't tell if I am having a nightmare that I am seeing my doorknob rattle, or if I am actually seeing it. Did I add my extra security lock when Polly and I came in? I thought I did. Should I go check?

Polly stirs. I stare at the doorknob. I swear it looks like it's moving. Am I hallucinating? I think I might be dreaming.

She pulls me over her. I climb on top of her outstretched

body like she is a wooden cross, and I am being nailed to her. I am holding her wrists and bowing my head over her face. We kiss and it tastes like sour wine from dinner.

We didn't brush our teeth. I didn't have a spare toothbrush to offer her, so I said, "I won't brush my teeth either, so it's even," and she thought that was funny. I didn't realize she'd want to hook up. I would have approached this differently.

I thought she wanted to go out with me to better assess Joan's affair, but now I wonder if this is her trying to get over her marriage. Maybe I am a convenient stepping stone out of that stage in her life, on to something else.

I feel like a voyeur again, only like I have escalated and come inside to touch her things. I am watching her cycle through the private process required to get over someone. I am a participant in this personal crisis that I have no right to be involved in but have somehow inserted myself into. I feel like I am hiding in her closet and watching her have sex with me through the cracks in the door.

All the while, I feel simultaneously paranoid that someone is turning my doorknob. I look over my shoulder at the door while Polly bites my neck. The doorknob still looks as if it's turning slightly. Is that a trick of the light? Am I imagining it?

I say out loud, "Am I dreaming?"

Polly mistakes the question for bewilderment that she is hooking up with me, and is flattered. She laughs and says, "No, you're not."

❋

I dream that my childhood house is on fire. I am in my bedroom, putting my palms up against the door. I learned in school to touch doors before you open them when there is a fire. If they

are hot, don't open them. I hear my mom crying in her bedroom. I touch the door but it is hot, so I pause. I do not know
whether I should open it.

I think I will. I think I have to, right?

"I have to go to work." Polly's voice swims into my dream.

I open my eyes. She is standing next to the bed. "Thanks for
having me over. It was fun. I'll let myself out, okay?"

"Okay," I say, groggy.

I start to fall back asleep, but the second I hear the door shut
behind her I widen my eyes. I whip my blankets off and climb
out of my bed to lock the door. I rush to it, terrified by every
millisecond that passes with the door unlocked.

✳

"There she is!" Maveric shouts as Vin and I enter the break room.

We both stall in the doorframe as if we have come upon a
bear.

"I've got a bone to pick with you!" he says.

"What?" I ask.

"I went on a date last night with this chick who said she
used to see someone who works here. I thought she was going
to say Brad or Ralphie, but she said you! I couldn't believe it."

Vin scowls. "What couldn't you believe about that?"

"It's just a crazy small world," he says.

"What's her name?" I ask.

"Julie."

I'm not sure if I heard him right. I don't recall a Julie.

"What's her name?" I confirm.

"Julie," he repeats.

"What does she look like?"

"She's Cambodian. Has a short haircut. Tattoo of a duck on her wrist."

I don't recall her.

"Are you sure she said my name?"

"Yeah, she said you broke her heart."

Vin rolls his eyes. I can sense that he is annoyed that Maveric knows someone I dated, despite the fact that I do not remember her.

"It's going to be an awkward holiday work party this year, eh?" Maveric jostles my shoulder. I flinch at the unexpected physical contact. He laughs. "I'm just kidding. But I hope it's cool I'm seeing her?"

"It's fine," I say. "Godspeed."

Vin and I sit down, and Maveric leans above our table.

"So, do you remember what she likes?" he asks.

"What?" I look at him.

"Like, do you have any tips for dating her? Does she have a favorite flower or something?"

"I don't remember her."

He opens his phone and shows me a photo.

I squint at it.

"Oh," I say as I place her. We dated years ago. It was brief. "I remember her, yeah. She's nice. I didn't get to know her very well. I'm not sure what she likes. Sorry."

"What do you remember about her?" He sits down at the table.

Vin sighs loudly.

"Uh," I say. "We went to a live show of a true crime podcast we both liked once."

"Oh God." Maveric cringes.

"What?" I say.

"I hate that shit. What is it with you women and that? I feel like every female I talk to mentions she's into true crime like it's some original quirk. Like, we get it—"

Vin and I exchange a look.

I add both "Maveric" and "men who use the word 'female'" to my list of grievances.

I say, "You think the reason women have interests is to be quirky?"

"What? No, I didn't say that. I just mean liking true crime in particular isn't some oddity—"

"But why do you think a woman's objective in being into true crime is to be unique?"

He stammers, "Why are you yelling?"

I wasn't yelling.

"Are you into sports to be unique?" Vin asks.

He frowns. "You're both missing my point."

"I'm not," I say.

He looks at me. "You really think being interested in true crime is like being interested in sports? That's sick."

Vin says, "I've read women are into it because it's like a dress rehearsal. They're more fearful of violent crime than us because they're victims of it more often. They're taught not to walk alone at night or trust strangers. They have a reason to pay attention to those stories."

"Oh wow. I didn't know that," Maveric says.

Vin continues. "I think it also gives people a sense of relief that they aren't the victim."

Maveric looks at me. "Is that why you like it? Because you're happy you're not the victim?"

"Yeah," I say. "But it's also because I'm happy I'm not the perpetrator."

He laughs. He thinks I'm joking.

＊

Vin slides the shirts in front of him across the bar aggressively. We are at a thrift store. He invited me to shop with him after work.

"Maveric is the worst. Are you upset that someone you dated is seeing him? I would be devastated," he says.

I am inspecting a jacket that says BUCKETS, for some reason, on the arm.

I put the jacket down. "I barely remember the person he mentioned."

Is Buckets a surname?

"Still," he says.

I sense hostility from Vin. I think he is trying to insult me underhandedly for dating someone Maveric would, as a defense mechanism.

I hold up a T-shirt that says MISANDRIST on it in comic sans. Vin barely looks at it.

"It's got to bother you that someone who was into you is into him now, right? Like, what a nightmare. We should take bets on how long it takes him to crack a threesome joke." He makes a gagging gesture.

"Did you read this?" I ask, holding the shirt up again.

"Yeah, it's funny," he says, but he doesn't laugh. "You know who Maveric reminds me of? Every boy who bullied me for being gay growing up. Does he make you feel the same way? He has that vibe about him, doesn't he? Or is it just me? Does he remind you of the kids who bullied you for being deaf?"

I put the shirt down. "Yeah. Kind of."

A voice behind me says, "Enid? Is that you?"

I spin around. I see my sisters. Edna has her arms full of

baby clothes. Kira is pushing a cart with a wooden rocking horse in it.

Edna hugs me. Her stomach has popped. I feel it press into mine. Kira hugs me after. For both embraces, I am consumed with concern that I have BO.

"Shopping for the little one?" I ask.

Why did I say *little one*?

"You know it." Edna holds up a pink baby tutu. "Look at this. Isn't it sweet? It just kills me."

Kira holds out overalls with little sunflower patches sewn into the knees. "And check out this little getup. Isn't it cute?"

I smile. "Yeah, adorable—"

Vin clears his throat.

I look at him. He raises his eyebrows.

"Sorry," I say. I turn to my sisters. "This is my cowork— I mean, my friend. This is Vin."

He reaches his arm across the rack of clothes between us. They all shake hands. "I'm her best friend. And I assume one of you is an ex?"

They both laugh, confused. "What? We're her sisters."

Vin's face falls. "Oh. Of course you are. That was, uh, just a weird joke. I like to crack weird gay jokes. I'm gay, so don't worry. It's not like I'm being homophobic or anything. Not that gay people can't have like internalized homophobia or anything. I'm just— Uh."

I do not know whether my sisters are aware I am gay, and Vin knows that. He is afraid that he just spilled the beans.

I am gripping my toes in my shoes and my face feels warm. I look at the girls. I can't tell what they are thinking.

"So, you're pregnant?" Vin attempts to redirect the conversation. "And I hear it's a girl, right? Congratulations."

Edna rubs her belly. "Yes, a little girl. Thank you. We're all so excited."

"We are a big family of girls," Kira adds, nudging me.

"Jealous," Vin says while sopping sweat off his forehead with his jacket sleeve.

"It's so nice to see you out in the wild." Edna grins at me. "And to meet people in your life." She smiles at Vin.

I don't know how to reply, so I stammer, "T-thank you."

"I love meeting people in her life too," Vin says. "She's quite private, isn't she?"

I tune out while they all talk about me being quiet. I pretend to listen. I smile when they smile.

I wish I could call my mom.

✳

"I am so fucking sorry," Vin whispers in the housewares section.

"For what?" I ask. I pretend to inspect a glass figurine of a frog, but really, I am looking through the hole in the shelves at my sisters. They are across the store at the cash register.

"For asking if they were an ex of yours. Do you think I outed you?" he asks.

"Oh no, I don't think so," I say while watching them pay. "I don't think it registered. And they might already know. I'm not sure."

He exhales. "Well, that's a relief. I could have died. That's why I was rambling to them after. I always ramble after I put my foot in my mouth. I think I can bury something stupid I said by saying a thousand more things. I should have known who they were. You've described them to me. They look just like you said. I just wasn't thinking. I'm really sorry."

"Don't sweat it." I watch the girls push their cart out the exit.

I used to look for my sisters everywhere. In the same way some people are on guard for their exes, I used to go into grocery stores and glance around for them. I wanted to see them. I wanted to know what they looked like in real life. I also *didn't* want to see them. I knew spotting them would make me feel bad. I felt this deep fascination, an intense draw, mixed with sadness and a sort of rejection. I still feel a shadow of that now when I see them. It makes it hard for me to talk to them. I'm afraid they can tell.

"They're just like you described," he says again while scrutinizing a teapot shaped like a mushroom. "Sort of chirpy and bland, but nice."

Despite being the source of Vin's disparagement, I feel offended by it.

"I didn't say bland, did I? When did I say that?"

"Yeah." He clinks the mushroom cap lid against its pot. "I think we had been drinking. Or you said they're insipid, I think. Or vapid? Something like that. But they're also nice, right? You said they're nice."

I feel my face heat. "Yeah, they are nice."

✳

"Are those your sisters again?" Vin asks as we carry our shopping bags out into the dusky parking lot. The sun is setting.

Edna and Kira are standing in front of their car with its hood up.

Kira notices us and waves.

"Are you having car trouble?" Vin shouts.

"Yes, are either of you any good with cars?" Edna says. "It won't start."

"No, I'm useless. Sorry," Vin answers.

We're standing by their car now.

"I'm useless too," I say. "My mom is good with them, though."

I always take my car to my mom before I go see a mechanic. She grew up on a farm and learned about machinery. She usually accompanies me when I do things like get my oil changed, to make sure no one tries to fleece me. There have been a few times when people tried, and my mom surprised them with her car knowledge.

"Do you think you could call her?" Kira asks.

I look at her like she just suggested I sever my own foot off. Why did I mention my mom to them? What was I thinking? When I hear someone talk about car trouble, I think of her. I should never have mentioned her. I just open my mouth.

Kira looks confused.

"S-sure," I sputter.

I dial my mom's number. My palms are sweating.

When she answers, I realize I should have pretended to call her. I should have had a fake conversation in front of my sisters and lied and said my mom was busy, or that she didn't answer.

"Hi Mom."

"Hi honey. What's up?"

"Um." I inhale. "I'm just at, uh, the thrift store off Elm—"

I wish I didn't call her. I feel sick.

"Oh, did you see something I might like? Sometimes they have nice fabrics—"

"No, um, well, I actually ran into—uh. Well, I ran into Edna and Kira."

Whenever I mention Edna or Kira to my mom, her voice changes.

"Oh?" Her voice changes.

"Yeah, they're, uh, having car trouble actually. I wondered if maybe, um. Are you able to come to the parking lot? You don't have to if you're busy. We could call a mechanic, or something. It's no problem. I just thought maybe, um, if you have a spare minute. They'd understand if you can't, of course. I just mentioned you're good with cars and uh—"

"Sure. I'll be right there."

✳

I feel like I am aboard the space shuttle *Challenger*. I am moments away from being propelled 46,000 feet into the air, breaking apart, and dying. Vin had to leave. Omar was coming over. I told him it was fine to go, but it wasn't. Kira and Edna are talking about the color of the sky. The sun is setting. I am pretending to listen to them while I watch cars drive by in the dimming pink light, feeling deeply rattled at the thought of my mom pulling in.

My stomach drops every time I see a car that looks like hers.

My mind is racing. Maybe I should pretend I have to go to the bathroom, call my mom from a stall, and tell her not to come. I could say never mind; the car started working. Then I could tell Edna and Kira that she got in a car accident on the way here, and they'll have to call a mechanic. I'd say it was a minor accident, nothing to be worried about, but she can't come. Or I could say her friend got hurt. She unexpectedly has other plans. Or maybe I could—

Fuck.

She is pulling in. I put on a brave face. I pretend my intestines aren't knotted in my throat. I wave her down.

While she climbs out of the driver's seat, I say, "Hi Mom. This is Edna and Kira."

My voice sounds higher than it's supposed to.

"Hi girls," she says.

I watch her face. I watch her eyes change while she examines them. Her pupils get bigger.

They all shake hands. They say, "Hello," and "Thanks so much for coming."

Though they are all smiling, I sense they are looking at each other the way caged zoo animals might across the path. Like confused tropical toucans might eye a desert camel. Like creatures who would have no business ever seeing each other if not for someone's meddling and arrogant caging of them.

"Let's take a look at this thing," my mom says while positioning herself in front of the hood.

She starts tinkering with the engine. She is wearing a long, pleated skirt, and she has a yellow scarf tied around her neck.

I'm standing behind her. I feel nauseous.

"It's so cool you know how to fix cars," Kira says.

Edna grins. "Yeah, so cool."

I'm clenching my toes in my shoes. I feel like I'm watching a crossover between two TV shows that have nothing to do with each other. It feels bizarre and concerning, like two galaxies have crashed.

There is so much space in galaxies. Most of space is empty. When galaxies collide, it's unlikely for stars to crash into each other even though they're colossal. Collisions tend not to result in any planets or stars touching. The space between stars, the gas and dust, collides and creates new stars, and there are shock waves, but objects are unlikely to crash.

I watch my mom and glance at my sisters. I remind myself that they are unlikely to collide. This is just dust and gas.

"Thanks again for helping us," Kira says.

"Oh, I'm happy to," Mom says in a voice that isn't really hers. It sounds a bit like her phone voice. It's sweeter than usual.

"Our dad always used to help with our cars," Edna says.

That statement feels like a crate of bricks falling from the sky onto the cement beside us. I feel my heart jolt.

I watch my mom for her reaction. After a brief pause, she says, "He was always good with cars, wasn't he?"

"What about your husband, Edna? Is he any good with cars?" I say, afraid if I don't interject, the conversation will derail. I worry my mom will make it weird. She might start sharing all her memories. She might talk too much. She might reveal that she has harbored this strange obsession for their father, or that she was always in love with him.

"No, he's not a very handy guy," she says. "He's not a lot like Dad at all, actually."

My mom twists something. "I think I found the problem. Could you please try starting the car again, honey?"

Edna walks around the car and sits in the driver's seat. She starts the car.

"There we go," Mom says when it starts.

"Wow! Thank you so much again for your help," Kira says.

My mom looks into Kira's face a little too long.

"You have your dad's smile," she says.

Fuck. She's going to make this weird. I've been trying so hard not to seem weird to them.

She adds, "I hope you don't mind me saying."

Kira smiles wider. "Do I? Thank you."

I exhale. It's interesting that Kira interprets that as a compliment. Whenever my mom says that something about me reminds her of my dad, I feel slighted. It feels underhanded. I've always interpreted those comments as her way of saying something like, *I love you, but you're horrible.*

"You must be so excited for the baby," Mom says to Edna as she returns to us.

Edna touches her stomach. "We are, yes. It's an exciting time."

"I'm so sorry your dad isn't here for it," Mom says.

I clench my toes again.

"Me too," says Edna.

✳

"They look so much like him, don't they?" Mom says.

We're sitting on her couch.

"I don't know," I say.

I barely know what he looked like. My mom always says he was handsome.

"It's so different to see someone in person versus a photo, isn't it? In real life, they have his expressions, don't they? Like the way the muscles in their faces move. Their posture. They really look like him. Don't you think?"

I close my eyes. She's been going on and on since we came home. I wish I had gone to my apartment instead of coming here.

"Genetics are so strange, aren't they?" she continues. "I really wished I wore something nicer. I was wearing that skirt all day. It was sort of wrinkly. I hope they don't think I'm a slob. Do you think they'll think I'm sloppy? I hope I didn't look—"

"You were fixing a car," I say.

I repress an urge to tell her she sounds crazy. I can feel my parasite crawling around in my skull, muttering that my mother is nuts.

"Still. I always imagined myself looking more put together when I met them."

I look at her. "You imagined meeting them?"

She sighs. "Yes, of course. I always wanted to meet them."

I make a disapproving face and roll my eyes, despite the fact that I always imagined meeting them too.

*

Rather than sleep over at my mom's, and suffer more conversation about my sisters, I decided to go home. I am on the bus watching YouTube on my phone. I have the volume off. I'm just reading the closed captions. My apartment is six stops away. In this video, I am taking my audience on a tour of my childhood bedroom, introducing them to my cat, my stuffed animals, and showing them inside my closet. I think I must be about twelve. I had posters of Dalmatians and golden retrievers plastered on my walls. My comforter is covered in images of little cartoon robots.

I hold up a book titled *Ghost Stories*.

"*I used to be super afraid of ghosts,*" I tell the camera, which is pointed way too close to my face. "*I got over it when I learned more about them.*"

The camera is pointed at my mouth. One of my front teeth is missing. My new adult tooth is partly grown in.

"*Ghosts just have unfinished business. They don't have to be scary. Casper, for example, is a friendly ghost. My mom showed me cartoons of Casper and she got me some Casper books. He's not scary at all. Trust me.*

"*The thing is,*" child-me continues, "*ghosts aren't any more scary than people are. Think about it. Ghosts just used to be people. Some people are really scary, like murderers, and bullies. There's no reason to single out ghosts for being scary when everyone can be just as scary as a ghost."*

I feel a chill. I look up from my phone at the other passengers on the bus. It's dark, and the lights on the ceiling blink when we drive over bumps. I watch the people around me fade into shadows and then light up.

I zero in on an old woman sitting at the front. She has her hair tucked under a rain cap, and both hands gripping her purse. She looks uneasy, as if she is concerned that someone might snatch her bag. I watch her for a while. When the bus is lit, I wonder about the scariest thing that has ever happened to her. Maybe she has been mugged before. When the bus goes dark, and she is in shadow, I wonder about the worst thing she has ever done.

"DO YOU HAVE THE TIME?" the man sitting across from me screams.

I look at him, startled. His face is red.

"I'm hard of hearing," I say, realizing he must have been asking me earlier and I didn't reply.

His face remains red, but presumably out of embarrassment now rather than anger.

"It's 8:23," I say.

CHAPTER FIVE

My fingers leave prints in the condensation on my window. It is after seven p.m. and the sun has set. I am looking at the alley, watching the shadows between the garbage cans for movement.

"Do you believe in ghosts?" I ask.

My mom is here. I invited her over. I felt bad about how I left her house yesterday. I think she sensed I was annoyed by her. We are going to watch a scary movie. I felt like watching something frightening so I could exert power over it. I want to eat popcorn while I watch it and laugh while it tries to scare me.

"Oh, not this again," she says.

"What?" I turn around.

She is standing in front of my closet, feeling the fabric of my clothes. She looks over her shoulder. "When you were younger, you used to talk my ear off about ghosts. Don't you remember?"

"Did I?"

"Yes, you did, but talk about them to your heart's content, honey. I was just kidding. I like hearing about what fascinates you. You always have interesting things to say."

I resist the urge to accuse her of pumping my tires. Instead, I ask again, "Do you believe in ghosts?"

"I don't know. Do you?"

"I'm not sure—"

Her eyes dart behind me and widen. She points and says, "Oh my God, who is that?"

I jump away from the window like I have just touched an electric fence.

Is the bald face back?

"Got you," she says while I suffer heart palpitations. I put a hand to my chest. "What about aliens?" she asks, not realizing she has thrown me off a cliff into a panic. "Are you in on that at work? Is there life beyond Earth? Or are we alone? What do your sisters think? Have you ever talked with them about this?"

I don't reply. My heart is racing. I can feel it beat in my throat.

"Enid?"

"Earth to Enid?"

"Do you believe in aliens, honey?"

✳

I am watching a YouTube video of myself trying on a formal dress. I am a teenager in the video. The dress is long and black.

I squint at the screen, wondering if it is really me. I don't remember the dress I'm wearing. In the video, I say my mom made it. It takes a long time to make a dress like that. I don't remember her making it.

When I watch myself on YouTube, around this age, I wonder if someone had a voodoo doll of me then. I wonder if I was asleep and moving because someone was moving my doll. It doesn't feel like I am watching myself. It feels like I am watching a possessed mannequin that looks like me, but off.

In the video, I am asking my audience how I should do my hair.

"*Up or down?*" I ask the camera while gathering my hair in my fist.

I have no memory of being this person.

"*I think Ben would prefer it down,*" I say.

I pause the video. Ben was my boyfriend.

I feel something dark move in my stomach.

I press play again and watch myself put my hair up, then down, then up again.

❋

The search tool is still malfunctioning. If I restart the crawl and use a specific browser, it returns the correct results. When I search "exoplanet," however, it returns results as if I have searched my own name.

Rather than continue to comb the tool for bugs, I have spent my afternoon branding it. It now sports the agency's logo and a little favicon.

"That's looking good," my boss says over my shoulder.

I did not hear him approach, so I jump.

"Sorry," he says. "Did I startle you?"

I feel my heart in my throat again.

"No," I lie.

"We should present this to the management team again soon, eh?" he says.

"It's still buggy," I say.

"Is it? It looks good. Should we meet with George again?"

"No," I say immediately. "No. I can figure it out."

"You should use George. He knows his stuff. He's a good resource. Just book a meeting with him."

I grit my teeth. "Okay, sure. I will."

I won't.

※

"I think you're going to like him. He's a lot like us," Vin says.

I am sitting on his couch waiting to meet Omar. I declined a glass of water earlier and regret it now. My throat feels dry.

I look around his apartment. He has art books stacked on his coffee table and plants arranged by his windows.

"Did you clean up for us?" I ask.

"No, not really. I cleaned yesterday. My mom came by."

"Oh, how's she?"

"She's stopped taking her medicine."

"Again?"

He frowns. "It's like always. She thinks she's cured. Is your mom taking her medicine?"

"Good question," I say. "She came to my house yesterday. She seemed okay."

Near the beginning of our friendship, Vin invited me over. We had been having lunch together at work for weeks. He had just moved into this building and wanted to show me his new couch. We had discussed the couch during our lunches. He showed me the couches he was considering and consulted me regarding which one to buy. He landed on a contemporary mid-century sofa made of tan vegan leather.

I came over after work to see it in person. We sat on it and watched a comedy special. We both laughed at the same jokes. He had to pause it when he got a call from his mom. I heard her through the phone, crying, saying something was wrong. He reassured her, "It's fine, Ma. You're fine. Do you want me to come over?"

She ultimately settled down, he hung up, and apologized. I told him not to. I asked him about his mom. He told me she has bipolar disorder and that he has to check in on her a lot. I told him about my mom. We then looked at each other the way two animals of the same species might when crossing paths in the woods.

There is a loud knock. I jump.

"You're so skittish lately," Vin says as he answers his door. He opens it without looking out his peephole first. I hear the baritone of Omar's voice as he enters the apartment. The two kiss on the mouth before Vin leads Omar over to me by the hand.

"I'm so happy for you two to finally meet." Vin beams.

I smile at Omar. He has a friendly face and a full head of hair.

He says, "It is so lovely to finally put a face to the name. I have heard nothing but praise about you."

"He lies about me," I say while shaking his hand.

They both laugh.

✳

"Did Vin tell you how we met?" Omar asks.

He is sitting beside me on the couch. Vin is puttering around the room, watering his plants.

"Yes," I say. "At a bookstore, right?"

"Close. The library."

Vin interjects. "I said the library. She just has a bad memory."

I nod. I do have a bad memory.

Omar grins. "I love telling people how we met. I'm a librarian—so I'm not sure I could make up a better place to meet someone than in the stacks. Our hands touched reaching for the same book. It was like a movie."

I watch Vin examining a yellowing leaf on one of his plants. Despite his face being mostly turned away, I can tell that he is smiling.

I smile too. "That is a nice way to meet. Though, I would have thought working at the library would turn you off from finding the place romantic. You must like your job."

Omar says, "Sometimes I do. What about you? Do you like your job?"

"I think so," I say. "I like working with information about space. I like that I can do a lot of my work alone at my desk. I don't like the office small talk or going to meetings, but mostly, it's a decent job for me, I think."

When I was younger, I thought I wanted to be a nurse. Despite feeling squeamish around needles and blood, having weak social skills, and no interest in biology or gym class—I thought becoming a nurse was right for me. I think I wanted to become a nurse in the same way I wanted to become a man's wife, or a mother. I thought it would look good on paper. I thought people would think favorably of me if I was a nurse. It would prove something. I thought of it as a feminine career that required higher education and that attracted the type of girls who I felt judged by, and who I judged. I think I considered becoming a nurse synonymous with becoming normal.

I'm not sure what my job now is synonymous with. I don't know whether it's really right for me, or not. I'm not sure I care. I managed to overcome aspiring to appear normal but never really figured out what I should aspire to be. I have a feeling that what I should try to become has nothing to do with my job, though. If I had to guess, I'd bet I should be aspiring to become happy, or a good person, or something. That's probably what enlightened people do.

"There are bad parts to every job," says Omar. "We've had some atrocious things happen at the library. A man died in the washrooms last month, for example."

I laugh, then cover my mouth. I should have assessed whether he meant to be funny before letting myself react. Sometimes when I hear something shocking and dark, my impulse is to laugh. It might be because I listen to too many murder stories. It might be because of my parasite.

Omar is a good sport. He smiles. "Come on, Enid. A man is dead."

Vin cackles. "She's heartless."

I say, "Sorry. Uh. Rest in peace man."

Omar lifts his glass of water up in memoriam. He takes a sip, then asks, "So, what about you two? How did you pals meet?"

"At work, actually," I say. "We were in a training session together. We were both hired at the same time. We bonded over a shared disdain for our instructor—"

Vin is walking to the bathroom. He says, "Oh God, I forgot about that guy. He kept joking about how much he hated his wife."

I say, "Yeah, he was the worst," as Vin shuts the bathroom door.

Omar and I are alone now. I feel uncomfortable without our buffer, but I'm sure Vin won't be long. We just need to make it through a few moments. Maybe I should ask him a question. Maybe I'll ask him what he wanted to be when he was a kid. Or what he thinks enlightened people want to be—

"You know"—Omar leans in—"Vin really loves you."

I look at him. I don't know how to respond.

I squirm. "Oh, h-he hates me."

He laughs. "No, he loves you. You are important to him."

I feel my parasite twitch. I know Omar is saying this because he doesn't know me, and he thinks hearing that will make me feel good, but it doesn't. It makes me feel stressed. I don't know how to reply.

The bathroom door opens. Thank God.

Omar changes the subject. "So, what about you? Are you seeing anyone?"

"Uh," I say. "I went out the other night with a girl named Polly."

Vin is now sitting between us, smiling like a puppy hearing his humans talk about bones or balls.

"You did? You didn't tell me that," Vin says. "Who is she? What's she like? Can I meet her?"

"We just went out once. Well, before that she came to my house once. We had a shower."

Omar and Vin both make a noise like a hen coop waking up.

"It wasn't like that," I say. "It was actually a very solemn shower."

"This was the first time you two had ever met?" Omar clarifies.

"Yeah. I don't think anything will come of it."

"But you like her?" Vin asks, eyes eager.

"I think so, yeah, but I also kind of hope I never see her again. Do you know what I mean?"

"Totally," Omar says, but I sense he doesn't. I think he's pretending he relates to me because I'm Vin's friend, and he wants me to like him.

Vin squints. "*What?* You get what she means? I don't get that at all. That's not normal, Enid. If you like her, you should want to see her again. And can we please backtrack to the shower? Why was the shower solemn?"

"Oh," I say. "Because she was crying."

He tilts his head. "What? Why was she crying?"

"Her wife cheated on her."

He gasps. "She's married?"

"She's getting a divorce. Her wife cheated on her—"

"Why did this woman who you've never met before come cry in your shower after being cheated on?"

I look at him. "Well, because I was who her wife cheated on her with."

Omar snorts. He covers his mouth. "Sorry."

"Jesus Christ." Vin exhales. "And you like this person? What's her name again?"

I sip my drink. "Yeah, I do. Her name is Polly."

"Can I meet her?"

I shake my head. "No. I just said I kind of hope I never see her again."

He narrows his eyes. "You make no fucking sense."

✳

Sometimes, when I have a nice interaction with someone, I hope I never see them again. Occasionally, I have a nice chat with a cashier, for example. I leave the store thinking, *I hope I never see them again*. I avoid their register if I do. Sometimes, when I visit extended family, like my mom's cousins, or a great aunt, I think it's a shame they saw me now at my age. I think it might have been better for them to have last seen me as a kid. I think seeing me now might ruin the memory of when I was little. I often stop texting people I'm seeing after having a nice time with them. I wish I could have one nice interaction with everyone and then disappear.

✳

I met a girl named Talia when I was nineteen. We were outside a shawarma stand. The bars had closed. It was after two a.m. I was in my first year at university. I was alone and she was alone. I told the girls I went out with that I had a ride, but I didn't. I just wanted to eat pickled turnips and walk home by myself. I found it exhausting going out with them. I wore this heavy, happy mask the entire time despite feeling uncomfortable and out of place. I wanted to have friends. They were my first friends. The muscles in my face hurt after a few hours of fake smiling. I had this phony laugh. They thought I was someone I wasn't; someone energetic, who liked to drink, and laughed loudly. I was mimicking them.

I thought I was evolving. I had accepted parts of myself. I was openly gay, I dressed how I felt comfortable, but socially— I was still trying to figure it out. I didn't know how to have friends. I still don't. I was faking it.

As my friendship with them progressed, I started taking up smoking and doing coke recreationally just for an excuse to get away. I remember standing still in a bar of moving people, the lights flashing red, and thinking, *I would definitely rather have chronic obstructive pulmonary disease than remain in here.* I begged people for cigarettes. I would go to the bathroom with rolled paper money and my driver's license, not truly desiring any high besides the one I got leaving a room.

I am not friends with any of those people anymore. I have them on social media and am invited to the occasional wedding, but I don't hang out with them. We don't keep in touch. I rarely think of them. I think of Talia.

I only met her once. She was in front of me in line at the shawarma stand. She had lost her wallet. She was crying and drunk. Her high school boyfriend had just dumped her, and she could not pay for her sandwich. Nothing was going right. She hated all her classes. Her roommates were mean to her. She was falling apart under the fluorescent light at the window.

I said I would pay for her sandwich. I said, "It's on me, don't worry about it."

As I punched the debit card machine, she said I was the nicest person she had ever met. I assured her she was mistaken.

We left the shawarma stand and walked in the same direction. It turned out she lived near me, so we walked together. I wanted to be alone, but it would have been rude, so instead I walked with her with my happy mask off. I sighed loudly and told her I lied to my friends so I could walk home alone. I told her I didn't have friends when I was younger and wanted them. I smelled like cigarettes and was overly alert because of the coke. I felt mentally exhausted. I told her, "I don't know who I am. I don't know who I want to be. I wish I were someone different."

She sat on a bench to eat. She kept telling me not to wish I was someone different. She said she liked me as I was. I was nice. I told her I wasn't nice. I'm not nice.

She said, "You paid for my sandwich."

I told her that was just so the line would move.

She said she had good intuition and that she was sure I was nice.

I told her to be careful because she is wrong. I warned her there are people like Ted Bundy.

She asked why I thought I was a bad person.

I told her I've done terrible things.

She said, "Like what?"

I said, "Never mind," and we chewed.

She said, "You know, recently I realized that to my parents, I am someone different than to my friends. To my teachers, I am someone different than to my coworkers. Between my friends, ex-boyfriend, and roommates, I am someone totally different. I think if you picked two people from my life and asked them to describe me, they would describe two completely different people."

I thought of the people I went to school with. I thought of my new friends at university, the people I had dated, my mom, and my dad. I said, "I feel that way too."

She said, "To some of them, I'm bad."

I nodded. "Me too."

"Do you know who we really are? Do you know which person is right?"

"None of them?" I guessed.

"No, they all are," she said.

I ate my pickled turnips and stewed with that thought.

"Hey, for me, you will always be a nice person who paid for my food and walked me home."

"Okay, and for me you'll always be someone nice who listened to me complain."

"Let's promise to never meet again so we can't ruin it. Let's stay nice people to each other to balance out how we're bad for other people."

✳

"Did you have a chance to meet with George yet?" my boss asks.

He appeared behind me unexpectedly. I had just said "fuck" and slammed my mouse down after the search tool failed another test.

I look at him. "Uh, no. I haven't been able to get ahold of him. I think he must be busy doing new employee things. Orientation, and all that. I've been working on other things too. I've been helping the team in HR with another project."

He nods. "Ah, that makes sense. Well, keep trying to reach George. I think he can help us with this."

✳

I think of Polly as I hook up with a stranger. They have the same hair color and a similar build. If I narrow my eyes, she looks like her.

"Do you wear glasses?" the stranger asks.

"No, why?"

"You're squinting."

"Oh, sorry."

"It's okay."

She throws my pillows off my bed. While she ties her hair up, I look at the window.

"I think we need to shut your curtain better," she says.

"Why?" I sit up. "Did you see something?"

"No, but you're right on the ground level. Do you ever worry someone might look in?"

✳

I dream about the bald face in my window, but the window in
my dream is in my bathroom. It is right beside where I sit in the
tub. The logistics of the dream are confusing; I bathe with the
window open to the street. People walk by and see me. They do
not behave as if it is abnormal. However, the bald man does. He
spots me from across the street and moves quickly toward me
until his face is pressed right up against the glass.

I've been touching your things, he mouths.

✳

*"Sexual predators usually start out small. They begin by looking into
people's windows while they undress at night. Not all Peeping Toms
are rapists; however, most rapists were Peeping Toms . . ."*

An episode of my podcast is playing while I get ready for
work. This one is detailing the warning signs sexual predators
exhibit before attacking people. Ted Bundy, Dennis Rader (the
BTK Killer), and Joseph DeAngelo (the Golden State Killer)
were all voyeurs when they were teenagers.

*"It's a power thing. It's about control. Most of them don't attack
until they're in their twenties. When they're younger, they build up
their confidence by doing things like watching people without their
consent. Sadistic rapists don't usually rape or kill people before testing the waters. First, they walk into people's backyards without their
permission. They get a taste of what it feels like to do something in-
vasive. They watch people through their windows. Sometimes, they
start doing it naked. DeAngelo was chased by some victims when he
was naked from the waist down. Imagine trying to chase down that
creep, dressed like a perverted Winnie the Pooh? They start going*

*inside people's houses, watching them sleep, stealing their under-
wear . . ."*

When I was in university, I recall more than one instance
when men were caught peeping into windows. I remember
watching the local news when a reporter explained that one
man's behavior had started to escalate. He had begun entering
homes to watch young women sleep. All the girls at my university had to tuck in at night with that fear looming over us.

I lived in a house with three other girls. They suggested
that I might be able to protect them, presumably because I am
a lesbian. I was at the time especially weak. I didn't exercise,
and I subsisted almost entirely on white bread. I considered
explaining that the source of men's physical strength does not
actually come from their attraction to women, and that I was
probably weaker than most of them because they did Pilates.
I decided instead that because it comforted them to think my
presence was somehow helpful, to let them think it. I said,
"Don't worry, ladies. I'll protect you," but the truth was that I
was scared too.

*"Russel Maurice Johnson was known as the Bedroom Strangler.
He was described as being obsessed with cleanliness. He would com-
pulsively wash his hands. He started raping women in the 1960s but
didn't murder anyone until the seventies. He would stalk his victims
first. He would break into their homes and watch them sleep for
hours. He was able to crawl up the sides of apartment buildings and
enter through balcony doors. He suffocated his victims with their
pillows. At first their deaths were attributed to causes like hardened
arteries, allergic reactions, and overdoses because there were no signs
of violence, and because he methodically cleaned up afterward . . ."*

I glance around my apartment. I look at the window.

"Johnson followed his victims prior to attacking them. A lot

of these guys stalk their victims first. Ladies, if you ever feel like you're being stalked, or that someone is treating you oddly, speak up. Women are conditioned to be polite to people. We do things like help Ted Bundy because his arm is in a sling. If you ever feel like something is off, scream."

I touch the back of my neck. I glance at the books on my bookshelf. I notice a row of paperbacks have been toppled over and are lying sideways on the shelf. How did those fall?

"Don't talk yourself out of fear. Fear is important. It keeps us safe. There is a reason we feel fear."

✳

Polly texted me.

Hey.

I read the message twice. I feel electrocuted by it. I did not think that we would speak again. I write back,

Hi.

I wait five minutes, then write,

Did you know bed bugs have infested the international space station?

After hitting send, I feel regret. I should have just said,

What's up?

She replies.

You're kidding! That's going to be a nightmare. The females can lay five hundred eggs.

I smile and write,

They have particularly infested the toilet.

I reread my message after sending it and feel my smile fade. Why did I say that? Why would I mention the toilet—

She replies,

That makes sense. They live far away from light.

We text for an hour about bugs, until Polly stops replying. I think she fell asleep.

While I lie awake waiting for her to reply, I search her name on Instagram. I look at her profile. After examining every photo, I decide to look up my sisters. I find the photo that I was in at the gender reveal party. I look at myself smiling next to them.

Before I fall asleep, I text my mom.

Hey mom, just letting you know Jupiter has sixty-seven moons.

✳

I dream again about the bald man in my window. He is standing in the frame, with his head cocked to the side, and his forehead pressed up against the glass. I have pulled the curtains open, and I am facing him. I am looking him dead in the eyes.

"Are you a ghost or a person?" I ask through the glass.

"Aren't ghosts people?" he replies.

"Are you real?" I ask.

He says, "No, you're dreaming."

"But are you real outside my dream?" I ask.

"How the hell would I know? I am a figment of your dream. I have no idea what's real."

✳

I wake up and immediately check if Polly texted me.

I feel oddly relieved and oddly disappointed to see she hasn't. I simultaneously hope she never texts me again, while also hoping that she writes me right now.

I reread our text conversation. Maybe I should write her. I could say, *Good morning*.

Or maybe I should block her.

I close our conversation and google "evidence of ghosts" and click the search results. I watch a video of a ghost sighting that looks fake. I read a blog about an old hotel in Quebec City. It says a man died there and asked for his heart to be mailed to his girlfriend. She refused to accept it, the organ was returned, and now the man haunts the hotel's ballroom.

I shift gears and open a new window. I search "how to know if you're the target of a pervert." I read an article titled "Ten Signs You're Being Stalked." It mentions repeated phone calls and receiving inappropriate gifts. It says nothing about seeing bald faces in your window.

I google "how to tell if someone has been inside your apartment," and scan the results.

Are things missing?

Are lights left on?

Has your underwear been tampered with?

✳

"Did you know astronomers found a planet without a star?" I ask my mom. I called her on my lunch break after looking at Kira's and Edna's Instagram profiles again. I began by looking at Polly's, and got sidetracked.

"Did they? Had they ever seen something like that before?"

"No. Well, they have found some they thought might be failed stars, but this one is a planet. They think it probably formed around a star but was shot out of orbit."

"What's a failed star?" she asks.

"It's a celestial body that's like a star but doesn't produce light."

"Why doesn't it?"

"It doesn't have the mass to."

✳

When I write "brown dwarf" in the search tool, it returns results about the moon. I would prefer it return nothing. I search "Polly" as a test, just to see what happens, and receive an error message that reads: "CATASTROPHIC FAILURE."

I think there is some sort of permissions problem. I screenshot the message and email it to Vin. I write, "This error message is me."

He writes back, "I see what you queried."

Embarrassed to have been busted, I change the subject. I write, "Hey, do you believe in ghosts?"

✳

I hum the tune to "Do Your Ears Hang Low?" while trying to unlock my apartment. While I tug at the sticky door, I hear a creak in the hall.

I try to move faster, but before I can, the woman from the unit across from mine enters the hallway. I exhale as she reaches her arm into her apartment to shut off her lights. She says, "Oh, hi. Do you live in that unit?"

I look at her. "Yes, I do."

"I think someone has been looking for you," she says.

"Sorry?"

"I might be wrong, but I noticed a man is often standing by your door. He was there earlier, but he left."

I smell smoke.

"A man?"

"Yes."

"What does he look like? Is he . . . bald?"

She considers the question. "I think he wears a hat. I'm not sure. I've seen him a few times. Do you know who I'm talking about?"

My chest hurts. "D-does he," I stammer. "D-do you ever see him enter my apartment? Or does he just wait by the door?"

She thinks, then says, "I feel like I have seen him leaving, to be honest. Is that weird? I assumed he was your boyfriend or something?"

"I'm a lesbian."

"Oh, are you? Good for you." She looks down at her phone. "Sorry, my Uber is here. I'll have to catch you later, okay? If I see the guy, I'll let him know I told you he was looking for you."

"Don't," I manage to say. "I . . . I'll get in touch with him."

"Okay," she says. "Catch you later."

※

"Someone has been following me," I tell the 911 dispatcher.

"Are you in immediate danger?"

"I don't think so."

"You need to call the nonemergency line," she says.

"Oh, okay. Sorry."

※

"Someone has been following me," I tell the nonemergency line dispatcher.

"Are you in immediate danger?"

"I don't think so."

"What's the name of the person who has been following you?"

"I don't know."

"Okay. What makes you think they have been following you?"

"My neighbor saw them. And I think I saw them in my window."

"You think?"

"I'm not sure."

"Have you been threatened by them?"

"No."

"Have they been repeatedly communicating with you?"

"No."

The dispatcher is quiet.

"Is there anything I can do?" I ask.

"I am afraid you need evidence."

✳

I scream. A framed picture just fell off my wall.

I put a hand to my chest. *Jesus Christ.* The noise startled me. I thought someone was in here.

I walk to the picture. It's a recent one of me and my mom. I hung it up poorly. I used a thumbtack. I couldn't find any nails.

I look at the picture. The glass cracked when it fell. I take the photo out of the frame and throw the rest out. I stick it to my fridge with a magnet shaped like Saturn.

I stand in front of my fridge and look at the photo. My mom is smiling with teeth. She has a red scarf in her hair and dark lipstick on. My smile is muted, and I look tired. It's not a very flattering photo of me, actually. I put it up because my mom looked so happy. I look sort of sick.

A door in the hallway slams. I jump.

Fuck. What is wrong with me?

I text Vin.

Something is wrong with me. I think I'm going crazy.

You are crazy, he replies.

Then later,

Are you okay, though?

＊

The more I think about what my neighbor said, the more I question my sanity. The person she mentioned could be anyone. Maybe he is a process server, trying to serve me a legal document. Maybe I am being targeted by some church for recruitment. Maybe he has the wrong address. Maybe I am being confused for someone. She said she *felt like* she saw him leave my apartment. Not that she saw him, that she *felt like* she did. Maybe she didn't. Maybe this is a misunderstanding.

＊

I place a single grape by my front door on the ground. I position it strategically so that if the door is opened, the grape will be knocked over and roll. If someone comes here, they probably will not notice the grape. They will inadvertently knock it over.

If they do notice that they knocked the grape—they will have to reposition it, and so I will be able to tell. If the grape is moved, that will prove that someone has been coming into my apartment. If the grape does not move, that means everything is okay.

I place the grape by the door before leaving for work. I position it so I can open the door slightly and slide through, but so it would roll if anyone opened the door properly. I take a photo of it with my phone. This way I will know exactly where and how it was placed.

*

There is a blood moon tonight. It is a lunar eclipse. My mom and I are parked on the outskirts of the city. I am sitting on the hood of my car, and she is climbing up beside me. She wore high-heeled boots and is struggling to get up. I offered her a hand, but she insisted that she is not that old yet. After a difficult two minutes, she finally positions herself next to me. The metal hood makes a clunking noise beneath her.

We throw our orange blanket over our laps and lean our heads back on the windshield.

The moon is bright red.

"Why is it red?" she asks.

She is wearing lipstick.

"It's a trick of the light. When the Earth lines up with the moon and the sun, it hides the moon from sunlight. The only light that can reach the moon when that happens comes from the edges of Earth's atmosphere."

"Why does that make it red, though? Wouldn't it be blue because Earth is blue?"

"It's because the molecules from Earth's atmosphere scatter out the blue light and the light that remains reflects onto the moon and makes it look red."

We both look up at the red face in the moon.

My mom inhales and exhales loudly. "He looks sort of like he's blushing, doesn't he?"

I squint. It is strange that the moon has such an identifiable face. Billions of years ago, before humans existed, asteroids flew into it and there were volcanic eruptions. Molten magma spewed out, then cooled and created dark patches that now look like a face. If I were disconnected from society and lived alone somewhere in a forest, I would definitely think that the moon is God.

"Did I ever tell you about the boy who I went camping with as a teen? Gregory?"

"No," I lie. "Tell me about him."

"Well, our families drove us up north for a week one summer. He had two sisters. I forget their names now. Lovely girls, though. My dad was a real outdoorsman, and their dad was too. I forget how they knew each other. Church, probably. Anyways. They were the type to love making fires. Chopping wood, that sort of thing. So, they decided they ought to take us all camping. Now, I was about fourteen, and I had, of course, planned out all my outfits for the week. I had this beautiful crimson-colored summer dress, and this lovely sage-green hat. I had a floral scarf I pictured myself wearing while we canoed. My parents lectured me about how we were just camping. They said I should just bring rags, but you know me. I think clothes are meant to be worn. No matter the occasion, there is an outfit. So, of course, I overpacked, picturing myself in all these possible scenarios camping. I know I brought my kitten heels. I had multiple hat options, and my lovely canoe scarf. But, of course, I managed to forget my bathing suit."

"Oh dear."

"Oh dear, indeed. Now, Gregory and I had a little romance. I got to wear my canoe scarf while he paddled us along the river. It was quite the scene. Me running my fingers along the water, making ripples, as he hummed behind me. We went out every day. One evening, he and I went out in the canoe around dusk, and despite his best efforts, we managed to capsize the boat. I wouldn't be surprised if it were my fault. I probably reached for some lily pad and unsteadied us, but all to say—we fell in. As I mentioned, I had no bathing suit, but landing in the water was such a relief because I'd been so hot in my ill-advised scarf. So, we swam along together, me fully dressed, him in his swimsuit, under the darkening sky. I remember hearing frogs and crickets and splashing Gregory, laughing. The sky was really clear there, of course. We were in the woods. All the stars were out. Now, after a while, I ended up finding my way to the shore, where I got butt naked out of my drenched things—"

"Okay, Mom, maybe this story isn't appropriate for me—"

She chuckles. "No, no. So, I had the genius idea to leverage my canoe scarf as a sort of towel. I wrapped it around myself. Gregory ended up coming to shore shortly after to find me, and despite the scarf providing perfect modesty in my opinion—it was quite a large scarf—he nonetheless looked a lot like the man in the moon does tonight."

I look at the man in the moon. He looks bald.

She sighs. "He ended up marrying a friend of mine. Elizabeth. I might have introduced them. They made a lovely pair. I went to the wedding. They had two sons, I think. I can't recall their names. Nice boys, though. Lizzie wore an off-white lace wedding gown. I remember thinking it looked so nice on her, it suited her coloring, but our church ladies had a lot to say about it not being pure white. They were such prudes. You can't imagine what I went through having you without a wedding ring on, honey. My mother hardly survived it."

I stare into the moon's red eyes.

"All well worth it though, of course." She knocks my knee with her leg. "I wouldn't trade you."

✳

My mom's kitchen is clean today. It is cluttered and decorated in knickknacks, but there are no dishes in the sink, and the counter isn't sticky. I look at her fridge. She has a school photo of me on it. I have no front teeth.

"Does Edna have a name picked out?" she asks.

I came back to her house after watching the red moon. I did not tell her that I am afraid to go home. Instead, I said I wanted to make lemon muffins.

She tries to bring Edna, Gina, and Kira up casually, but whenever she mentions them, there is a weight to their names.

"She mentioned Amelia," I say, watching her face for the response.

Her eyebrows raise. "Amelia," she repeats, registering the information with interest. "When did you find that out?"

"She mentioned it at a party at Gina's house," I say.

She looks at me. "You went to a party at her house?"

I nod.

She positions her stool in front of the oven.

After sitting down on it and staring into the oven, she says, "Your dad sure made a long line of women, didn't he?"

"I guess so."

"Gina must be so excited."

"I think she is, yeah."

"I always thought Gina sort of wanted a boy though," she says. "She seems like the type to want a boy, doesn't she?"

I am not sure what that means, so I don't reply.

"Your dad always wanted a boy," she continues.

Again, I don't reply.

"Was my dad ever balding?" I ask.

The image of my dad's face is foggy in my memory. When I see a photo of him, I know it's him, but without a picture in front of me, he exists as a faceless silhouette of a man.

"No," she says. "He always had a full head of hair. I don't think he even went gray. Why?"

"I just wondered."

"How is her house?" she asks. She means Gina's.

"Beige," I say.

She snorts. "Of course it is."

I start to tidy the small mess we made while making muffins. As I fill the sink with soapy water, she stands up. She says, "Excuse me, honey," and goes upstairs.

*

When I was a kid, I went through my mom's closet looking for clothing I could repurpose. My mom loves thrift shopping, knitting, and sewing, and has amassed an eclectic wardrobe. She wears drapey, colorful skirts, vests, and sweaters. She likes mismatching layered patterns. She ties scarves around her neck and in her hair. Among her vintage smocks, I found a box full of notes from my dad. They were written before I was born. He wrote her these sappy love letters. He penned little poems and drew sketches of her. I remember seeing the box out on her bed often. She looked through it a lot.

✳

I have turned off the oven and popped the last of the muffins out of their tray to cool. I bite into one. It glues itself to my palette and scorches the roof of my mouth. I spit into the sink, desperate to dislodge it.

My mom has not come back downstairs. I think she went to bed.

I tiptoe upstairs. The steps creak under me. I stand on the second floor, at the landing between the bedrooms and the bathroom. I turn the hall light on and look into my mom's bedroom. She is under her covers, snoring.

I go into her bathroom and open the medicine cabinet. I find the orange pill bottles behind her mirror and check the labels to see if they were prescribed recently. She also has a pill organizer, with the weekdays on it. I check whether she has taken what she should have this week.

She hasn't. It's Thursday and the last pills taken are from a Sunday.

✳

My mom's bathtub is pink. I ran the faucet too long. The waterline is above the overflow drain. It's making a loud, slurping noise. The water is also too hot. My legs look red beneath it. I have my phone in my hand. It's playing the last video published on my YouTube channel. The video is of me lighting a match. It shows the match striking the red strip on the side of its matchbox. I used a sepia tone and filmed until the match burned out. It has the most views of any video on my channel. It has been watched hundreds of thousands of times.

I click report video.

It asks me why.

I click "Violence."

I want to delete it. I try to log in to the account and remove it. I try to guess my password. I write, "Lou."

Lou was the name of my cat when I was growing up.

I write, "Edna."

I write, "Kira."

I write, "Mom," "Mom1," "Mom2."

✳

The second time I ever spoke to my sisters in person was at Edna's wedding. It was a year ago. Edna sent me an invitation. I felt weird about going but decided to go anyway. She seemed to want me to. She married a man who looks identical to all white, bearded, brunette men. I have said hello to more than one stranger since, mistakenly believing that the stranger was Edna's husband.

Gina walked her down the aisle and the crowd cried because the moment stressed that her—*our*—dad is dead.

I then listened to a minister explain that marriage is the union of a man and a woman, emphasis on man and woman, and watched oblivious Edna kiss her groom and smile, bright-eyed.

At the reception, she sat me at a table with her friends. I didn't tell them that I was her half sister because I didn't know if they knew the backstory. I said I was a friend of the family. My seat was near the podium where they gave the speeches. Gina talked again about what a sweet father Elmer was, and how much he would have loved to be there. Almost every speech mentioned Elmer and how proud he would be of Edna and her new husband. I intentionally shifted how I was sitting so that my deaf ear bore the brunt of the speeches.

My mom called me the next morning, asking for every detail. *What was Edna's dress like? What did Gina wear? What did Gina say? Was your grandma there?* I told her the wedding was boring and normal, and that Gina's dress made a roll of fat on her back. It really did do that, but I regretted telling her. She fixated on it and discussed it at length for days. She still brings it up sometimes.

"Imagine having a back roll out at your daughter's wedding!"

It brought out the worst in her.

✳

Vin is helping me with the search tool. In our attempts to fix it, we have made the problem worse. Now it always returns the same search results no matter what we query. I can search "black hole," "nebula," or "fuck my life," and the search results are always the same.

"Hey guys." Maveric appears behind us.

We both jump.

He sits down on the edge of my desk. "Julie and I are going to dinner tonight, so I've come for your advice. Any hot tips?"

Vin rolls his eyes.

"I don't remember Julie well," I remind him.

"I've got a hot tip," Vin pipes up. "Don't interrupt people who are working."

Maveric laughs, not grasping that Vin is being serious. He stretches, exposing sweat stains in his armpits and a bit of his pale midriff. "So, did you guys see how well Matthews played last night? The guy is a beast. He has the Hart trophy in the bag this year."

Neither of us reply.

"The guy is an absolute beauty, just like you two. What are you guys working on, anyways?"

Vin says, "We don't watch sports."

"What? You're kidding! Not even hockey?"

"Especially not hockey," Vin says.

✳

I unlock the door to my apartment. I haven't been here since yesterday. I slept at my mom's last night and went to work all day. As I open the door, I hum, "Do Your Ears Hang Low?"

I push my door open and look at the ground for the grape I left.

I gasp. It's gone.

I get on my knees. I look around to see if it was knocked under something. I put my cheek to the floor and look beneath my bookcase. I don't see it anywhere.

Holy shit. Someone must have been in here.

Wait. Could they still be here?

I hold my keys in the hammer grip and walk forward slowly. I find my metal baseball bat and hold it, braced to hit. I walk slowly through the rooms, checking behind doors, curtains, under my bed, and in the shower.

"If someone is in here, get out," I shout, hoping my faked bravery might scare off a prospective killer. "I have a gun," I add, which is a lie. "And I've killed before."

After searching everywhere, including—for some reason—inside all my drawers and under my rug, it becomes clear that I am alone. Whoever was here is gone now.

I lock my door. I add my additional security lock and check the window.

CHAPTER SIX

"Peter Holt speaking," my landlord answers his phone.

I have my baseball bat clutched in my hands.

"Hi Peter, this is Enid calling. I live at eighty-seven Frank Street, unit four. I am just calling to ask if you entered my unit in the last couple of days?"

"Which unit?" he says.

"Unit four."

"No, I don't think so."

"You don't think so? Is there any way you could confirm for sure, please? I have reason to believe someone was in my unit and if it wasn't you—"

"What unit did you say again?"

"Four."

"Oh, four? You know you're not allowed pets in there, right?"

I scowl. "I don't have any pets, Peter. I need to know if you were in my unit or if I should call the police. Someone was in my unit. I'm at my door with a baseball bat, terrified someone has been in here. Can you please tell me if you were?"

"What makes you think someone has been inside your unit?"

"There is a grape missing."

"Excuse me?"

"Never mind. Could I please ask you to provide twenty-four-hour notice before entering my apartment going forward?"

"Sure."

"And could you please tell me whether you were in here recently?"

"I was not in your unit recently," he says.

I can't tell whether he is lying because he knows it's illegal to go in my unit without notice, or if he really has not been in here.

"Is that everything?" he asks.

"Yes," I reply, annoyed.

"Okay cheers. And remember, no pets—got it?"

＊

I am installing a Ring camera. It will film the front of my door, by the peephole. Using it, I will be able to monitor who enters my apartment. I am mounting it frantically. I am afraid my bald neighbor or someone worse will enter the hallway while I am here. My hands are sweating, and my screwdriver keeps slipping out of the treads in the screws.

I hear a door creak and my heart races. I try to shuffle inside.

"Has someone been stealing your packages too?" The woman who lives in the unit across from mine peeks her head into the hall.

"What? Someone's been stealing your packages?"

"Yes." She opens her door wider. She is in a robe. She holds it closed tight to her body. "Is that why you're installing a camera?"

I look at her.

"Yes," I lie.

She tuts. "Someone stole a pressure cooker I ordered. There is a criminal getting in the building. You make sure to always lock your door, right?"

I nod.

She adds, "Also, have you noticed pests?"

"What do you mean?" I ask.

"I think the building has mice," she says.

"Oh," I say. "Did you see one?"

"No, but I've noticed little bites in things. I had to throw out all the fruit in my fruit bowl."

I gasp. "Do mice eat grapes?"

She looks visibly confused.

She says, "What? I'm sure they do, yes. Of course. Why?"

Did a mouse eat my grape? I should have used a marble to do the test with.

"I'm missing a grape," I explain.

She narrows her eyes. "You're missing a single grape? You noticed a single missing grape? Do you count your grapes?"

"No, no, I, uh," I say. "I dropped a grape and um. I haven't been able to find it. It rolled under my couch and disappeared. I keep picturing it rotting somewhere, but maybe I can't find it because a mouse ate it. I'm just a bit of a clean freak."

She nods. "Ah, I see. Well, I'm especially sorry to break the dirty mouse news, then."

✳

The camera I installed comes with an app. I can watch footage from my phone. Through it, I can view the hallway. Every time a neighbor walks by, I feel startled.

My phone dings. I jump.

I hope Polly texted me.

She didn't. It's from Kira.

Hey sis, we're planning a surprise baby shower for Edna. Would love it if you could come.

I sit up. I try to be careful not to make typing errors when I text Kira or Edna. I want to phrase myself well. I feel jittery and off right now, because of the grape situation. I try to focus on my fingers while I type.

Thank you so much for the invitation. Of course, yes, I will be there. Please let me know if there is anything I can do to help.

After tapping send, I text my mom.

Mom, just so you know, a day on Venus is longer than a year on Venus.

✳

I discovered I had a sister while snooping through the box my mom keeps in her closet. She had cut out Edna's birth announcement from the paper. By the time I had unearthed it, Edna was already one. The clipping included a newborn photo of her. It was black and white. Her face looked wrinkled, and she was wearing a hat. The announcement read:

*Proud parents Elmer and Gina Hughes are delighted
to announce the birth of their first sweet daughter,
Edna. Born on December 10 at the Riverside Hospital, Edna was seven pounds and eighteen inches long.*

I zeroed in on the words, "*first sweet daughter.*" Edna was
their first daughter together, but I was my dad's first daughter. Explicitly dubbing Edna the first felt pointed. I thought the
word "sweet" must be there to clarify that Edna wasn't the first
daughter, but she was the first *sweet* one.

✳

I did not disclose immediately to my mom that I knew about
Edna. Instead, I regularly creeped into her bedroom to look at
the clipping. If I heard her coming upstairs while I indulged in
that private hobby, I would scamper to my bed like the toilet
monster had been roused.

I knew about Edna for months before my mom was aware I
knew. She found out during an argument. I was refusing to go
to school. She told me that I had to. I told her I had no intention of it. She insisted that I had to go, so I said, "Does Edna
have to go to school?"

She replied, "Does who?" in the same tone she would use if
I had just revealed that an elderly lady who she had been having
lunch with had been dead for fifty years.

"Edna Hughes," I repeated. I knew that mentioning her
would feel like using the F word. There was a gravitational pull
to her name.

My mom did not make me go to school that day, but I
wished I had gone. I wished I hadn't mentioned Edna.

＊

A year later, my mom told me Kira was born. She knocked on my bedroom door and said, "Honey, I have some news. You have a new little sister."

I was playing at the time. I recall chewing on my Polly Pocket's clothes. I looked at her, confused, with a slobbery doll's rubbery dress hanging from my mouth.

"I have a new sister?"

"Yes," she said. "Her name is Kira. She was born on May 19."

The room felt eerie during the conversation. I felt how I imagine I would on the moon, sort of weightless, captivated, and afraid. I could tell my mom was wearing the mask of someone happy to announce a baby. I saw it slipping, so it felt more like a death notice.

"Will I meet her?" I asked.

I had never met Edna. At that point, she would have been two.

"Maybe someday," she said. "For now, it's just important that you know she exists. You want to know she exists, right?"

"Yes."

＊

"Do you think it's more likely that a mouse, a ghost, or a burglar would take a grape?" I ask Vin. There is live footage of my apartment's hallway playing on my phone. We are sitting at his desk at work.

He turns from his monitor to look at me. "Do I think *what*?"

I pretend I never asked.

"Should we just leave it like this?" He gestures to the search tool. The tool is now returning relatively good results, but if someone searches "white dwarf," it is game over. That query triggers a strongly worded error message. It reads, in bold capital letters, "CALL YOUR ADMINISTRATOR NOW."

Vin and I are both administrators.

He says, "How often is someone searching 'white dwarf,'" anyways? They've got nothing to do with the Rover project. Why don't we just avoid the term?"

I consider that suggestion, then say, "No. I think if 'white dwarf' does this, something else will too. The root cause of the problem isn't 'white dwarf.' The root cause of the problem is a bug."

✳

I am watching my old YouTube channel and pausing periodically to check my security camera app. The woman across the hall just brought in groceries.

In the YouTube video, I am talking about my middle school English teacher. I am doing so with a level of zeal that I now recognize is mortifying. My English teacher was a quirky woman in her late twenties who had short hair that she wore butterfly clips in. She wore overalls, beaded necklaces, and colorful eye shadow. It is painfully obvious in retrospect that I was in love with her.

"*Ms. Lemon taught me about haikus,*" I tell my audience adoringly. "*She is so smart and creative. She is my favorite teacher, for sure. She gave Chelsea detention for writing mean things on the cover of my notebook. I have literally never had such a nice teacher . . .*"

I put my hands over my face. I watch the video through my fingers like it is a snuff film.

"*Anyways,*" I say in a singsong voice, "*I wrote a poem for Ms. Lemon. Well, for her class, I mean. I am going to read it for you now.*"

Child-me clears her throat while now-me cringes.

Very solemnly, I recite:

"*I will be a ghost*
when I am not a child
I will frighten you."

The video ends.

What the fuck? Did I think that creepy-ass poem would woo Ms. Lemon?

I click "report video."

✳

Water spurts from my rusty faucet into my bathtub. I have lathered a bar of soap all over my body and am writing my name with my fingernails into the coating of soap on my chest. I play tic-tac-toe with myself on my legs and write "Hello" on my forearm.

I texted Polly hello yesterday, but she did not reply. That is for the best, I think. I wish I never texted.

I submerge my face in the bathwater.

I have a date with a polyamorous couple later. Their names are Eliza and Emma. I was a little put off by the alliteration because my name is Enid, and a throuple of queer women with similar names is a bit much; however, I discovered they own a restaurant and Emma is a chef. She is making us lemon tagliarini.

I lather rose shampoo in my hair while I listen to a podcast episode about the Toy Box Killer. The Toy Box Killer had a soundproofed truck trailer that he called his "toy box." He would kidnap, torture, rape, and kill women in it. He used things like saws, syringes, electricity, and dogs to torture the people he trapped. He often targeted lesbians. The worst part of the torture are the audiotape recordings of his voice that he would play for his victims.

The podcast is playing part of the recording. It starts with "*Hello there, bitch . . .*" then goes on to warn the listener what they are about to endure. I look up a picture of his ugly face while listening to him go on and on about what he plans to do to the listener. He is dead now, so the joke is on him because I am listening.

❋

"Can I pour you a glass of wine?" Eliza offers.

She and Emma live in a house with floor-to-ceiling windows. They have oversized surreal art hung on their walls, and their front yard is entirely a garden. They have no grass, just rows of snapdragons and violets.

I hold my cup out and say, "Yes. Thank you."

"So, you work for the Space Agency?" Eliza asks, clinking the mouth of the wine bottle on the lip of my glass.

I nod, watching my glass fill with foamy white wine.

"Do you know a lot about space?" she asks.

I swallow a sip of wine. "My job has less to do with space than it does with making information organized, but yes. I know some things."

"What's something cool I might not know?" she probes.

I consider the question.

"There's no sound in space."

She raises her eyebrows. "Really?"

I nod. Space is a vacuum, so it doesn't carry sound waves like air on earth does. We have probes in space though that capture radio emissions. The radio emissions have been converted into sound waves. In them, Saturn sounds like a robot in a windstorm crying for help, and the magnetic field around Jupiter hums like a frozen lake.

I say, "And you two own a restaurant?"

She smiles. "Yes."

"That's interesting, tell me more about that."

Emma shouts from the kitchen, "We should take you sometime! It's called the Cupboard. It's downtown. Have you been?"

"Not yet," I say. "I've heard good things though."

Eliza beams. She has a gummy smile and straight, bleached teeth. "Tell me about you, Enid. What do you do for fun?"

I pause.

"I've been getting into photography," I lie.

"That's cool," she says.

My phone vibrates. "Excuse me," I say, looking down at it. There is a notification coming from my security camera app. I open the app. It says someone is at my door.

"Is everything okay?" Eliza asks.

"I think so." I look at the camera. No one is there. "I have a new Ring camera at my apartment, and it says it senses motion, but I don't see anything."

"We have cameras in the restaurant. They can be very touchy. A fly has set ours off before."

"Really?" I look up from my phone.

"Yes. I'm sure it's nothing. Would you like to go check? It's fine if you need to—"

"No, no." I bat the air around me. "I'm sure it's just a ghost. Thank you."

✳

"Have you ever been in a poly relationship before?" Emma asks.

I have salad in my mouth. It involves seeds, citrus, and flavors I am unfamiliar with. I cover my mouth to say, "Briefly."

They flash smiles at each other. They are happy that I have been in a poly relationship, because it means I know what I am in for, but I don't. I don't know much about relationships regardless of the number of people involved. I had a very brief relationship with a woman in a poly relationship last year. I never met her other partner.

"Are you in therapy?" Eliza asks.

I am struggling to get a piece of lettuce on my fork. Each stab I attempt leaves four puncture marks in the leaf but does not result in the lettuce transferring onto my fork.

"Sorry if that's personal," she adds. "I have a hard time gauging what's appropriate first-date conversation. I've heard bisexual women often joke that on first dates with men they make awkward small talk, but with women they talk about their childhood trauma."

Emma and Eliza both laugh.

I laugh too, even though that has not been my experience.

"I am in between therapists right now," I lie.

I have never gone to therapy before.

Emma brings out bowls of lemon tagliarini. She has plated the pasta artfully with little mint leaves and lemon zest.

"Thank you," I say. "This looks beautiful."

The three of us begin spinning pasta on our forks.

After a few bites, they start telling me more about themselves. Emma quickly shares that her father is an alcoholic, and her mother enables him. She and her siblings were emotionally neglected, and they grew up very poor. She ate so much split pea soup and cinnamon sugar toast that the smell of either nauseates her now. Apparently, this is a big part of why she became a chef. She tells me that because she is the child of an alcoholic, she is afraid of authority figures, carries an overwhelming sense of responsibility, and constantly seeks approval. She also lets me know that she is working on all of this in therapy and is mindful about her own alcohol consumption.

I nod, pretending that I find it normal to hear someone overshare so much so fast.

Eliza quickly pipes in. She tells me that she grew up with a brother who had special needs. He died when they were teenagers, and her parents divorced shortly after. Her mother is now devotedly religious. Her father lives alone, seems depressed, and struggles to care for himself. She had behavioral problems as a child that she now understands stemmed from being the sibling of a child with a disability. She also has complicated grief, and post-traumatic stress disorder.

I eat my entire plate of pasta while the two of them continue to share all the hairy details of their private therapy sessions. They tell me what their attachment styles are, the sexual trauma both have endured, and what medications they take. Eliza is on Lexapro, Lamictal, and Naltrexone. Emma uses a lot of CBD and medical marijuana as well as Clonazepam, when needed.

Once in a while I say *Wow* or *Yikes* or *That's interesting. Tell me more about that.* But mostly I just eat my pasta and nod.

After all the food is eaten, Eliza takes our empty plates to the kitchen. Emma and I sip our wine while we listen to the clamor of trays and plates in the next room.

Eliza returns with small ramekins of soufflé and little cups of espresso.

I begin eating my dessert when Eliza says, "Now what about you, Enid?"

I swallow. "What about me?"

"Yes, what about you?" she repeats.

"U-um." I don't know what to tell them. I didn't realize this was the kind of date we were on. I thought we were just having pasta.

"Well." I clear my throat. "I am a Libra."

"What?"

"That's my horoscope," I clarify.

"Oh," they say. "We're not really big into horoscopes. Are you?"

I look at my dessert. "No, not really."

"What was your childhood like?" Eliza asks.

Jesus.

"Uh," I say. "It was good."

They both look at me. My answer was clearly unacceptable. They want the dirt.

"I-I was bullied?" I offer.

"Oh, for what?" Emma asks.

"Uh," I say. "I couldn't tell you. I was weird, maybe? I don't know. I'm a lesbian?"

They laugh.

"I'm also deaf in one ear." I touch my ear. "That was the source of some bullying for sure. I was insecure about it when I was a kid. I couldn't always hear my teachers, and I often missed parts of conversations. I think it impacted how I interacted with people."

"I couldn't tell you had a disability," Emma says.

I don't know how to reply. I've never considered it a disability.

"What about your home life?" Eliza continues to probe.

I look at their faces. They are staring at me, waiting for me to repay them for their secrets with mine. I swallow. "Well. My dad left my mom when I was a kid for another woman?"

I say this as if it is an offering. As if I am saying, *Is this good enough?* I am uncomfortable discussing personal topics with strangers, or anyone really. I also feel like their trauma is so much worse than mine, I feel embarrassed to even discuss mine.

They both look at me sympathetically. I almost wince at their expressions.

"That must have been awful," Eliza says, sipping her espresso.

"It really wasn't that bad. He didn't stay in contact with me, though. He started a whole new family. He ended up having two daughters. He named the first Edna, which is weird because that's pretty close to my name, don't you think? It's like he realized he was close on his first try at a daughter. He almost had it but needed some revisions." I laugh.

Neither of them laugh with me. They continue to look at me sympathetically.

"That's horrible," Emma says.

"That's really fucked-up," Eliza agrees.

I sip my drink. My face feels hot.

Maybe I should leave.

"How did your mom handle all of that?" Eliza asks.

I am sure that I did something terrible to deserve this conversation. I wish I could stand up and leave but I have eaten the food they artfully prepared for me. I listened to them talk about their lives. I wish I were capable of being rude enough to leave. I wish I were a different person.

Instead, I consider the question. I think of my mom waking me up at night, asking me to come sleep in her bed with her.

"She was okay," I lie.

Both women are eating their desserts, staring at me, rapt.

I can tell they want me to continue.

I exhale. "Um. So, my mom is sort of a romantic person. She loves romance novels and movies. She likes to tell me about dates she went on when she was younger. I think she really loved my dad. She seemed to pine for him after he left. I remember hearing her talk to friends on the phone about how maybe he would come back. When I was really little, I thought maybe he might. I had to figure out for myself that he wouldn't. Whenever we watched romantic comedies, she'd say the male lead reminded her of my dad. I don't know if she ever saw him for what he really was. They didn't date that long, and I'm sure I was an accident. I think she saw him as if he were her life's big love, or something."

Emma says, "Your poor mom. But poor you, too. That must have been so hard for you. Why did he cut off all contact with you? It's one thing to end a relationship with your mom, but his own kid?"

"Yeah, that was fucked-up. Your guess is as good as mine. When I was a kid, I thought he just didn't like me."

I watched a YouTube video of myself recently explain to my audience why I had no dad. I said, "*I do have a dad, he just doesn't like me.*"

Both women make a sad *aw* noise.

I feel uncomfortable. I wish we were discussing something else. I wonder if I can drive this conversation back to their trauma.

Eliza sips her espresso. "Some people compartmentalize

things, and it's unforgivable, but maybe he did it because it was easier for him to not address it."

We are all quiet for a moment.

"How was your mom in terms of your disability?" Emma asks.

"Uh," I say. "She was good, I think. It was, uh, never really a big deal. She had me go to a speech pathologist. I think a lot of kids do that, though. We talked about getting me a hearing aid, but I didn't want one. I thought I'd get made fun of, and it didn't feel necessary. I could hear. Besides that, I think I may have watched T.V. and listened to music kind of loudly, but my mom never asked me to turn it down. I actually didn't realize until I'd moved out and lived with roommates that I listened to things loudly. My roommates told me I did. My mom never complained about it. I remember always seeing ear plugs on her bedstand, but it never occured to me why she had them until I reflected on it later."

"That's sweet." Emma smiles.

"That is sweet, yeah. How was your high school experience?" Eliza asks.

I want to be grateful for the topic change; however, this subject isn't my preferred choice either.

"I can't remember it," I say.

"At all?" Emma asks.

I shrug. I think if I tried hard enough, I could remember. When I watch my YouTube channel, it jogs my memory. I have videos of myself as a teenager, but I was more guarded then. I didn't share as much. I just filmed myself applying makeup and trying on clothes.

I think the reason I don't remember high school is because I don't want to. Whenever it occurs to me to consider that time period, it's as if I close my mind's eye tightly so I can't see it.

"I don't remember much about it," I say. "I think it was just uneventful."

"Did you come out in high school?" she asks.

I pinch my leg under the table. I'm uncomfortable.

"No," I say. I came out after I graduated. "What about you two?"

"I didn't," Emma says. "I was almost twenty-four when I came out. It took me a little while to realize. Not like Eliza here—"

"I was thirteen." Eliza laughs. "I dated the one other queer girl at my school. We were a terrible match. We're still friends, though. She's married."

I find it impressive when queer people knew they were queer as kids or teenagers. I think it reflects a strong sense of self-awareness. I was not self-aware when I was a teenager. I can tell from my YouTube channel that I did not know who I was at all. I presented myself with no consideration toward my true personal tastes or interests. I wore the clothing I did, bought the things I did, and behaved how I did purely to protect myself from negative attention.

"Did you have boyfriends?" Eliza asks.

My memories of high school are shut behind a big ominous door in my mind. If I wanted to, I could open the door. I just don't want to. To answer Eliza's question, I approach the door and put an ear to it. Rather than look inside, I listen. I ask the door, "Did I have a boyfriend?" and the noise behind the door confirms, *yes, I did.*

"Yeah, I had one. His name was Ben. We only really dated for a month or two, though. Maybe three."

I have never dated anyone, regardless of gender, for more than a few months. I won't share that, however.

Both women laugh.

Despite being gay, I used to think about boys a lot. I wanted boyfriends when I was a teenager. I felt unsafe socially as a kid. I was insecure about my hearing, and something just felt off about me. I didn't feel like a normal person. I remember walking on the outskirts of the schoolyard, near the fence, trying to avoid the crowds. Once kids threw snowballs at me that had ice in them. They cut my upper lip and one of my eyelids. Another time, Chelsea Molloy cut my hair when she was sitting behind me in class.

I was louder when I was little. I would yell back, and it made it worse. I remember punching a boy who tripped me. We were both suspended for two days.

By the time Ben entered the picture, I had become quiet and agreeable. That lent itself to some teenaged boys liking me. The memory of who I was when I was younger faded slightly, and I was desperate to be liked so I could go to school without wanting to kill myself.

"It didn't occur to me that I was gay until right after finishing high school," I say. "I knew I was gay when I graduated. My high school was pretty toxic in terms of queerness. I don't remember much else about my high school, though. I was too preoccupied, I guess, pretending to be straight. What about you two? What were your experiences like?"

Emma says, "I smoked too much weed and had a lot of short-term boyfriends. I was busy pretending to be straight too, I guess."

Eliza says, "Not me. I was busy with my one girlfriend. I was also busy binge drinking and managing my eating disorder."

Emma interjects to share, "Eliza is a recovering anorexic."

I look at Eliza. I don't know what to say. I land on, "Good for you for owning a restaurant."

"Thank you." She smiles. She begins talking about diet culture. She says, "Women are oppressed by it. We are conditioned to run on a hamster wheel, constantly pursuing a tiny, thin body, so we don't have time to think about anything that's actually worthwhile. We just hate ourselves and occupy our minds with diet, diet, diet, and spend money on SlimFast and Atkins. It's oppressive."

I put the last portion of my dessert in my mouth. My spoon clanks against my teeth. I say, "I think it's also to keep us weak."

"What?" Eliza says. "What do you mean?"

"Like women are easier prey to murderers because we're all malnourished." I wipe my mouth off on my napkin.

They eye each other.

Eliza says, cautiously, "Right."

✳

Motion was detected again on my camera, but I don't see anyone there. I am walking home with my keys in my fist, in the hammer grip. I think a thunderstorm is coming. The air smells like rain and there's rumbling in the clouds. I am rushing home to avoid the downpour and to see what's making my camera go off. I turn the corner of my street and the sky lights up. I look up to see a lightning rod being thrown from one cloud to the other. I hear a delayed boom. The clouds tear open and heavy rain starts to plummet to the road. Each drop falling splats on the concrete loudly. It sounds like a clapping audience. I rush in the front door of my building, drenched. I hurry down the hall to my apartment, my keys still in the hammer grip. I turn the corner and spot my bald neighbor.

He is standing in the hall, right beside my door. I smell

something burning. His hand is very close to my doorknob. It looks almost as if he just left my unit. I stand still, gripping my keys. He furrows his brow and shuffles forward into his apartment, like a rat hiding in a kitchen when the light switch is flipped.

I rush into my unit and lock the door behind me. I add the extra security lock.

I look around my apartment. I open my top dresser drawer and survey my underwear. Nothing is missing. I study my belongings. I look at my boots and coats by my front door, at the mismatched plates in my cupboards and the books and tchotchkes on my shelves. I make an inventory in my head. I want to notice if anything goes missing or is moved.

I open my security camera app. I rewind through the footage and watch when he approaches my door. He stands in front of it. He stays there for a while. He opens his phone right in front of it, and looks at the door, as if he's writing my address down.

I sit on my couch, still surveying my belongings. One of my walls is covered in busy, yellow patterned wallpaper. I glance at it. I always see faces in it. The pattern looks like little Picasso eyes and mouths.

"Did you guys see anything?" I ask the flowers.

My phone goes off. It startles me.

I put a hand to my chest before looking down at the notification.

Polly texted me.

Would you like to go for a drive?

CHAPTER SEVEN

Polly and I are parked at a lookout that faces the river. When we arrived, the rain stopped, but the sky was still dark gray and ominous. As the sun set, orange light cracked along the horizon and is now reflecting in the water. Polly brought us peppermint tea in large take-out cups. We are sipping our drinks and looking out at the water. There are mallard ducks coupled and bobbling along together, occasionally dunking their heads. Today is the first official day of fall.

After a few peaceful moments of watching the ducks, I consider asking Polly why she wanted to go for a drive. I didn't think we would see each other again. While planning how to phrase myself, I glance at the car parked next to us. I realize that a couple is having sex in it. I choke on my most recent swig of tea and nudge Polly. She looks over just in time to spot the male participant's pale butt in the window. She cackles at the sight of it. After the initial shock and some laughing, we decide to be polite and pretend it isn't happening. We stare forward at the darkening sky and offer our neighbors the courtesy of not glancing at them.

"What do your tattoos mean?" she asks, touching one of the rats on my arm.

"Oh, they don't really mean anything," I say, looking down at them. "I just like them."

When I was younger, I thought tattoos were ugly. I had an epiphany as I aged that I loved them, so I covered myself in them. I have my rat tattoos, a tattoo of Gary from *SpongeBob*, and my mom's first name, Dawn, written above my knee.

"Do you have any tattoos?" I ask.

She shakes her head. "No, I'm too afraid of needles. I have thought of getting a tattoo of a bug, though. I was thinking of a cricket. They're a sign of good luck, and I love how they sound."

"It doesn't really feel like getting a needle in your skin," I say. "It feels more like scratching. You should get a cricket."

I can hear murmurs coming from the car next to us. I glance at it, then lean closer to Polly. "You don't think they want us to notice, do you?" I say under my breath, thinking of the podcast episodes I have listened to lately about perverts.

She makes a face. "I hope not. Should we leave?"

Before I can say yes, I notice red and blue flashing lights in the rearview mirror. A cop just pulled up behind us. Polly adjusts her seat so she is sitting more upright while the police officer exits his car. He slams his door, walks toward us, and raps his knuckles on the driver's-side window. I glance at the car next to us. The couple are shuffling into the front seats. I spot the man's butt again.

"What's going on in here?" the cop asks, shining a light into the car.

"We were just watching the sunset," Polly says, gesturing to the horizon.

The cop makes a face, as if Polly's lying. He mutters, "The sunset is long gone, ma'am. Are you aware that people come here for nefarious reasons?"

"Oh, like what?"

I stifle a laugh.

He looks in the car at me. "Are you both women?"

"Yes, why?"

He doesn't explain why. He says, "Cars are not allowed here after eight p.m., ladies. It's trespassing. Move it along."

Polly raises her eyebrows. "Okay. No problem."

He walks away from the window slowly, crunching the gravel below his feet. He walks around the back of our car and approaches the car next to us. Polly mutters, "That man's a dick," and I suppress another laugh. We can't back out yet because his trooper is behind us, so instead we watch him knock on our neighbor's window. After the window is rolled down, I notice a discernibly more chipper tone to his voice.

"Got a girl in here, young man?" he asks.

I listen to them laugh. I hear the happy murmur of their conversation. The girl in the car is giggling. I hear the cop say, "Don't let her dad find you." I then watch his hand make a fist and bump it against the driver's.

＊

Polly and I are now parked in a superstore parking lot. The store is closed. We are the only car here. There is a towering, bright streetlight above us. It sheds a white light down on us and the car. Polly is discussing how abhorrent she found that police officer. She rants. "I bet he just prowls around there every night, trying to catch a glimpse of teenagers having sex. Like what was he doing there? Who sneaks up on cars parked at a lookout?"

I laugh. She is very impassioned. She uses her hands a lot as she speaks.

"You know, I bet he is a pervert. And did you hear how he asked if we were both women? Was he being homophobic? What was that?"

"I don't know," I say. "I doubt it occurred to him that we could be lesbians. I've worn a T-shirt that literally says 'lesbian' on it around middle-aged men who ask me if I've got a boyfriend. I think you're right. He was just disappointed that we weren't teenagers having sex. Let's just catalog him in our minds in the place where we track our grievances."

She exhales. "Okay. Let's stop talking about him. Do you want to play a game?"

She shifts in her seat to face me.

"Sure." I turn toward her.

She touches my arm and says, "Okay, I'll say a word, and then you say the first thing you think of, okay?"

"Okay."

She says, "Red."

I say, "Blood."

She says, "Water."

I say, "Drowning."

She says, "Mother."

I say, "Psycho."

She laughs. "What the hell? Drowning? Why psycho? Is your mom psycho? Your answers were all fucked!"

I laugh. "Sorry. No, my mom isn't psycho. She has some issues, but no, I wouldn't call her that. I was thinking of Ed Gein."

"Of who?"

"Ed Gein, you know. The murderer who the movie *Psycho* is based on. He killed women who looked like his dead mother. He made shrines out of their skin and bones."

She stares at me.

"Sorry," I say. "I keep bringing up weird murderer things in situations when it's inappropriate. I don't know why I—"

"Do it with me," she interrupts, tapping my arm.

"Do what? The word association game?"

"Yeah." She smiles.

I say, "Okay. Red."

"Fire ants."

I say, "Water."

"Mayflies."

"Psycho."

"You."

We laugh.

She reaches across the center console between us to squeeze my leg. She grins. "I like you. You're weird."

I smile. A feeling similar to fear buds in my chest.

She looks at me. I find she often looks at me for longer than is normal, as if she is searching my face for something.

She looks away and puts her keys in the ignition. I buckle my seat belt. We pull out of the parking lot and turn down a dark street. It is after midnight and there are few cars on the road.

My skull bobbles against the headrest. We start driving over a bridge, which scares me. I can't help but picture bridges collapsing whenever I am on them. I roll down my window in case it does, to make it easier for me to escape the car underwater.

She has the radio on. A Janis Joplin song is playing. She sings along to the lyrics with zeal. My eyes are closed.

"Take another little piece of my heart now, baby!"

"Break it!"

We have passed the bridge, so I open my eyes.

I start to think of returning to my apartment. I picture watching myself on my security camera. I see me opening the door, tossing my keys in a dish, and standing face-to-face with a bald man.

I smell burning.

I glance at Polly. I watch her hair whip her face as she belts along to the song.

I start singing with her despite having a terrible singing voice.

When the song is over, I ask, "Can I sleep over at your house?"

✳

There is a piano in Polly's living room. It is made of dark oak, and it is covered in black tapered candles. Polly is in the kitchen pouring us glasses of water. I stand in front of the piano and wonder if it is Polly or Joan who plays. Would it be inappropriate to ask? If it's Joan's piano, it might be a sore subject—

"Do you play?" Polly asks.

I jump. I didn't realize she had reentered the room.

"No," I say. She hands me a glass of water. "Do you?"

"Yeah, obviously. This is my house. I own that piano."

"Yeah, well, I just wondered if . . ." I trail off.

"What?"

"If it was, uh, a decoration," I say, rather than mention Joan.

She says, "No, I play it. My mom is a piano teacher. Well, she's retired. So, I learned to play when I was very little. I hated practicing when I was a kid, but I love to play it now."

"Let's hear a song."

She smirks. "You don't really want me to play it, do you?"

"Yeah. Why not?"

"Really?"

"Yeah."

She sits down on the bench. She plays *Twinkle, Twinkle Little Star* quickly; her fingers press into the keys so rapidly the song sounds as if it is being fast-forwarded. She starts to shut the tray that covers the keys, but I stop her. I say, "Wait. Play another."

She looks at me. "Have you ever been at a party where someone picks up a guitar despite no one asking them to and starts playing 'Wonderwall' against everyone's will? I would hate to be that person. I don't want to force you to listen to me play the piano—"

"This isn't like that," I say. "I want to hear you play. I'm asking you to."

She looks at me. She says, "Fine."

She maintains eye contact with me as her fingers rush along the keys.

"How's this?" she asks.

She looks at me and not at her hands. She plays a song that I assume is Mozart, but I do not know much about music. It sounds complicated and fast, like the soundtrack to a bug being hunted through the sky by a bat, twirling through tree branches, plummeting to the ground, zigzagging. Soaring upward. Escaping.

"Is this good for you?" she asks, still playing without looking at her hands.

She bows her head with concentration. She hunches over the keys. Her hair falls into her face as she reaches her arms and presses down with strength. The house vibrates with the noise. She seems almost angry as the song intensifies. Her eyes are closed tightly. She moves rapidly, her fingers stretched and twisting, jumping from key to key. As she finishes the song she bangs her hands into the keys, making a clashing noise that sounds somehow both intentional and like a cat being chased across the piano. She slams the keys, then exhales loudly, and I stand stunned in the quiet ringing that reverberates through her house.

"Are you impressed?" she asks.

I wonder if I appreciated that as well as someone with good hearing.

"A little," I joke.

✳

Polly is in the shower. I am sitting cross-legged on her bed, listening to the water run. She has a king-sized mattress with oatmeal-colored blankets and pillows.

I roam around the room like a stalker who snuck in to rummage through her things. I feel like I am not supposed to be here. There is a framed display case of dead butterflies above her bed, a candle shaped like the headless bust of a woman on her dresser, and a little TV mounted to the wall. I look at a red-and-white-striped sweater hanging over the door of the closet and wonder, *Is that Polly's or Joan's?*

Her bedside tables are both piled with books. I look at their spines; there is an antique book of fairy tales, a book about the

Salem witch trails, and an encyclopedia of insects. Next to the books, there is a little ceramic plate with a gold wedding band and an engagement ring in it. I stare at the plate. A bit of light reflects from the stone in the engagement ring and shines a white spot on the wall.

I wonder what their wedding was like. I wonder if they wrote their own vows, and if they had a honeymoon. Maybe they eloped.

Her curtains have a floral pattern in them. They look sort of like my yellow wallpaper. They are covered in flower buds and vines. The way the petals fold look sort of like eyelids. The way the vines curve looks like little mouths. I sit, looking into the pattern in the curtains, as if looking at a crowd of faces who are all wondering what I am doing in this room.

I take off all my clothes and crawl under the oatmeal covers. The sheets are thick, and the pillows smell like lavender.

✳

Polly leans over me in the same way she does a piano. She has a sort of angry talent. She seems both practiced and sloppy; banging on the keys, her hair in her face, her shoulders slouched over me. I look at her strained neck; at the veins that connect her head to her heart. I think of murderers cutting throats open. I think of heads being chopped off and people being strangled to death. I wrap my fingers around her throat. She rolls so I am on top of her. She stretches her neck while I keep my hand wrung around her. She does nothing to free her breathing. She trusts me to choke her.

✳

Polly braids her legs into mine and presses herself against my back. The heat from her body warms mine until her feet touch me.

I shriek. "Why are your feet so cold?"

"I'm a vampire," she replies. "I'm dead. Is that cool?"

I say, "No, it's not."

She cackles and puts her face in the groove of my neck and my shoulder. She falls asleep quickly, but I don't. I lie wide awake with her attached to my back like a jet pack, thinking of bugs being chased by bats through the sky.

✳

Joan and I were seeing each other casually for about a month. Every time we met up, it was at my house, and we barely spoke.

While Polly sleeps, I scroll through my old texts with Joan. The texts reveal very little. They mostly say things like, Are you free? and I'm here. I leaf through my memories as I scroll, trying to pull out what I can to better understand Joan and Polly's relationship.

I met up with a lot of other people from dating apps while I was seeing Joan. I don't remember her well. She has sort of blended into the other people.

I see that I messaged her first. I suggested she come over. She was hesitant. Maybe I thought she was just playing hard to get. When she came over, I remember it was midafternoon. Maybe she didn't think she would have an affair. Maybe she was just toeing the line. Maybe she was having a hard time; Polly mentioned she and Joan had been struggling. Joan's dad died, she said. Maybe she had been depressed. Maybe that drove her to do this.

I think of her hands. I don't think she wore a wedding ring. Did she take it off before coming over?

I glance at Polly snoring beside me. Her arms are stretched across the bed.

I wonder if Joan is devastated by this breakup. I wonder if she has a box of Polly's old love letters that she looks through at night. Maybe she hopes they will get back together.

I hate thinking of someone feeling like that.

I look down at my phone.

I text my mom.

Hey mom, just letting you know it rains diamonds on Jupiter and Saturn.

✳

In the morning, I reach across the bed, feeling the heat of the unfilled space where Polly slept. She must have gotten up already. I open one eye to confirm she is not here.

I fish through the blankets for my phone. When I finally find it, I check to see whether my mom has replied to my fun fact yet. I see that she hasn't, but it's early. She might be sleeping in.

I open my security camera app. I rewind through the footage to see if anyone came into my apartment last night. I see people walk by, but no one stops.

I sit up, stretch, and climb out of the bed. I take the red-and-white sweater off the closet door. Polly reenters the room as I pull it over my face.

"I tried to wake you up," she says. "I spoke right into your ear. I said, *Rise and shine!* but you kept snoozing. You must have been really tired."

I look at her.

"I'm deaf in one ear," I admit. "You were probably on my bad side."

"Are you really?" she says.

I nod.

She has two mugs of coffee in her hands. She tells me she put sugar and cream in mine, but if I don't like that she can remake it. I say, "Thank you, I like it this way."

We sit on the edge of her bed, sipping our coffee together. I feel out of place.

I turn to her. "Do you mind if I play an episode of a true crime podcast? I normally listen to it when I wake up."

She says, "Sure," and crawls further into her bed. She stuffs pillows behind her back to lean comfortably against her headboard.

*

After spending the morning lying in Polly's bed, listening to episode after episode of my podcast, we got hungry. We are now at the grocery store buying the ingredients to make tacos.

"Excuse me!" an angry woman shouts at me. She shoves my shoulder.

This startles me but I realize as she storms off that she probably attempted a more polite encounter first on my deaf side. Though of course it is possible that I have just been the target of gratuitous antagonism.

Polly is standing nearby inspecting a bag of jalapeños. She looks at me. She mouths, *Did that woman just shove you?*

I nod. "Yeah, but it's probably because—"

She marches after her. I watch as she confronts the lady. The spray that is released on the cabbages is misting me.

Polly is shouting. "She's deaf in an ear! She didn't hear you!"

Every time the woman tries to get a word in, Polly raises her voice.

"Even if she had heard you, shoving people is unacceptable! You're in a society!"

✳

My hands are folded in my lap. Polly is driving. The podcast is playing, but I can't hear it. There is a guest host, and I think their voice is too high-pitched. I wish I could hear it. I don't like driving in silence. I find myself thinking too much. There's something about looking at the world blur by without noise that makes me pensive. I don't like being alone with my thoughts. I can see that the podcast is playing on the console. Maybe the volume is too low.

"Can you please turn the volume up?" I ask.

"What?" Polly shouts.

It must be playing loudly already. I don't want to ask her to blare it if it's already loud.

I'll just sit here.

I look out my window. I watch rows of pine trees blur into each other. I close one eye. I wonder what it's like to be half-blind.

I glance at Polly with one eye shut. Her eyes are on the road. I stare at her, like a pirate, and think about how she stood up for me in the grocery store. I wonder why she did that. I wonder if she does that for everyone.

"Why are you staring at me?" I read her lips. She is still focused on the road.

"I'm not," I lie.

"What?" She leans forward and turns the podcast volume down. I watch how far she turns the dial down and note it must have been on loud.

"What did you say?" she says.

I open my mouth.

"Nothing. I said, uh. Thank you."

"For what?"

"For . . ." I trail off. "For stopping at my mom's house."

"What?"

"I was just thanking you preemptively for stopping at my mom's house. Do you mind if I drop some stuff for her? I told her I'd stop by today."

This is a lie. The truth is that she hasn't replied to my interesting fact yet, and I saw stroopwafel cookies in the store. She likes those and I can't always find them.

"Oh. Sure. Of course." She puts her hand on my leg.

I direct her to my mom's house while we listen to more of the murder podcast. She gasps at the shocking parts in the story. I still can't hear it. I can only hear her. She makes comments like, "Are you kidding me?" and "No way!"

When we park outside my mom's house, she pauses the podcast. She says, "I'll wait here for you, okay?"

I try not to seem panicked as I unbuckle my seat belt. I feel my usual compulsion to bolt into the house, but I temper it. I don't want Polly to think I'm strange.

I amble up the lawn toward the front door. I take steady paces up the steps. I unlock the door and flick the light switch. The light fixture is out.

I inhale as I shut the door behind me. The house smells like something rotting. I shout, "Mom?"

"Mom?"

I feel my heartbeat migrate into my throat. I scream, "MOM?"

"MOM?"

I smell smoke. I stumble to the stairs in a panic. I clutch the railing with wet hands and almost slip.

I catch myself, inhale deeply, and think:

If Jupiter disappeared, Earth would be hit by more asteroids. Jupiter's gravitational pull grabs a lot of space trash heading toward us.

If the moon disappeared, the Earth would tilt. Our ocean tides would weaken. The sky would be darker at night.

"MOM!" I shriek again.

"Is everything okay?" Her voice bounces off the walls in the stairwell. When it reaches my ear, there is an echo. "Is everything okay?" I hear again.

I look up and see her standing on the landing in a nightgown. I exhale, relieved to see her—but by the time I inhale again, I feel angry.

I shout, "You tell me!"

"What's wrong?" she asks. "What's wrong?" the echo asks again.

"Your house is a fucking disaster! It smells like smoke!" I yell. There are garbage bags sitting by the front door, waiting to be brought out but forgotten. There are multiple sodden washcloths on her staircase. They look as if they were thrown down for the laundry but never picked up. The light is burned out.

"Like smoke?" she asks. "I don't smell smoke—"

"Put on your lipstick!" I scream from the bottom of the stairs.

She looks confused. I feel like crying. I feel like my parasite took over.

She stammers, "Y-you just caught me at a bad time—"

I make a noise like she just punched me and spin around.

I throw her cookies into the belly of her dark house before I leave. I try to slam the storm door behind me, but it has that hardware that prevents it from banging.

✳

I position my head at the foot of Polly's bed, and my feet in the pillows. Polly flips through her book about bugs and pauses to ask me questions about the podcast. She becomes especially interested in the death of JonBenét Ramsey, who was a six-year-old beauty queen who was suspiciously killed in her family's home. No one has ever been charged with her murder.

After listening to more than three podcast episodes about JonBenét, Polly says, "Okay, there is absolutely no reasonable explanation that makes any intruder theory make even remote sense."

I say, "You're right."

She has reading glasses on the edge of her nose. She puts her open book down on her chest and says, impassioned, "Was it her dad? Or her brother? Or her mom? Was it Patsy? Do you think Patsy did it?"

✳

Polly and I toil diligently to solve the murder of JonBenét. She says, "What I can't get over, is that no one has been charged. It's not like this was some masterful murder. It was sloppy. How the hell could no one be charged?"

I nod. "I agree. The ransom letter was careless. It was amateur."

"And it's not as if they didn't find her body. She was right there. If someone kills you, who should I suspect?"

"What?"

"Who should I suspect killed you if you randomly get murdered? This whole thing is making me think that everyone should keep a running list of the people they think should be looked into if they're murdered. For me, it's Joan, obviously. I don't think she'd kill me, but we're going through a divorce, so if I die, definitely look into her. There was also a girl I was best friends with as a kid who I think was a sociopath. She would lie to me about having boyfriends from other schools, and she'd weave these weird, complicated webs about how people hated me and thought I was ugly and stupid. She wrote me a letter once and pretended a boy in our class wrote it, saying basically *Everyone hates you*. Her name's Theodora Kline. She goes by Tea. I have her blocked on all social media."

I think about Joan. I consider how she followed me and Polly to a restaurant. I think of how she threw water in my face.

"Who should I look into for you?" she asks.

I look at her. "Do you think Joan would follow me?"

*

After spending the weekend at Polly's, she drives me home. I am wearing her gym clothes and carrying what I wore to her house in a white plastic bag with a yellow smiley face on it. My hair feels flatter than usual because I have been using her unfamiliar hair products. I smell like her lavender pillows and coconut shampoo.

She pulls up in front of my apartment building. I unbuckle my seat belt and thank her for the ride. She reaches for me across the center console to kiss me goodbye and as I lean back, she says, "It was Burke."

"What?"

"Burke, JonBenét's brother. I think he killed her."

I say, "What about that investigator?"

"He was suspicious too, you're right. Damn. Can we hang out again later to solve it?" she asks.

I look at her. "Sure."

She smiles while I exit the car.

I walk up to the front door of my building. As I step forward, my knees start to feel weak. I'm nervous to go inside. I haven't been here in two days.

I turn around to see if Polly is idling, but she has already driven off.

I look at my phone. Vin's texted me a lot. I read the messages. They say, "Hey," and above that:

Hello? Reply. Where are you? Why are you ignoring me?

I didn't reply to him all weekend. I was preoccupied at Polly's.

I open my security camera app on my phone. I check that no one is outside my door.

I continue up the steps. My hands are sweating. I swing open the heavy metal door. I rush through the hallway, afraid of seeing anyone. I look over my shoulder and my hands shake as I unlock my door.

I finally scuttle inside. I slam and lock my door behind me. I add my security lock, then turn around. A cold chill travels down my back.

Someone has been inside my apartment. My closet door is open. Lights I know I turned off are on.

I open my app and rewind through the footage until I see it. My heart starts beating in my throat.

Someone came in. The footage shows them approaching the door, unlocking it, and swinging it open. They exit later. It doesn't capture their face clearly. I have paused and zoomed in, but they are wearing a hoodie and moving too quickly. Their face is a blur.

CHAPTER EIGHT

"Hello, Joan, this is Enid," I say into my phone.

"What the hell do you want?"

"I need to know, have you been inside my apartment?"

"What?"

"Have you been inside my apartment? Have you been following me?"

"What the fuck? No. How dare you? I'm not a stalker."

I remain silent to give her more of an opportunity to fess up.

I say, "I'm sorry, but please tell me the truth. I'm freaked out. Someone has been in my apartment, and I've felt like someone's been following me for a while now. You showed up at that restaurant Polly and I went to. You were following us—"

"I'm not fucking following you. I followed Polly once. I went to one restaurant. Give me a break. I don't give a shit what you do. I don't give a shit what Polly does anymore either, by the way—"

"Are you being honest?" I interrupt.

"Yes. Why would I lie?"

I pause. "I don't know."

"Get a fucking dog."

"What?"

"If you feel like someone has been following you, get a dog. I'm going to hang up now."

"Okay."

"Bye."

✴

I can't get a dog. My landlord is obsessed with ensuring that there are no pets in his building. This morning I received another less-than-subtle email reminder from him about that. It had a red exclamation mark next to it and it was titled "PETS ARE NOT ALLOWED IN THE BUILDING UNDER ANY CIRCUMSTANCES."

Wait. Maybe it was him. Maybe he was in my apartment.

I dial his number.

"Peter Holt speaking," he answers after one ring.

"Hi, have you been in my apartment this weekend?"

"Who is this? Which apartment?"

"Enid Hughes. I live at eighty-seven Frank Street, unit four. Someone was in here. Was it you?"

"No, I haven't been there. Why do you think someone was in there? Is there a mess? Do you have a pet? Pets can cause messes if you leave them unattended. That is why they are not allowed under any—"

"I don't have any pets. I have a Ring camera and saw someone enter. Can you please tell me if it was you?"

"No, it wasn't me. You should call the police."

✳

"Hello, what's your emergency?"

"Hi," I say. "Could you please send someone? My apartment has been broken into."

"Okay, are you in immediate danger?"

I glance around. "I hope not."

I saw the person leave on my camera. I wish I bought a more expensive camera so I could tell who it was. The footage is black and white, pixelated, and blurry because the criminal was moving too much. They must have been rushing to get inside. If it wasn't Joan, and it wasn't my landlord, who was it? My gut is telling me it was the bald face I saw in my window. That it was my neighbor coming in here to cut my throat in my sleep.

"An officer will only attend if you are afraid to enter the premises. Are you afraid to enter?"

I open my mouth. "Y-yes," I say hesitantly, despite already being inside the premises.

He says, "Okay, what's the address?"

"Eighty-seven Frank Street, unit four."

"Someone will be there shortly."

"Thank you." I hang up.

✳

"You should change the locks," the detective says.

He and I are in my kitchen. I am trying to veil that I am in distress. I think that I am having an anxiety attack. I had to call in to work. "Are you sure nothing is missing?" he asks.

"I don't think so." Before he arrived, I rifled through my belongings to check if anything is gone. Nothing is. Whoever came in here didn't come to rob me. Perhaps I'm feeling a little frantic, but the only other motive left, that I can think of, is that they came to murder me.

I showed him the footage on my camera. As he examines my apartment, I wander behind him, tapping on my pressure points. I point out the security bar in my window. I say, "Look, I put that there for safety," as if fishing for him to compliment my attempts to save myself.

I put two fingers on my neck, monitoring my pulse, while he inspects my vents to assess whether they could fit a person. He says they couldn't. He jokes, "Maybe a baby?"

"I don't know any babies," I say. My pulse is out of control. "My sister is pregnant, though. My half sister, I should say. It's a girl."

He says, "I don't really think a baby came in here."

I realize by his expression that I have exposed myself as insane; however, I don't care. His stupid joke was poorly timed. I am the victim of a crime.

I say, "No, I know."

"Are you feeling okay?" he asks.

I look at him.

"It's normal to feel uneasy after a break-in."

"Is it?"

"Of course. Do you have any idea who might have come in here? Is there anyone in your life that you suspect?"

"I'm not sure," I say. "There's a woman named Joan, but I called her and she said it wasn't her. Maybe my landlord, but he said it wasn't him. I have a neighbor." I pause. "He's b-bald."

"What's he done to make you suspect him?"

I consider the question. "Nothing really, I guess. I've seen him around. I thought I saw him or someone who looked like him in my window . . ."

"Does he look like the person in the footage?"

"I can't tell. The footage is too blurry."

"The person in the video looks to be about five eleven. Is that how tall your neighbor is?"

"I don't know."

He hums. "Okay. Well, I have to ask a strange question now. Forgive me, but did you check your underwear? Sometimes perverts take women's underwear."

I resist the urge to inform him that I am well aware of that. Instead, I say, "Yes, I checked. No underwear is missing. Why? Is somebody out there stealing women's underwear right now?"

He nods. "Yes, there always is."

Great.

✷

Vin keeps texting me.

Why aren't you at work?

Where are you?

The doors to my car are locked. I am trying to soothe myself with my calming murder stories.

I write,

Someone broke into my apartment.

He replies immediately.

There you are!

I close my eyes and listen to the story of a woman escaping a murderer. He locked her in her bathroom while he prepared a tarp to kill her on, as if it were a picnic blanket, but she shimmied out the skylight.

He texts me again.

Are you okay?

Yes.

Good. Why didn't you reply to me all weekend?

I was at a girls house.

Oh.

He writes.

Then,

What's her name?

I don't reply.

Is it Polly?

Can I meet her?

✳

Polly and I are having coffee on a patio. I did not tell her about the break-in. I would prefer she did not know. She texted me, asking if I would like to hang out again after work. I said yes. Now, I am pretending that I worked today.

"Nothing like a coffee at the end of a long day's work, right?" I sip my Americano. The caffeine is mixing with my preexisting panic. Coffee drops spurt from my cup onto my shaking hand. "How was your day?"

"I get to help name a park," she tells me. "Got any creative suggestions?"

I think, and then suggest, "Jurassic? Abusement?" I look at my arms. "Something to do with rats?"

"Enid?" I hear someone address me.

I look over my shoulder.

"Is that you Enid, honey?"

It's Gina. She is approaching our table. She has shopping bags in her arms.

"Hi," I say, unhappy to see her unexpectedly.

"Hi. Who is this?" She smiles at Polly.

Polly shakes her hand. "I'm Polly. Enid's date."

Gina squirms and Polly notices.

I look down at my drink.

"So, two friends out getting coffee?" Gina tries to drive the conversation back to where she is comfortable.

Polly says, "Two friends? No. We're on a date. It's a romantic date. We're lesbians."

Gina's face flushes. So does mine. She laughs, batting the air around her as if swatting what was said away. "Well, it's lovely to see you, Enid." She squeezes the top of my arm. "I just wanted to say hello, since I saw you. You are coming to Edna's baby shower I hope?"

I nod.

"Wonderful," she says through a pained smile.

She starts to walk away and Polly scowls.

"Who was that woman?" She slurps her coffee. "She's a bitch."

Gina hears and pauses. My eyes widen. Is she going to pretend she didn't hear?

"Excuse me?" Gina turns around.

Fuck.

Polly glares. "You were just so weird about us being lesbians."

"I didn't say anything." Gina puts a hand to her chest, outraged.

"Okay, well, I did. I said you're a bitch."

Gina looks at me. "This is an extremely disrespectful friend, Enid. I don't think your father would approve—"

"My father?" I repeat, shocked.

"I'm not her friend," Polly interjects. "I'm her date. What's so hard about that?"

Gina is faltering. She keeps opening her mouth and closing it. "I-I just want to have a nice relationship with you, Enid. I'm trying really hard. The girls want to be friends. They care a lot about you." She starts crying. Her voice is breaking. "It's a lot to expect of me. This is a very difficult relationship for me—"

"Because she's gay?" Polly asks.

"No, because she's my late husband's daughter, and a point of serious contention in our relationship, and I am a grieving widow. I miss my husband and I want my daughters to be happy. I am trying really hard to make this all work for everyone, but I'm extremely upset, and it is uncomfortable for me, and I can't—"

"This woman is fucking crazy." Polly looks at me. "Is she your mom?"

"No." I look at Gina.

"Please. Go home." I try to calm her down. "It's okay. We can pretend this never happened."

Gina wipes tears from her cheeks and says, "Okay."

I watch her leave.

"Do you want to go to a movie later?" Polly asks as if nothing happened.

I frown. "What the fuck?"

"What?" she says.

"You can't just—" I pause. "You can't just call people I know 'bitches.'"

I'm worried about Gina talking to my sisters. I'm worried about them disliking me. I don't want her to tell them I'm awful, or to stay away from me. I don't want to be someone they dislike. I have been trying to be careful with them.

Polly looks taken aback. "What? You didn't think she was being a bitch?"

"Obviously I think she was being a bitch. She's the worst, but we could have ignored that. I don't want to be in arguments with that woman. Who wants that needless stress? Just nod and smile."

"You wanted me to ignore that? I don't just nod and smile. I always speak up when someone is being rude—"

"And you can't just tell middle-aged women that I'm a lesbian," I interrupt her. "What if that were a secret? What if she were my homophobic boss? That was really careless of you."

"Oh," she says. "Sorry. Was she your boss? I wasn't trying to be careless—"

"No, she's my sisters' mom, but no one tries to be careless. The whole point is that you didn't consider the repercussions of your behavior. You know, it can be unpleasant to be non-consensually in the firing range of you yelling at someone. Sometimes the intensity of your reaction is out of proportion with the injustice that you're reacting to."

She scowls. "Fuck you. You think it's out of proportion to call someone a bitch for refusing to acknowledge we're on a date? I don't want to be passive-aggressive just because she is. I'm not going to bother cloaking my delivery in niceties for her. That's exhausting."

"That's what people do," I say. "That's normal behavior."

"Normal behavior?" she says. "Are you a stickler for that? I didn't realize."

I look at her. "Are you calling me weird?"

"Yes," she says. "You are weird."

"Okay." I stand up. I brush crumbs from my pants. I ate a muffin earlier. "I'm having a terrible day. I can't do this. Someone broke into my apartment this weekend. I've been dealing with cops all day. I'm pretty sure I'm being targeted by someone. And Gina knows I'm a lesbian. She's clearly not cool with that, and now you're calling me weird? I'm exhausted. I am not interested in any additional problems—"

"What? Someone broke into your apartment?"

"Yes." I stop trying to hide my tremors. My arms are shaking. "I think a bald man has been following me."

"Oh my God. Are you okay?"

"I'm fine." I look at her. I sneer, "I'm a little weird, but I think I'll be okay."

She breathes air out of her nose. "I'm sorry for calling you weird, Enid. You're right, it was careless of me to call that woman a bitch. I have a hard time veiling my real feelings. I say what occurs to me, but I shouldn't always do that. I'm sorry, okay?"

I don't feel well.

I exhale. "No, I'm sorry. It's fine. I'm just having a bad day. I'm not really thinking through what I'm saying."

Our eyes connect.

I look away. "I actually like that you say what you're thinking. I don't know why I said otherwise. I'm not feeling like myself."

I look at her again. "I'm still going to leave now though, okay? But I'm not mad. I just don't feel right. We're fine, right?"

She says, "Yes. We're fine. I'm sorry you're having a bad day."

I push my chair in. "Thank you."

✳

"I think you're overreacting about this break-in," Vin says.

He invited me to stay over at his house. I told him I did not want to stay at mine until the locks are changed. Perhaps even then.

I look at him. "Wouldn't you be afraid to sleep at your place if someone burglarized it?"

He sighs. "I guess. I don't know. I just think it's a stretch to say burglarized. No one stole anything. It was probably just your landlord. I really think you're blowing this out of proportion. I don't think you should overreact—"

"I called my landlord. He said it wasn't him—"

"He probably lied."

Vin is using the same voice he uses on the phone with his mom. I sense he feels frustrated by me. He must think I'm being rash and unreasonable, but I'm not.

I frown. "Why would he lie?"

"Because he's a landlord! He's always sending you those animal emails. He's probably just illegally inspecting his property. I've had landlords that came into my house without notice all the time. I really think you're being paranoid."

I exhale. "Well, we are two very different people."

"What do you mean?"

"You assume the best and I assume the worst. Imagine you say all that, you tell me not to worry, I go home, tuck into bed, and then I'm murdered in cold blood. Wouldn't you find it hard to live with yourself?"

He rolls his eyes. "You're not going to be murdered."

"People get murdered, Vin."

"I know people get murdered, Enid, but you're not going to get murdered. You're being paranoid. You consume too much true crime content. You're driving yourself insane."

I don't say anything. He starts putting sheets on his couch for me. Despite feeling annoyed by me, he is fluffing my pillow.

I wonder if I am imposing. Maybe it's true that I am over-reacting. Maybe it's annoying to hear someone exaggerate. I know he has his own problems.

"How is your mom?" I ask.

"My mom? Oh, she's okay," he says. "I have to check on her, you know. Like you do with your mom. Lately she's been fine, but not great. She's taking her medicine. I had to devote a solid four hours of my life to begging her to, but she promised she's back on them. I'm sure it'll be an issue again in a few months, but for now, she's stable. But I think we'll have to have this fight forever, until she dies."

Our eyes connect. The reality of having mothers like ours is that the only possible reprieve from worrying about finding them dead is them dying. As long as they are alive, the threat that they might die persists. Of course, anyone's mother can die, but this is different. In this case, they might not have if we had just argued with them to take their medicine, or if we ran into their house faster and got inside in time.

"How is your mom?" he asks.

I look at him. "She isn't wearing lipstick."

"I'm sorry to hear that," he says.

✳

Vin's sofa is my bed tonight. I dream that my mom is dead and I feel happy. I am throwing a party. There are balloons, streamers, and I am making a cake. I do not watch it bake. I decide that I don't need to. The cake starts burning. Flames are growing and engulfing the room. People are screaming. "Who started this fire?"

"What kind of sick freak would do this?"

"This is horrible!"

"Someone is dead!"

✳

"Enid speaking," I answer the phone on my desk.

"Hi Enid, this is George Fox."

My heart drops.

"Sorry to bug you," he says. "But I heard you're the person to call if folks have questions about taxonomy. Is that true? Are you the taxonomy person?"

I inhale. "Uh."

I close my eyes. I tell myself to pretend he has hair. I can't see him on the phone. Just picture him with hair.

He says, "Are you busy right now? Would it be easier for me to come by your desk?"

"No," I say quickly. "No. I am busy right now, sorry, but I prefer phone calls. Maybe, uh. Maybe you could call me later?"

"Sure, no problem. How's tomorrow at eleven?"

"Fine, sure." I hang up.

✳

My Ring camera app alerts me that someone is at my door. I am in a meeting with my boss, but I open the app anyways. I look at my phone in my lap to see who is at the door and gasp.

"What's wrong?" my boss asks.

It is my bald neighbor. He is knocking on my door.

"Is everything okay?"

∗

"Peter," I say, out of breath. I just ran to the bathroom to call my landlord. I lean on the inside of a stall. "Did you do a criminal background check on my new neighbor? T-the . . . the *bald* man?"

"Of course I did."

"Did anything come back? He was just knocking on my door. Someone broke into my apartment, and now he's knocking on my door—"

"What? Just because he's knocking on your door doesn't mean he's who broke in."

"He's a creep!" I yell. "Unless it was you who came in, I think it was him. Does he have a record? Is he lying about who he is? Has he ever attacked anyone? Has he—"

"What? Are you okay? What are you talking about? He's a perfectly nice man! He's an accountant."

I think of John List, a bald mass murdering accountant who shot everyone in his family in the back of their heads.

"How tall is he? Five eleven? If he's five eleven—"

"I don't know how tall he is. Pull yourself together," he says. "The locks are being changed today. Everything is fine. Break-ins happen all the time. Just remember that pets are not allowed in the building, and keep your door locked. I've been getting complaints about stolen packages, and now this has happened, so I plan to send out a mass email today about letting people who don't live in the building piggyback in when the door is unlocked. We just need to follow better security practices."

＊

I am inside my apartment despite every atom in my body compelling me to leave. The locks have been changed and I deluded myself in the hour following that everything was fine. Everyone I consulted—my landlord, the police, Vin—all said it was safe to return here. They all said, "Go home, you're paranoid, don't let your fear fester, it's safe, you're safe."

I'm not. I am wielding my baseball bat. My murder podcast is playing. I pace the kitchen, imagining my bald neighbor opening my door, running at me, and assaulting me like a rabid loup-garou.

I practice swinging the bat, imagining he is in front of me. I picture the bat striking his head, and it flying off him like a softball into space.

The podcast is telling the story of a taxidermist being murdered. He was killed with a plastic bag and stuffed like one of his squirrels. When his body was found, investigators speculated whether the bag was placed postmortem.

"*Plastic bag deaths are rare,*" the podcast host says. "*They are usually accidental. Children kill themselves. Deaths in autoerotic situations have also been noted. In this case, the autopsy found, however, that the taxidermist was, in fact, suffocated with the bag.*"

I grab the bag that I keep all my other plastic bags in from beneath my sink. I eye the rest of my kitchen for other weapons I could brandish. My frying pans. My knives.

He is underestimating me. I am more capable than he suspects. I can do damage. I have a parasite.

I swing the bat again.

If he comes in here, I think I could kill him. I am capable of it.

There's a knock on my door. I duck, despite there being no conceivable way that I could be seen here. I open my phone to the security camera app.

It's him. He's standing at my door. He's knocking.

What the fuck?

My chest is pounding. An electric current runs through my entire body. It's in the strands of my hair. I reach into the depths of my gut for the bravery to shout, "How tall are you?"

I watch his face through the peephole. I read his lips. He says, "What the fuck?"

"How tall are you?" I repeat, louder. "Answer the question!"

He says, "What the fuck?" again.

"I can figure out by how tall you are in relation to my door! You might as well just tell me! Are you five eleven, mother-fucker?"

He leaves.

✳

I crouch down on the floor in my kitchen and call Polly.

"Hey," she answers.

"Hi. How tall is the average door?"

"What?"

"If a man were, say, a little over eye level with the average peephole, how tall would you say he is?"

"Uh. I think I need more context. Are you okay?"

"Yeah. Can I sleep over?"

"Sure."

"Thank you," I say, while looking beyond my cabinets at my living room as if I am in a trench at war.

She laughs. "Thank you?"

"I mean," I say, "cool. I meant cool. Great."

She laughs again. "Are you okay? You sound a little frantic."

"Oh yeah. I'm totally okay."

I am clutching a butcher knife.

"What about you?" I ask. "How are you?"

✳

I watch my security camera app for forty minutes before mustering the courage to exit my apartment. I open the door as if I am opening the entrance to hell. I hold my biggest knife under my sweater and run down the hall as if I am being chased with an axe.

✳

"I found your YouTube channel," Polly says.

I have my security camera app open on my phone. I look up.

"You what?"

"Your YouTube channel," she repeats, as if in slow motion. "I found it."

I feel my face flush.

"You were so cute," she says. "I can't believe how creative you were. You had such a big personality. You were so precocious! And you were so different as a teenager, too. It's so cute to see you grow up—"

I feel as if she just pushed me into my grave. Every statement she makes is a shovel of dirt added on my rotting body.

"And you loved Casper, eh?"

I watched the nineties version of the movie *Casper* on repeat as a kid. In retrospect, I think I had a crush on Christina Ricci. I remember hating the part when Casper became a real boy because I liked it better when he was an androgynous ghost. At the time, I don't think I had any idea why this appealed to me. Now I think it's because there was no romantic content for girls who like girls. I guess it's weird for there to be any romantic content for children, but there is. Boy cartoon characters like girl cartoon characters all the time. Heterosexuality is really shoved down children's throats.

In my videos, for about a year, I am often wearing *Casper*-themed apparel. I had a hoodie and multiple T-shirts. Some videos feature me reciting lines from the film.

"*What's it like to die?*" I ask the camera in an almost whisper.

The screen flashes to me with white face paint on. "*Like . . . being born, only backward.*"

I cringe. "Please pretend you never saw that."

"Why? It's so cute. I love how imaginative your makeup looks were. Why did you stop?"

"Wearing makeup?" I ask, defensive.

"No, YouTube," she says. "Do you remember why you stopped?"

*

To hurt myself, I am rewatching all my *Casper*-related YouTube videos. Polly is sprawled asleep next to me. Now that I know she has watched at least one of these, they sting especially sharply. I stare into my chubby face as I discuss at length why I prefer Fatso the ghost to Casper's other uncles. I give an impassioned justification for this opinion.

"*I know some people won't agree,*" I say, putting my hands up, as if I am being arrested, "*but the fact of the matter is, Fatso is the superior ghost in the trio.*"

I scroll down to look at the comments beneath the video. I learn as I read them that there is quite the Casper community, and that my view is controversial. There are many comments arguing against my point, all stating remarks along the lines of: "Fatso sucks and so do you."

A lot of the comments include fire symbols. I scroll through more of my videos, jumping down to the comments. I roll through blocks and blocks of fire symbols. I wonder if Polly noticed these.

✳

My phone is ringing. It is lost in the sea of blankets on Polly's bed. We shake out her pillows and reach our arms through the mattress trying to locate it. Polly finally does. She hands it to me just in time for me to answer.

"Hello?" I put it to my good ear.

It's my mom.

"Are you okay?" I ask.

"Yes," she says. "I'm fine. I just wondered if you had any interesting facts about space?"

"Oh, loads," I say. "Do you know much about black holes?"

"No. Do tell."

"Okay, we think they're usually formed when massive stars die. When a huge star runs out of fuel, it collapses under its own gravity."

"Wow, that's interesting."

"And we can't see black holes with our naked eyes. We can just see what surrounds them. We can see a star that's close enough to one falling in, for example."

"That would be a marvel, wouldn't it?"

"Yeah, it would."

"Thanks Enid."

"No problem."

She hangs up.

"Who was that?" Polly asks.

"Oh, no one." I exhale.

"Another woman?" she jokes.

I breathe air out of my nose. "It was my mom."

"Oh," she says. "So, not someone else you're seeing?"

I laugh. "No."

"Okay, perfect. Should I worry about anyone else?"

"N-no," I stammer. "Well, are you asking me if I am seeing anyone else?"

"Are you?"

"Uh. Well, I went on a few dates around the time I met you. I went on a date with a polyamorous couple not too long ago. Although we just had pasta and talked about our childhood trauma. I don't know if I'd consider it a date in retrospect, actually. It was platonic."

"Did that really happen?"

"Yes."

She looks at me. "You've never told *me* about your childhood trauma."

"What?"

"What's your childhood trauma?" she asks.

I look at her. I picture the ominous door that I keep shut. The door is not locked. I could open it. It has a giant latch bolt that I could lift if I wanted to.

"Do you really want me to talk about that?" I ask. I see it in darkness, with light glowing through the cracks surrounding it.

"Yes," she says.

I approach the door. I put a hand up to it and feel heat. It blisters my palm. I jump back.

I say, "Uh. Okay, um. I was bullied. My dad left my mom. I told you about that too, when we first met, remember?"

"Yeah, and you have two half sisters."

I nod. "Yeah, exactly."

"Is there anything else?" she asks.

I pretend there isn't. "No," I say.

She looks at me. "Okay, and why haven't you ever asked me about my childhood trauma?"

"I . . . I'm sorry. I didn't realize you wanted me to."

I can't tell if she's being serious.

"Are you being serious?" I ask.

Rather than answer, she says, "My parents are divorced. My grandma has histrionic personality disorder, which has wreaked havoc on everyone in my extended family. My sister was in a car accident when we were teenagers, but she's okay now. She can't work in a job where she has to sit too long, or lift much, but for a minute there we thought she might die—so it's all good, considering. Um. I had a boyfriend who punched me in the face when I was fifteen—"

"Oh God. Really?"

"Yes, it was after I refused to go to a house party with him. I had to file a police report and go to school with a black eye. Um. What else? My first girlfriend cheated on me. I think I told you about that. For a while I had a bit of an eating disorder, and even now I have some issues with that. Oh and!" She gives me a warningly sad look and says, "I saw a cat get hit by a car once. It was awful. Really traumatizing."

Once it is clear to me that she has finished, I say, "Thank you for sharing all of that with me."

She looks at me for longer than is normal.

"Tell me more things about you," she says.

She doesn't break eye contact. I feel like we are in a staring contest.

I don't know what to tell her.

When I was a kid, my mom told me that when I lied, she could see sparkles in my eyes. I believed her for too long. I was a preteen, still covering my eyes when I lied to her. I think that's affected my ability to keep eye contact now. I have been trained to be genuine when someone can see whether my eyes twinkle.

"Um," I say, looking directly into the black of her pupils.

She doesn't blink.

I sputter, "I-I have a phobia of bald men."

"You what?"

I blink. "I have an irrational fear of bald men."

She laughs. "Are you being serious?"

I nod.

"That's ridiculous. Why are you afraid of bald men? I know lots of very nice, handsome bald men."

"I know, it's not that," I try to explain. "I don't know what it is. But I think the person who broke into my house was my neighbor, who is bald, and I can't tell if I think it was him because of my phobia, or if he's been genuinely strange. He knocks on my door all the time. I think I saw his face in my window once. I can't tell if I'm being crazy, or if his behavior has actually been off. I think it has been off. But if it isn't him, who is it? It could be my landlord. He is weirdly obsessed with making sure I don't have a pet, but he said it wasn't him. He told me to call the cops when I told him someone was in there. It would be so bizarre for it to be him, right? Everyone seems to think I am overreacting. Am I? Do you think I am? I feel insane. Am I insane? Do I sound insane?"

She listens intently. When I stop rambling, she says, "No, you're not being insane. That is strange. Let's get to the bottom of it."

✳

Polly and I are now researching. We both took sick days. I google "how to get over a phobia," while Polly looks into whether similar break-ins have happened near my apartment. She told me to focus on my phobia and said she will focus on the break-in. She is also trying to find the name of my neighbor, and to look into him.

The comforting lull of our murder podcast plays in the background. This episode is about John Wayne Gacy, a classic true crime story about a man who dressed as a clown and tortured, raped, and killed at least thirty-three boys and men.

Most of the search results about overcoming a phobia recommend that I gradually expose myself to my fear. This is, of course, what I was afraid of. Some go even further to suggest a horrible technique they call "flooding," which involves immersing yourself in the fear. A claustrophobic person might, for example, lock themselves in a small space until they emerge— apparently, cured.

Reading even the suggestion of this approach prompts my mind's eye to picture: me, drowning in a sea of bald man. My shoulders involuntarily jump to my ears, I flinch, and I close one eye.

Polly looks at me. "Are you okay?"

I nod.

The podcast host mentions that John Wayne Gacy lured one of his victims from a Greyhound bus station, which solidifies my belief that Greyhound bus stations are just fronts for hell mouths.

A lot of people are afraid of clowns. I hope no one who John Wayne Gacy killed was. Being tortured, raped, and murdered is bad enough. Having a phobia of clowns and being raped and killed by a clown would be unimaginable.

I know it is ridiculous, but for some reason, bald men are sitting in the same room in my mind as murderers, monsters, and John Wayne Gacy. I do not know why they are in there. It is not a choice I made.

I turn to Polly. "Maybe I'm afraid of bald men because I have some sort of intuition that someday one will kill me. Maybe I'm not paranoid, maybe I'm psychic."

Polly entertains the idea. She adds, "Maybe it stems from something in a past life. Maybe you were a mosquito smacked by a bald man. Maybe you were a dog with an abusive, bald owner. Or a flower plucked by a bald man?"

We sit quietly. The podcast is discussing John's childhood. The host says, "*His dad was abusive. He'd hit him for no reason and demean him. He called him a sissy and said he would 'probably grow up queer.' Gacy had a heart condition and frequent black-outs. He spent a lot of time in the hospital when he was a teenager. His dad accused him of faking it to gain attention. Despite all his father's mistreatment, however, Gacy said he still loved him—*"

"Can you turn that off?" I ask.

I think listening to this story is bad for me. Maybe listening to this podcast at all is unhealthy. I feel like I'm giving my parasite an outlet, and distracting myself, but maybe I'm not supposed to do that.

What am I supposed to do?

The room is quiet. Polly turned the podcast off.

"I think I need to go to therapy," I say.

She agrees. "Yeah, you do."

＊

"So, tell me about yourself," the therapist says from across the room.

I contacted the therapist recommended to me by the poly couple.

I am sitting on a chair with my backpack in my lap. I am cradling it like I am a lizard, and it is my egg.

"I have a weird phobia of bald men," I confess.

"Sorry?" She leans in.

"I have a weird phobia of bald men," I say again, louder.

"That's what's brought you in?"

I nod. "Yes. I've stopped going to my doctor because he's bald. I can't work with a coworker because he's bald. And I feel like I am being followed by a bald man. Someone broke into my apartment recently. I think the culprit is my bald neighbor, but I can't tell if I suspect him because of my phobia, or if I have legitimate grounds to be suspicious of him. I feel paranoid. I should probably mention I listen to a lot of true crime podcasts. That might be contributing to my paranoia. How much true crime content is normal?"

Before she can answer, I add, "I listen to like two hours a day. That's way too much, isn't it?"

I actually listen to it more than two hours a day, but I'm worried she'll judge me.

She starts, "Well, that is quite a bit, yes—"

I interrupt her again. "Yeah, it's gross too, right? It's un-ethical, I think. It's horrible of me to listen to that, isn't it? Real people have died, or been attacked, and I'm out here listening to their stories as if it's entertainment. I'm sick, I think. Something is wrong with me—"

She says, "I understand you're feeling concerned. Can we please circle back to your comment about someone following you? Can you tell me more about that?"

"Yes. Um. Well, I think I am actually being followed. Some-one *really* has broken into my apartment. The police are in-volved. I have camera footage. That really did happen. I didn't make that up. I'm not hallucinating."

She says, "Okay, good to know. And you don't have a history of hallucinating, right?"

I purse my lips. "Well. Actually, I once thought I saw a ghost."

She folds her hands. "Okay."

I'm worried she is going to diagnose me with early-onset dementia or some other disorder that involves hallucinating.

"Sometimes I can't remember if I imagined something or if it really happened. That's normal, though, right? Is that bad? I think I'm too in my head."

Before she can answer, I reiterate. "Someone *really* broke into my apartment. I can give you the cop's number to prove it. I have footage. I'm not insane. I mean, I might be insane. Sorry. I shouldn't be saying 'insane,' right? Should I call myself 'mentally ill'? I'm not mentally ill. Well, no—I am, obviously. I have this phobia thing. That's mental illness, right? I just mean, I'm not seeing things. Someone broke into my apartment—"

"I believe you," she says.

"Thank you." I exhale.

"How long has this fear been an issue?"

"I don't know. I have a terrible memory."

She's going to say I have dementia for sure.

"That's okay. Can you remember any other instances when your fear disrupted your life?" she asks. "What's the earliest instance you can think of?"

I trace my mind. Before recently, it was not that big of an issue. It's been something I could avoid. It is not as if I am agoraphobic, afraid of pigeons, or of some pervasive plant. I am not afraid of grass, or birds, or rain. Until recently, it has not been that disruptive. My dad isn't in the picture to go bald. I am a lesbian. I have one friend, and he has lots of hair. None of my coworkers have been bald until George. I have been able to navigate around the fear.

"It just started to disrupt my life," I say. "I remember crossing the road when I saw bald men years ago. In college, I avoided a Subway sandwich shop that had a bald sandwich artist. It wasn't really disruptive to my life, but I remember it being a little problem. I think it's gotten worse recently."

She writes notes down. "Okay, interesting, and do you have any idea why you have this fear?"

I shake my head. "No, I have no clue."

"Do you think it stems from some trauma?"

I shrug. "Do you?"

✳

Since leaving my last therapy session, I have been trying to pinpoint my earliest memory of my phobia. I remember one night, in college, I went out with my roommates. I usually snuck away when we went out. I absconded home alone. I pretended I was going to buy a drink, or use the washroom, but secretly, I'd sneak out the exit.

I was almost busted once. My roommate Sarah caught me by the door. She said, "Hey! Are you skulking off?"

I said, "What? No. I'm—uh. I'm just going to smoke."

She said, "Oh, great. I'll join you."

I didn't have any cigarettes, so when we went outside, I approached a man who was smoking. I said, "Hey, could we please mooch two smokes?"

He said, "No."

I said, "Please?"

He sighed, "Fine," then complained about girls never buying cigarettes.

After he dispensed the cigarettes, we asked if we could please use his lighter. He wouldn't give it to us. Instead, he lit our cigarettes for us.

I wanted to be handed the lighter. I wanted to light my own cigarette, but I got the impression he thought we might run off with it. I don't know why he was so possessive of a fifty-cent Bic lighter.

After we smoked, I followed Sarah inside the bar. When her head was turned, I beelined back to the exit.

After starting my journey home, I noticed the man who we smoked with was walking behind me. We were on a well-lit road with a number of bars on it. It was common for people to hop from one bar to another. I noticed that he was behind me, and I made note of that, but I assumed he was just heading to another bar.

He started shouting, "Hey! Wait up!"

I pretended I didn't hear him.

"Wait up!" he called again.

I felt uneasy. I had seen enough *Dateline* to know that being trailed by inebriated men at night was dangerous. I worried that maybe he felt like I owed him something after giving me a cigarette and a spark of his lighter fluid. I told myself that maybe he didn't realize it's unnerving to follow girls at night. He was probably just drunk and wanted to talk to someone.

Still, I felt unsafe. I didn't want to turn onto dark side streets or lead him to my house. Eventually, I decided—out of an abundance of caution—to call a cab.

I asked the cab driver to pick me up a few blocks ahead of where I was. I did that so I could keep rushing forward, and hopefully shake off the man. He kept following me, though. I had passed about three bars, and he was still trudging behind me.

I remember him gaining on me when the yellow cab finally pulled over. I felt terrified. I opened the back door of the car, relieved to reach my getaway, when I noticed that the driver was bald. His head was smooth and oily. My heart jumped into my throat.

This is the first memory I have of being afraid of bald men. I remember feeling deeply, irrationally startled by the cab driver. I felt as afraid of him as I would if I found a man with a knife standing behind my shower curtain.

The driver said, "Cab for Enid?"

I looked at him, wide-eyed, then back at the man who was following me. I shook my head. I slammed the door shut.

Because I had paused by the cab for so long, the man following me finally caught up to me. As he approached, I braced myself. I felt sure that he was going to attack me.

Instead, he said, "I've been chasing you for like six blocks! Didn't you hear me? You dropped your debit card."

✳

My therapist told me to stop listening to true crime, and she gave me a stack of pictures of bald men. She had them printed and told me to go through them every day. She said, "The best way to overcome a phobia is by gradually and repeatedly exposing yourself to the fear in a safe and controlled way."

She asked if I felt comfortable with this approach, and I said "Yes"; however, I lied. The truth is that knowing there are photos of bald men in my possession makes me feel like I possess a cursed book bound in human flesh. I feel burdened by a dark, malevolent energy.

✳

"Hi Enid, I've been trying to reach you, but I can't seem to get ahold of you. Can you please give me a call back when you get this?"

I shudder. George tried to call me while I was away from work. He left that message and sent me an email saying the same thing.

My cubicle feels smaller than usual. My leg is shaking. What if he shows up here?

I get up and walk to the bathroom. I stay in the stall for forty minutes. I'm tempted to listen to my podcast, to distract myself, but my therapist told me not to—so I don't listen to anything.

I go back to my desk. I move my mouse, then walk back to the bathroom.

My boss sees me walking. I wave at him.

After forty minutes, I go back to my desk. I move my mouse, then go back to the bathroom.

My boss sees me again. He probably thinks I'm sick.

After another thirty silent minutes in the bathroom, I give in and play an episode of my podcast.

※

"You're crazy," Vin says. He is sitting on my couch, and we are listening to another episode of my murder podcast. I ran into him on my last trip to the bathroom today. I told him I'm feeling scared, so he offered to sleep over here with me tonight, to help me adjust to returning.

"I want to give notice," I say. "I don't want to keep living here. I'm terrified."

"Jesus. You shouldn't move out of your apartment just because of a break-in—"

"Why not? That feels like a great reason to move out. Also, I can't have a pet here. I'd like to get a cat. I had a cat growing up who I loved. Or I could get a dog. A big dog might help me feel safe."

"Did you ask your therapist if you should move out?" he asks.

I didn't ask because I was afraid that she might not agree.

I lie. "Yes. She said I should."

He gives me a look that means he knows I am lying.

"Do whatever you want," he sighs. "I think this is ridiculous. I don't think you should move. But if that is really what you want to do, I can't stop you."

"It is," I say while I begin drafting my notice for Peter.

He stands up and walks to the bathroom while I google "example notice to vacate."

He shouts, "Why is your backpack in your bathtub?"

The bald man photos are in my backpack. I put it there to keep them away from me.

"I don't know," I yell back.

There's a knock on my door. Vin pops his head out of the bathroom.

"If that's my fucking neighbor," I whisper.

He walks over to check the peephole.

He looks back at me from the door and gives me a stressed look that means it is.

"How tall would you say he looks?" I whisper.

"I don't know. Like my height?"

"How tall are you?"

"Five eleven."

Fuck.

He returns to the couch on his tiptoes. "Should I answer it?" he says. "Maybe if I answer, it'll scare him off."

"Just be quiet," I say. I turn off the podcast. "Maybe he'll leave."

He does.

✴

"Have you stopped listening to true crime podcasts?" Dr. Jeong asks.

I look at my shoes. I'm tempted to lie. I want her to think I'm a good patient. It's embarrassing I can't quit a podcast. I must have an addictive personality. It's a good thing I haven't been coping with alcohol or drugs, I guess.

"I've listened less," I lie. I've listened to it as much as I normally do.

"Did you try to stop?"

"I did try, yes."

Should I tell her I ended up hiding in a bathroom to avoid

my bald coworker and that I was so bored in there, I put it on? Or that I listened to the first half of an episode and wanted to hear the rest, so I listened to it later with Vin? Or that I fell asleep to another episode, or that I listened to another while traveling here, and another while sitting in her waiting room?

"Do you have any other interests besides true crime that bring you a source of comfort?"

I consider the question.

"Space."

"Space? What is it that you like about space?"

"It's interesting," I say.

"Is there anything that connects space and true crime?"

I brush my hair behind my ear. "Sorry, I'm deaf in one ear. Can you please repeat the question?"

She writes something down, then says, a little louder, "I'm curious if you see a connection between your interest in space and true crime."

I frown. "What do you mean? Do my interests have to be connected?"

"No, they don't have to be. I just wonder if they might be."

I consider what could possibly link space and true crime.

"I guess I used to find them both scary?" I suggest.

"And you like things that scare you?"

"No, I don't."

She looks at me like she wants me to say more.

"Uh, I guess maybe what I like is turning things that once scared me into things that comfort me. Does that make sense? I'm not afraid of true crime stories anymore. I used to be. I actually feel sort of consoled by them now. Is that gross? It is gross, isn't it? If someone I knew died in some terrible way, or was attacked, and their story entertained people, let alone comforted them, I'd be totally repulsed. But that's my truth. I guess I'm disgusting. And I used to be afraid of space, it made me feel meaningless, and like I could die at any minute, but I'm not afraid of it anymore. It's actually sort of soothing to think of how massive the universe is, and how I could be snuffed out at any minute. I guess I like tricking my brain into disarming things."

I pause. "Is that what I should be doing with bald men? Should I turn them into an interest like true crime or space? Do you think someday I'll find bald men entertaining or comforting?"

I shudder. The thought of that disturbs me.

She says, "Do you think feeling comforted by things that once scared you is healthy?"

I frown. "Isn't it? What else am I supposed to do?"

"Face your fears."

I blink. How am I supposed to face a fear of true crime? Am I supposed to get murdered, or to murder? Is that how people face it? And how exactly am I supposed to face a fear of space? Become an astronaut? Rocket into a black hole?

I know my fear of bald men is irrational. I know it's a phobia. It's stupid. But there are some fears that are rational. It's reasonable to be afraid of murder, or to feel troubled about existing as a speck on a space rock floating in colossal, silent darkness. Those are rational fears. They're both fears that can't really be faced. How am I supposed to cope with fears like that? I thought the only option was to be delusional. I thought everyone coped by imagining reality isn't what it is—by ignoring the threat of murder, or by forgetting we're in space—or by doing what I do. By repeatedly exposing yourself until the threats feel familiar, the shock wears off, and you've conditioned yourself to find what scares you pacifying.

"I'm supposed to face that we're in space? I'm supposed to face that people get raped and murdered?"

"Yes."

"Is that what you do?" I ask.

"What I do isn't important. We're talking about you."

"But do you do that? People do that? They walk around fully facing those things?"

"Yes," she says. She moves on. "I'd like to talk to you a bit about self-regulation, and how to manage your anxiety. Rather than listen to a true crime podcast when you feel stressed or anxious, it might be helpful to try some relaxation techniques . . ."

I tune her out while she talks about self-soothing and mindfulness. I'm still wondering how people face these sorts of fears.

"Breathing is important," she says.

In an attempt to be a good patient, I breathe in and out while she demonstrates deep breathing. Together, we inhale and exhale ten times.

＊

My mom, Vin, and I are at a sit-down pizza restaurant. It's my birthday. I briefed Vin. I told him not to tell my mom about the break-in or why I am moving. My mom is wearing a red dress with clay earrings. She has her lipstick on.

"I love the color of your lips," Vin says.

"Do you really?" she says. "Thank you. It's called Bloodrose."

"It looks great on you."

The restaurant serves the pizzas on little podiums with cake knives. The lighting in the dining room is warm. There is old wallpaper with pictures of tomatoes, cheese, and basil on it. We are eating ciabatta bread with oil, waiting for our pizzas to come.

"I wanted Enid to invite the girl she's seeing," Vin says.

My mom looks at me. "You didn't tell me you were seeing someone."

I glare at Vin. I guess I should have given him a longer briefing.

"It's not a big deal," I say.

"She never introduces me to the people she's dating," Vin says. "Do you ever get to meet them?"

"No," my mom says. "Why is that, Enid?"

I grimace. "Did you two forget it's actually my birthday? I'm not enjoying the conversation."

They laugh.

My mom says, "Okay, new topic. How about I tell your birth story?"

I sigh. "Sure."

Vin rests his chin on his hands to listen.

"It was a dark and stormy night," she says, as if it's a ghost story. "Your father and I had just finished an early dinner, and I was feeling just a little off. I went into the shower, thinking the warm water might help settle my stomach, until you made it evident that it was almost your birthday."

Vin says, "Uh-oh."

"Uh-oh, indeed. I remember your dad driving through stop signs and red lights." She chuckles. "And oh my God, the labor took seven and a half hours, but it felt like days. I couldn't get an epidural because of something to do with a birthmark on my back. I had no idea I wouldn't be able to get one. I was so upset. I was insisting they do it anyway, but they wouldn't. They refused. You were born one minute after midnight and your little noggin was all lumpy and weird, but look at it now—"

She touches my face across the table and beams.

"It looks normal."

Vin laughs.

✳

Polly invited me over to her house again tonight. I am standing at the entrance to her living room. She's decorated. There are multicolored balloons taped to her walls. She has a true crime documentary ready for us to watch. She's turned the closed captions on. I don't think I have the heart to tell her my doctor doesn't want me to consume true crime content anymore. It's paused on the opening title on her TV. It's about Jaycee Dugard, an eleven-year-old kid who was abducted by a convicted sex offender and his wife and kept for eighteen years.

I smell smoke. Is something on fire?

There is a *SpongeBob SquarePants*–shaped cake on Polly's table with little yellow candles in it.

"What do you think?" she asks.

My palms are sweaty.

"Did you burn something?" I ask.

"What?" she says. "No."

"Why'd you do this?" I ask.

"For your birthday!"

I feel like the room is cloudy.

"Are you okay?" she asks. "What's wrong?"

"Yeah, sorry, I'm just—I feel weird."

"Is it your stomach?"

I can't hear her.

"I'm sorry, I can't hear you," I tell her, watching her mouth open and close.

She's mouthing, *Are you okay? Do you need some water?*

✳

I am in Polly's bathroom, lying in her empty tub. I am reading the ingredients in her shampoo and kicking the pink loofah she keeps hanging from the bath spout.

I didn't realize Polly knew it was my birthday. I don't recall telling her my birth date. Maybe she saw it on social media. Or maybe I told her once, and she remembered.

I don't know when her birthday is. I hope it isn't soon. I wonder if it happened while we've been together, and I had no idea.

No, I doubt it. She would have said something. She'd have said, "*What the fuck? You forgot my birthday? That's fucked-up. I remember your birthday. What's your problem?*"

The thought of that imaginary scenario brings tears to my eyes. I put my face in my hands. I feel preemptively culpable for ruining her birthday.

She knocks on the door. "Are you okay in there?"

I shout, "Tummy troubles!" and my voice cracks. This is sort of true. My tummy does feel troubled.

✳

Despite being stuffed with pizza from earlier, I am now eating a wedge of SpongeBob's face. His blue eye is staring up at me from my plate as I consume his yellow flesh. I gathered the courage to exit the bathroom. Polly made me drink a glass of water and take two antacids.

She played me happy birthday on her piano. She has no idea why I don't feel well. She assumes it's something I ate.

"Did you have a happy birthday?" she asks.

"Yes," I say, even though I have spent the better part of this evening secretly harboring a peculiar heartbreak.

"Who did you go to dinner with?" she asks.

"My mom and my friend."

"Vin?"

"Yes. Vin."

"Maybe next year I can come." She nudges my leg.

I try to smile despite feeling like an arrow just punctured my chest.

She turns to the TV and becomes enraptured by the documentary. The room smells like blown-out candles. We have the lights off. She leans forward in her seat, watching. Her hand is on my knee.

"This makes me want to go out and look inside everyone's sheds," she says, angry.

Jaycee was trapped in her abductor's shed. She was handcuffed until she was conditioned to stay.

"I fucking hate this man. I hate him. I think I would kill him if I could," she says in a tone that suggests that surprises her. As if she didn't realize she could ever want to kill someone. "Honestly, Enid." She turns to me. The light from the TV casts shadows on her face. She looks me dead in the eyes. "I'm not kidding. If he were in front of me, I think I might kill him."

She turns back to the TV.

Fuck.

I am in love with Polly.

❋

Polly and I have our heads under her oatmeal-colored blankets. We are now watching a second documentary on the little TV in her room. This one is about Belle Gunness, who was a serial killer in the 1900s. She lured men with the promise of marriage. We are hiding our faces because an actress is reenacting murdering a man with a meat grinder. We are shielding our eyes from the gore.

Beneath the blankets, I can smell Polly's body lotion. We are holding each other's hands, terrified, and looking at each other while we listen to the sound of the TV for cues that it is safe to peek up again.

Polly often looks into my face for longer than is normal. She and I are staring into each other's eyes while listening to the TV's bloodcurdling screams.

After a loud clunk and a grinding sound, my parasite possesses me. I interrupt Polly's silent, extended staring to say, "You love me, don't you?" This is a leading question. It's phrased to guide the answer.

She looks at me, laughs, and says, "Oh no, what gave it away?"

She then says, "Yes, I love you."

My eyes sting, as if smoke is in them. I feel how I imagine stalkers do when they find their prey alone in a dark alley, or how a bat might feel right before it eats a fly.

I pull the blankets off our faces and joke, "I knew it. You sucker. You love me."

She cackles and I do not say it back.

✳

Polly falls asleep before I do. She is sprawled out in her bed like a dead butterfly in a display case, and I am cocooned next to her, watching her breathe.

I dream of Polly cutting herself open. I watch her slice herself down the middle, yank out the sausage links from her belly, and stand there, gutted, saying, "Look at these."

I do look at them. I look up close at the blood falling off their purplish-gray casing. As I examine them, Polly asks to see my hands. I have a paper cut she wants to look at.

I answer, "No."

"No. Absolutely not."

✳

"Why do you love me?" I ask her in the morning.

A pink light shines through her curtains.

"I just do," she says.

"Oh, so, it's for no reason?"

She laughs. "Do you want a list of reasons?"

I say, "Yes."

"Okay, um. I love how observant you are. I love how much you care about your mom. I love how knowledgeable you are about true crime and how interested you are in it. I love how you laugh at the same things I do and . . ."

I act as if I asked as a joke. I laugh at her answers, but each one feels like wood thrown on my fire. I feel myself gain heat and light.

"You didn't say anything about my appearance," I interject, my skin hot. "Am I hideous?"

She laughs loudly, throwing more kindling on me. "No, you're beautiful. I love how you look."

I crackle while she fans my flames with compliments.

"Why do you love me?" she asks.

I tease, spitting sparks, "I never said I did."

She laughs again and throws a pillow at me.

✳

I feel like I just did ten lines of coke. I feel out of my mind. I am an abductor. I have thrown Polly into the trunk of my car and driven her to my hideout. I feel as if I am about to light us on fire. I feel like I have tricked her into thinking that she loves me, but she doesn't really. She thinks she does, but she doesn't really.

✳

"Enid? Did you hear me? I asked if you could tell me about your upbringing."

Dr. Jeong's office has green walls. I came here after another day in the bathroom at work. There is a basketball-sized amethyst on the table in front of me. I was mesmerized looking at it. I wonder how much those things cost.

"Sorry." I rub my ears. "Yes. Uh. I had a single mom. She's nice. Um. I grew up in a new subdivision. Uh—"

I don't know what else to say. I feel uncomfortable. I have doubts that talking to her is going to cure me. I think whatever is wrong with me is permanent. I feel like I am wasting her time. I keep repressing an impulse to follow up her questions with ones about her. I want to say, *What about you, Dr. Jeong? Tell me about your upbringing?*

I keep thinking about Polly. I think maybe I deserve to have a fear of bald men. Maybe, if a bald man is after me, it's the universe's way of keeping other people safe. It's like the food chain; maybe Polly is a bug, I am a toad, and bald men are snakes. Perhaps this is just nature, and I shouldn't try to control it. Maybe the right thing to do is let the snake eat me before I can get the bug.

Dr. Jeong is writing things down. She asks, "Do you know much about your dad?"

"He wasn't bald," I say quickly. "If that's what you're thinking."

I can tell by the way she writes in her notebook that it was.

"Would you say you had a happy childhood?"

"For the most part, I think so," I say.

I consider mentioning the YouTube channel that documents a lot of my childhood, but I am afraid that would be a lot to ask a therapist to view. I don't want to assign a three-thousand-hour homework assignment to this poor woman.

"I had some issues," I admit. "I didn't have friends when I was little. I had social problems. I was a bit of an overachiever as I got older."

She writes more down.

"I was definitely affected by my dad leaving," I add. "More so than I wish I were. My mom had some problems, but she and I have always had a good relationship. I think overall I was pretty lucky. It could have been way worse."

"You know." She leans back in her chair. "One thing I always tell my patients is that everyone can say it could have been worse. Don't diminish the parts of your childhood that were difficult because they were comparatively better than others."

"Oh," I say while I register that comment. "Okay. Sorry."

She smiles. "And don't apologize."

Before we end our session, she reminds me to keep looking at the photos she gave me. She warns me that when I am ready, she wants me to sit with a bald man.

❋

George emailed me again.

> Hi Enid, I think your phone isn't working. Or
> maybe it's mine. I'm still getting used to things
> here. I am having a devil of a time trying to reach
> you. Can you please confirm whether you receive
> this email? I would love to set up a time to chat.
>
> Thank you,
> George Fox (He/Him)
> National Space Agency
> Senior Strategist

I delete the email.

✳

I am at Polly's. She has no idea that I am a toad, and that she is a bug. She is helping me with my fear. She went through five of the bald man photos with me. Every time she flipped to a new one, I closed my eyes. I am lying in her bed now, recovering from the exercise. I feel as if I just watched a slideshow of five violent crimes.

"Want to watch a documentary about aphids?" she asks.

"Sure," I say.

She turns it on. I watch as the screen zooms in on a cabbage infested with little, tiny insects. I learn there are thousands of different types of aphids; they all look different. Classical music plays while little green ones suck the sugary life out of plants and turn them yellow.

"*Aphids don't need mates,*" the narrator tells us. "*They clone*

INTERESTING FACTS ABOUT SPACE

themselves. *And their babies are born pregnant. All aphids are female. They give birth to both their daughters and their grand-daughters. That's why you only need one aphid to infest your garden.*"

✳

"I broke up with Julie."

I jump. Maveric just appeared behind me.

"Jesus. You scared me," I say.

My stomach is in my throat. I thought he was George.

He sits on my desk. "Just thought you ought to know. Julie is back on the market."

I breathe air out my nose. "Are you telling me to date the girl you just dumped?"

He shrugs. "If you want. Are you dating anyone?"

"Not really," I lie.

"Me either," he says. "Hey, we're both free agents. Too bad you're gay."

"Oh, you'd like to date me?" I laugh. I sincerely doubt that I am Maveric's type.

He laughs. "We're probably a bad match, I guess. But you know who might have been good for you, if you weren't into women? The new guy, George. I was chatting with him yesterday. He likes true crime, like you. He knows all about serial killers."

I put a hand over my mouth.

"What?" he says.

"Are you okay?"

✳

"What adjectives would you use to describe your mom?" Dr. Jeong asks.

I consider the question.

"Uh. Messy. Eccentric. Fashionable. Jealous. Depressed. Creative. Supportive . . ."

"You mentioned the word 'jealous.' Can I ask, is she jealous of you?"

"Oh no. She is jealous of the woman my dad left her for."

"Ah, I see. Well, that's reasonable. You also mentioned the word 'depressed.' Has she sought treatment?"

"She's on medication. She doesn't always take it though, which bothers me."

"Has she gone to therapy?"

"I doubt it. Should I ask her to? Do you think I should arrange it for her? Are you taking more patients? Should I book her—"

She stops me. "You can talk to her about it if you'd like to, of course, but your mother's mental health isn't your responsibility. Can you tell me more about her?"

I register the comment.

"Okay. Um. She was an early childhood educator. She's retired now, but she loves kids. She's good with cars. She is very creative. She loves fashion. She makes a lot of her own clothes. She often knits me sweaters. She made me this one, actually."

The sweater I am wearing has a letter *E* on it.

"She was raised quite religious. Catholic. She has always been very supportive of me being queer, though. Uh, what else? She was an only child, too. She and I have that in common. Well, I have sisters, sort of, I guess. We didn't grow up together though, so I feel like an only child. Her parents were much older. Her dad died before I was born, and her mom died when I was like four. It was just me and her. Overall, she's a good person. She loves cooking and baking and telling stories and—"

She interrupts me. "Did you turn to her when you were upset or scared?"

I consider the question.

I think of myself in my bedroom, lying under my blankets, muffling the sound of myself crying into my pillow.

"No."

＊

I associate my mom with the smell of sunscreen. I think of her when my hair is being brushed. When I was a kid, she would arrange elaborate crafts for me. We made a caterpillar out of an egg carton. We made a kaleidoscope out of a paper towel roll. I remember gluing popsicle sticks together at the kitchen table while she watched food broil in the oven.

I remember concerned teachers looking into students' lunch boxes to assess whether their parents were feeding them well enough. They would often remark after evaluating my lunch that it was an example of what a child's lunch should be.

She got me my kitten Lou for Christmas one year. She insisted Lou was from Santa to deflect my gratitude. I remember coming downstairs and seeing Lou with a red bow and feeling the same euphoric thrill I would now if I won a million dollars. I had tears in my eyes. My mom was laughing, so happy to see me so happy.

I had a colorful room full of toys, books, and art supplies. I remember she would pause to look at me at night, from the light switch of my bedroom, to say, "Sweet dreams."

She was a very devoted mom most days, but she often cried

in the bathroom, and every two months or so her energy would completely deplete, and she would not leave her room. Sometimes she stayed in there for full weekends, never leaving once. I would sit outside her door, scribbling pictures in sketchbooks of Lou, or of her and I, to gift her when she woke up. I would eat all the fruit and granola bars in the house. She would eventually emerge, still unwell, to bathe or to eat. I would pretend she hadn't been inside for days and show her my drawings. She would play along as if she had only been gone a minute.

Sometimes she would nudge me awake at night. "Come sleep in my room, honey." I remember the sound of my bare feet slapping against the floors as we walked from my room to hers. I would crawl into her bed, and she would lie across from me, brushing my hair behind my ears, and crying while I fell asleep. I tried to stay awake to comfort her. I would blink and see black, then my mother's crying face on her pillow, black, my mom's crying face, black. Sometimes now, when I blink quickly, I still see the burned image of her crying on the insides of my eyelids.

I remember sitting in the back seat of her van, watching rain roll down the window, while she cried in the front seat.

When I was thirteen, she holed up in her bedroom for four days. That was longer than she had ever done before. I knocked on her door after a while, but she ignored me. I said, "Mom, please open the door." She wouldn't. I had to pick the lock to get in. I uncoiled a metal clothes hanger to do it. I found her lying knotted in her sheets on the floor. She looked pale and plastic; she looked like the wax figure of herself. I had to call an ambulance.

The dispatcher kept me on the phone.

I told her, "I can hear the sirens."

She said, "Good, that's good. Stay on the line."

I was never told officially what happened, but the paramedics said I called just in time. That's when she started taking antidepressants. She never told me that, though. I just noticed. I found the orange pill bottles behind her mirror.

✳

Polly is holding up the photos of bald men again. She holds each up for five seconds before flipping to the next. I grimace at each portrait. I would rather see pictures of mangled dead bodies than these.

I cover my eyes when she holds up a photo of an especially frightening-looking bald man. He is very thin. His eyes look sunken and bloodshot. His skin is pale.

"Can I ask you something that might be upsetting?" she asks.

She puts the photos down.

"Sure," I say.

Nothing could be more upsetting than looking at those pictures.

"Do you think you might have been molested by a bald man?" she asks.

"I've thought of that," I say. "But I don't think so. I have no memory of anything like that ever happening."

She hums. "Sometimes people repress bad memories."

I look at her.

She adds, "You know . . . my dad is bald."

I shudder.

"You're never going to be able to meet my parents!" She laughs.

I laugh uncomfortably. "I guess not."

＊

"Enid, I am diagnosing you with post-traumatic stress disorder. You also show traits of being neurologically atypical. For that, I'm going to refer you to a specialist for a formal assessment. Some of your behavior is likely also related to your hearing. You mentioned you're deaf in one ear. Have you always been?"

I touch my ear. "Yeah. I was born with some nerve damage."

Dr. Jeong nods. "Sometimes deafness can manifest in social challenges. It's common to experience anxiety and hypervigilance when you have a hearing impairment."

She is handing me leaflets about mental health in deaf adults, autism, and PTSD.

She and I were just speaking about my childhood. She had me answer an extensive list of questions. This is the result. I feel like I just completed a warped personality quiz and instead of finding out which dog breed matches my soul I am being officially branded mentally ill, traumatized, and neurodivergent.

She explains, "So PTSD is a condition that occurs due to experiencing a traumatic event or a series of events that make you feel hopeless, trapped, or scared. It manifests differently in people. I believe your experience with it is also impacted by the way you process and learn."

I look at the leaflets in my hands. The top one is titled "PTSD & YOU."

She says, "Dissociation is one PTSD symptom I've noted you have. You mentioned nightmares, depersonalizing, brain fog. Hyperarousal is another symptom I see in you. You interpret situations as unsafe due to increased vigilance. That's not to say you aren't actually in some unsafe situations. Having someone break into your apartment is definitely grounds for concern.

But what you've mentioned—avoiding your coworker, avoiding your doctor—that's all a sign of this."

I look at the leaflets in my hands.

"You also have an exaggerated startle response. I've noted you're struggling with anxiety. This is likely partly due to your hearing. You also have mood changes; PTSD contributes to that. Depression and, again, anxiety are associated. You exhibit some emotional numbness, memory problems . . ."

I nod.

"And finally, the last PTSD symptom, which is what I'd like to talk about today if that's all right with you, is avoidance."

She points at the paper in my hands. There is a red heading that says, "WHAT ARE YOU AVOIDING?"

She says, "Many people with PTSD don't speak about the trauma event. You have blank spots in your memory, right?"

My mouth starts salivating the way it does before I throw up.

"Yeah, my memory is bad." I sit up.

My leg is shaking. Maybe this was a bad idea.

"Do you have any questions at this point?" she asks.

"Uh," I reply. "Yes. Do I have to know what happened to address the problem?"

"If your objective is to resolve your phobia, we can probably do that without digging into this with exposure therapy. However, you have PTSD, and I believe the best way that is treated is with cognitive processing therapy. This involves talking about the traumatic event, how it's affected you, and then writing about it."

Fuck.

She opens up a notebook. "Can you tell me more about yourself at eighteen?"

"At eighteen?"

"Yes, I've noticed you remember having some issues relating to your phobia after eighteen, but not before. I'd like to talk about that stage in your life to assess that time."

"I don't remember much," I say.

"It's totally blank?"

"Yeah, sort of."

"What do you mean by sort of?"

I swallow. "Um, to be honest, I think I don't remember because I don't like thinking about it. I used to ruminate when I was younger. I used to plan what I would say to people, and then think about what I had said. I used to enjoy doing that; it felt like playing, sort of. After high school, it felt unpleasant ruminating about past things, so I totally stopped. I didn't like doing it. I think you have to think back to things to remember them, right? You have to revisit memories to keep them? I don't let myself think about high school at all. There's like a block."

"Okay, that's interesting." She tilts her head. "And you said your mom was struggling with depression, right? You remember traumatic events relating to her when you were younger. But those occurred before high school, correct?"

I told her about the time I found my mom.

"Yes, that was before high school."

"Okay. Do you remember anything at all during the time that is blank? Can you remember a friend you had? Or classes you took? Anything like that? Anything that might jog your memory?"

I pinch my arm.

"Um," I say. "Well, I actually have a YouTube channel I filmed then," I confess. "I recorded videos when I was a kid and a teenager. When I watch those, it sometimes jogs my memory."

"Do you really? Can we watch some together? What's your account name?"

I cringe. "There are so many videos, Dr. Jeong."

"That's okay."

*

Dr. Jeong is now sitting with me on her office couch. It feels awkward to sit right next to each other now. She has opened a laptop in front of us. I had to type FlowerGirl69 into the YouTube search bar. My face is red, and we are watching as seventeen-year-old me applies blush to the apples of her cheeks.

"You presented a lot differently," she comments. "Style-wise, you've changed quite a bit."

I bite the insides of my cheeks. "Yeah."

"I bought this blush," my teenaged self says as I rub what looks like pink oil paint onto my cheeks. "Ben said he liked it on me."

She pauses the video. "Do you remember Ben?"

I look at her. "Yeah, he was my boyfriend."

"When did you date?"

"Um." I think. "It was the end of high school. The last semester."

"Okay, and how long were you an item?"

"I don't know." I pause. "A few months, I think. He was dating someone else right before me."

She nods. "Go on."

"Okay. Uh. Her name was Chelsea Molloy. They'd been together for like three years, I think. In classes I shared with her, I overheard her talking about how one day they'd get married and have kids. She'd be a nurse. He'd be a lawyer. She had their baby names picked out."

"Then you started dating him?"

"Yeah." I swallow.

This is something I don't usually let myself think about. "He cheated on her with me."

Saying that out loud triggers something in me. I feel like all the white noise in this office just muted.

"Okay," she says. "Do you have any feelings about that?"

I open my mouth. "Um. Yeah. I remember hating Chelsea. She was really mean to me when we were younger. She cut my hair once in class. I had to lie to my mom about what happened. I had to get a very short, unflattering haircut."

"That must have been difficult. Can you tell me more about that memory?"

"Sure, um." I race around my mind. "This wasn't high school, but, uh . . ." I look at her. "I remember, when I was about twelve, I wanted to kill myself rather than go to school with Chelsea and her friends. I would beg my mom to let me stay home."

Saying that out loud embarrasses me. Despite knowing that Dr. Jeong is a therapist and has probably heard lots of people discuss wanting to kill themselves, my face feels hot.

"You wanted to kill yourself? You had thoughts about that?"

My cheeks flushed. "Yeah. I did."

"Did you make any attempts?"

"No. Well, I remember I googled how to tie a noose once. I planned to hang myself in my closet. I remember opening the door with a leather belt in my hands."

I chew the insides of my cheeks.

"Do you remember what stopped you?" she asks.

I think of my open childhood closet. It had an accordion door.

"Yeah," I say. "My mom knits. She makes me sweaters. I remember seeing all the sweaters she knit me. I thought of her finding me in there with them, so I stopped."

She nods. "Ah, okay. So, would you say you pursued Ben when you were older because of your turbulent history with Chelsea?"

I consider the question.

"I don't know," I say. "Ben and I had to do a physics assignment together. I went over to his house. He told me he thought I was pretty, and we had sex in his basement. I didn't go there planning for that to happen, though. I don't think it would have occurred to me that it could. I went to do our science homework. I brought my textbook."

I remember his basement was wood paneled and smelled like dirty hockey equipment. I didn't like him. I didn't pursue him.

I think being a lesbian with no sincere interest in him accidentally manipulated him into infatuation. He wanted me to come over all the time. I often said no because I couldn't always stomach it. When I would go, I would suggest we have sex outside, drink a lot, or try positions where I didn't see his face or body because that lessened how unpleasant the experience was for me. I suspect that small amount of spice really flavored his limited teenaged sexual experience. He said he would break up with Chelsea for me. I didn't like him, obviously, but still— I told him to do it. I told him yes, let's date. I love you.

"But," I go on. "I was only with him because of Chelsea. I . . ." I pause. "I didn't like Ben, obviously. He was nice, though, I think. Besides cheating on his girlfriend. He was nice to me. I feel bad about him now. I just liked that being with him devastated Chelsea."

I loved dating him. I felt myself burn as his girlfriend. I

felt like I won a game that everyone pegged me for losing. I felt powerful and in control. I felt like a giant red star scorching Chelsea's world, boiling her oceans, turning her lifeless. I thought about how little I would care if Ben cheated on me next. I thought I must be invincible. That is the time when I think my parasite took over.

"That is a good example," I say, "of me being a bad person. I think that is something I struggle with. I don't like remembering things I did that prove I am a terrible person. Does that make sense?"

She nods. "It does, yes."

✳

It's nighttime. I'm in my old bedroom at my mom's house. The room is different than it was when I was little. My mom has a sewing machine in it, baskets of yarn, and a spool holder mounted to the wall. Most of my old things have been tossed out or donated. The bed is the same, though, and the walls are still painted yellow. My old books are still here.

I have a collection of poetry by Sylvia Plath. It actually belongs to my old school library. There is a stamp on the front page that says so. I never returned it. When I was sixteen, I was obsessed with this book. The school librarian recommended it to me. I loved it so much, I carried it around at school.

I got made fun of for that. A boy named Nick, or Rick, I don't remember, joked that I was going to put my head in the oven. I didn't know that was how Sylvia Plath died. At that point, I had stopped being the target of much bullying due to effort I put into being unobjectionable. I stopped reading the book. I pretended I didn't like it. I said I thought it was weird.

Whenever I see my mom watching her food cook in the oven, I sit next to her and look in. You can't kill yourself in modern ovens. Well, I'm sure you could. You could kill yourself with anything if you tried hard enough. When we sit there, though, I feel like we are moths drawn to the memory of what an oven can do to sad women.

I take the book off the shelf. I leaf through it. I get distracted as I thumb through the pages by the shape of my fingers. I look a lot like my mom, except for my hands. I must have my dad's hands.

I turn on my podcast to sleep to. I know I shouldn't. I am in the middle of an episode. The host was describing the commonalities between predators. She said they often suffered head injuries or were sexually assaulted as children.

She says, "*Of course not everyone who has a head injury or was abused as a kid grows up to murder or rape people. There's something else involved. There's another ingredient that some people are born with. Some people are predisposed to be predators.*"

✳

The covers of my old bed are heavy. The podcast stopped and I woke up to the silence. The room is dark. It has a distinct, familiar smell—like Barbie doll hair and sunscreen.

I close my eyes. I remember Ben being in this room. He sat on the foot of this bed when I told him we had to break up. He asked why, and I said, "We just have to." He didn't want to, he said he loved me. I insisted, saying, "We have to break up," and he cried. He said he wanted to kill himself.

"Don't kill yourself," I said. "People love you."

"Who?" He looked at me. "You don't. You said you did, but you don't really."

His chest was pounding up and down. I watched tears build and roll over his eyelashes before trickling down his cheeks.

✳

I spent a lot of time growing up trying to seem normal. Sometimes I worry I neglected doing the internal work most people do while they're developing; I was too preoccupied camouflaging. I think I might be stunted because of it. I think I missed a step.

I've dated girls before who told me gay people have two adolescences. The first is the one we're taught to have, where we suppress ourselves. In that time period, we're less likely to have experienced the growing pains associated with forming our true adult identities. We have our second adolescence late, after we realize who we are.

That rings true, but I feel like it's more than that for me. I realize I'm gay, but I don't realize much of who I am beyond that. I feel like I'm still missing some crucial information that I need to fully form myself. I feel half-developed. I'm worried that if I were cut open, I'd see all my organs were half-made. I think I'm missing parts.

I never want to cut myself open, though. In fact, I would rather be sealed shut. I'd rather be treated like a cursed tomb and have every orifice in my body cemented. I want all my half-baked organs to remain undisturbed. I never want them to become their full selves. I would rather they shrivel and rot. I want to linger here in the in-between, half-made, in some permanent adolescence, forever. I don't ever want to become my full self. There is no reality I can envision where myself now doubled is good. I think that if I were fully formed, I would be awful. I'd be even worse than I am now. I'd take after my dad. I'd be terrible.

I think I'm a bad person. I think I was born with the ingredient predators are born with. I don't trust myself. I think if I don't restrain myself, I become selfish, opportunistic, and dishonest. I am pretending to be someone normal, but I'm not. If I let my guard down, I am liable to hurt people.

I'm always fighting this impulse to find people who might love me. I make dating profiles and meet up with them to validate myself. It feels like a game. I feel like I'm playing with something dangerous—like an arsonist with matches. A murderer peeping in windows. I want to hold people's beating hearts in my hands. I want to see all their arteries. I want to study how fully formed and bloody they are. I want to get as close as I can to them; to touch all their things, to put my mouth on them. I want to trick them into loving me. I want to test whether I can be loved; however, I think the way to test whether I am capable of truly loving people back is by ending things. I think if I really loved someone, I would stay away from them.

※

I copy a block of writing I keep saved in my Notes app and I text it to Polly.

Hey, this has nothing to do with you, but I need a little space, so I am no longer dating. Sorry if this is weird, or coming out of the blue, I just wanted to let you know. Again, nothing to do with you. I really like you, and I would love to stay friends if you would.

CHAPTER NINE

Today is Edna's surprise baby shower. I have not returned to my apartment and have to assemble an outfit using my mother's closet. I am standing before the open doors, looking at her bright, eclectic wardrobe.

On the floor, beside a hamper of socks, I spot the cardboard box. It has a malevolent energy to it. I feel drawn to it, as if I am on the event horizon of a black hole—the spot you reach before you fall in.

I yank it out of the closet, sit on the floor, and root through it. I reread the notes my dad wrote. I examine his handwriting. There are drawings of my mom sporting a peacoat and a feathered hat. There is one of her in a fur vest. On the back of each piece of paper, I see my mom has written *"By Elmer"* and dated everything.

Looking through this box feels like revisiting a murder story that I first heard as a kid. It is familiar and strangely comforting, while simultaneously disturbing. Not just for its contents, but because of how it has melded with my memories and become somehow nostalgic to me. I feel rocked in a cradle by these papers that devastated my mom—that devastated me. This is my "turtle eating tulips" picture book. This is what he made me.

I read the notes that I read when I was little. They are the same papers I held then. The same notes I read when I was a teenager. Each time I revisit them, my eyes are older, and I understand them differently. I first thought, *These are confusing*, then *These are romantic*, then *These are absolutely vile*. He wrote lines like:

I love you like the sun. I will love you until the earth dies. I am sick without you. You are all I think about.

My mom would have been younger than me now when he wrote these. She would have been so easy to devastate.

I kick the box back into the closet with my foot. I shove it in as far as it will go.

I return to the hangers. While I slide clothing along the rack, I think about how I hope no one ever stores a box of things I give them. I hope I never write anyone a poem.

I find a yellow long-sleeved dress. It has white daisies on it. I try it on and pose in front of my mom's full-length mirror. I practice how I will stand in it. I fake smile at myself as if my reflection is Gina, Edna, or Kira.

"What a beautiful baby shower," I practice out loud in a whisper to myself. "Who made the cake? It's lovely."

I hear a noise and jump.

The bedroom door opens. My mom enters. "Why are you so jumpy?" she says. "Oh, that dress looks nice. It's cute, but it's not really you, is it?"

I say, "It's a costume for something."

"Oh, for what?"

"Nothing."

"Come on." She touches the dress. "Tell me what it's for."

I feel hot. The collar of the dress is too tight. It's choking me. I pull away from her. "It's none of your business."

She frowns. "What do you mean it's none of my business?"

"Mom," I glare. "Please. Just drop it."

She looks hurt. She asks, in her phone voice, "Is it for something to do with your sisters?"

I exhale. "Yes. Okay? It is. Is that a problem?"

"Of course it's not a problem. Why would you keep that from me—"

"Because you're weird about them," I snap. "Because every time I bring them up your face changes. You seem simultaneously captivated and distraught by the mention of them. I feel like I'm participating in something toxic and unhealthy whenever I bring them up. I don't like it. Okay? Do you understand? Do you get it?"

She looks taken aback.

"Are you shocked by that?" I project my voice. I think my parasite is taking over. "Did you think I didn't notice how weird you are about them? Did you think I had no idea my entire life that you had a strange fixation on their dad, on *my* dad, and on their family? Did you think that didn't affect me? Have you ever stopped to think that now, when I'm trying to build some relationship with these two people who I'm closely related to, that your feelings about them affect me? I feel like I'm doing something hurtful to you every time they talk to me. Do you want me to feel that way? Is that what you want?"

She stammers. "W-what? No. I didn't—"

"Never mind," I stop her. I feel angry. "I'm leaving. I wish you were normal."

✳

My car is hot. I'm fanning my face with a McDonald's coupon sheet. I arrived twenty minutes early so I am waiting here until it is reasonable for me to knock on the door. I feel like there is something crawling on me. I have the windows shut to ensure bugs can't get in, but I feel like one already is.

I wish I didn't yell at my mom.

Polly has not contacted me since I texted her. I keep opening my text conversation with her, tempted to write something. Sometimes I keep it open, watching to see if the text app shows that she is typing, but she never is.

I hope I never write her anything. I hope she meets someone who is genuinely nice. I hope they like bugs and are nice to their mom. I hope they can hear her play the piano perfectly. I hope she loves them, and that they love her. I hope they remember her birthday, and that they meet in some sweet way that doesn't involve her being cheated on, or crying in a dirty shower.

I hope I leave her alone. If you know you are capable of doing something abhorrent, like Ted Bundy, and you are unable to kill yourself because you have a mother, or a similar responsibility, then you should keep your distance. You should create space.

✳

I am kneeling on the floor behind Gina's beige sectional with Kira. We are waiting for Edna to arrive so we can surprise her.

The room is quiet apart from someone giggling. Gina keeps shushing them.

In the silence, it occurs to me that surprising a severely pregnant woman might be ill-advised. What if we alarm her into labor? Or what if she arrives wearing her husband's dirty T-shirt, hoping to spend a private evening alone?

I picture her entering the house and being so startled that she pees her pants. I picture everyone assuming her water broke. I see her playing it off as if her water did break to avoid the humiliation. I picture myself, somehow in the know, wrought with remorse.

"Do you think she suspects anything?" I ask Kira, secretly hoping she does. I hope she knows we are here, is dressed for the occasion, and has braced herself to pretend.

"No, she's oblivious," she whispers.

Great.

The door opens. Edna's belly enters before she does. The lights are turned on and everybody shouts, "Surprise!"

I do not yell "Surprise," I just mouth it. I don't want to contribute to the volume, or startle her.

She puts both hands up and screams, "Oh my God!"

I wince. I hope her water didn't break.

She grins. "I had no idea! Wow! I can't believe it, everybody's here!"

※

I dab my mouth with a napkin. The strawberry tart I am eating has a sort of gelatinous red filling. Kira is sitting next to me.

"Are you excited to be an aunt?" I ask.

"Yes," she says. "Are you?"

I take another bite. "Am I an aunt?" Tart crumbs spray out my mouth. I feel my cheeks burn, embarrassed to have spewed spit and pastry across the room.

"I think that's right, isn't it?" She politely ignores the tart situation. "You're Edna's sister. So, yeah, you're an aunt."

"Are you still an aunt if you're a half sister, though? Maybe I'm a half aunt."

"I don't know if asking the baby to refer to you as 'Half Aunt Enid' is practical. I think we should just go with aunt."

I brought a salad even though they told me not to bring anything. It has watermelon and feta in it. Gina keeps commenting that the salad is "queer," which I believe is her way of reminding me that she knows I am gay. I have taken note that she has not eaten any of the salad and have reasoned therefore that when she says something is "queer," that means she is not a fan. I feel relatively indifferent to this discovery because it is what I hypothesized.

I don't think that Gina told my sisters the hairy details of the interaction Polly and I shared with her recently. I do, however, know that she informed them that I am gay. I know that because Kira greeted me by screaming, "You should have brought your girlfriend!"

I spent the time in my car prior to entering this party regretting yelling at my mom and welling up at the thought of Polly. I looked in my rearview mirror before exiting my car to make sure my eyes weren't red. I approached the front door, repressing thoughts of my mom and Polly, with a phony smile plastered on my face. Kira's greeting hit me like a meteorite.

A woman in Alabama was hit by a meteorite in 1954. It streaked through the sky in a fireball in the early afternoon. It crashed through the roof of her farmhouse, bounced off a large wooden console radio, and woke her up from a nap on the couch. It didn't kill her, but it ruined her day.

"I don't have a girlfriend," I responded to Kira in the vicinity of Gina.

A meteorite will hit a person once every 180 years. That means the next time somebody will be hit is 2134, though of course, who knows?

"What?" Gina said. "The girl I ran into you with—you two insisted you weren't friends."

"We aren't, but we also aren't girlfriends."

She put her hands up and said, "I don't get it!"

An asteroid almost hit Earth in 2021. It went undetected because it came from a blind spot, where the sun is in our eyes.

"Do you think you're going to have kids someday?" a woman asks Kira. "Can we expect little cousins for this baby?"

Kira laughs. "Not anytime soon, but maybe. What about you, Enid? Do you think you'll give the baby cousins?"

Gina gets flustered. She says, "Oh Kira, honey! Um—"

I don't know if she is flustered because she would not consider my offspring her grandchildren's cousins, or if she thinks lesbians can't procreate and is mortified that Kira brought it up. I have an inkling it's the latter.

In an effort to help Gina not embarrass herself, I say, "Maybe."

✳

Edna opens my gift and beams. "This is so cute! Thank you so much!"

I bought the baby a yellow towel with a hood that will make her look like a duck. I also got baby shampoo and toiletries, and a little baby bathtub.

I hear Gina behind me somewhere say, "I saw that towel on sale the other day, too! That's so cute and what a bargain, right, Enid?"

✳

I have excused myself to the bathroom to look at my phone. I simultaneously want Polly to text me and for her to never speak to me again. I want to be hit by an asteroid.

I text my mom,

I'm sorry.

There is a knock on the bathroom door.

"Just a minute," I say.

I wipe my face off on a towel.

They keep knocking.

"Just a minute."

They knock again.

"Just a minute!"

I open the door.

It's Edna.

"Are you okay?" she asks.

"Yes, I'm fine," I lie.

She directs me back into the washroom, waddles in, and shuts the door behind us. She says, "My mom was rude to you. I'm sorry."

"It's okay. The towel *was* on sale."

"Not just today. I know she was rude earlier, when she ran into you and your girlfriend."

"She's not my girlfriend," I say. "But she told you about that?"

"Yes, she did. I'm mortified. So is Kira. We're both really sorry about how she behaved."

"Don't worry about it."

"She's being weird about you being gay, and it's embarrassing. I'm so sorry. We've been trying to talk to her about it."

"She's from an older generation. My mom can be weird too. I know they can't totally help it. I don't care—"

"Well, we care," she says. "It's unacceptable."

Something about that comment mixes with my preexisting sadness and triggers a weird gasp cry. I put a hand over my mouth to stifle it.

"It's okay." She hugs me. I feel the baby move. "It's really important to us that we know you. Something about you being around brings out the worst in our mom. She isn't as bad as she seems. She's just dealing with grief and with the fact that Dad made a lot of mistakes. I think you remind her of that."

I am crying more than the situation calls for.

"You remind Kira and me of the good things about him though."

"What?" I sob.

"You're a lot like him."

I close my eyes. "I don't want to be like him."

"No, you're not like the bad parts. You're both just quiet and then you say something surprising. You sit like him—you cross your legs like he did. You're always touching your hands the way he did. You have a similar laugh."

"Do my hands look like his?" I ask.

I show her my hands. They're shaking.

"Yes," she says, and I feel like I have been shot.

I close my eyes again.

She sits on the toilet. "I have to pee, sorry," she says.

I sniffle. "It's okay," even though I find this strange.

I notice the toilet paper roll beside her is empty. I rummage under the sink to find her a new one.

I hand it to her.

She says, "Thanks. So, did you and your girlfriend break up? Is that why you said she's not your girlfriend?"

"She was never really my girlfriend, but yeah," I say.

I look at my wet face in the mirror while I listen to Edna pee.

"Are you okay?" she asks as she flushes.

"To be honest . . ." I exhale. "I think I have a parasite. I didn't want you to know."

"A parasite?"

I grimace. "Yeah, like I think there's something bad in me that I can't control. I feel like I have some bug that other people don't."

"I understand," she says as she washes her hands. "I totally get it."

"Really?"

She nods. "Yes. I think I have one too."

"You do?"

She dries her hands. "Yes. I feel that way all the time. I'm worried about being a mom because of it. I think, *How could I be someone's mom? I'm a terrible person. I'll be a terrible mother.* I'm going to accidentally scream at her when I'm angry. What if I shake her? I'm terrified. I keep picturing her as a little girl, and me treating her like I treated Kira. She and I were always fighting—"

"You were?"

"God yes, we were awful to each other. It was a nightmare. I'm worried that I'm pretending to be this put-together adult mom, but that it's all a show, and that when I'm left alone with

this poor little baby my true horrible self is going to come out.
I'm going to wreak havoc on her. I am beside myself about it.
I'm more worried about that than I am about delivering this
baby, and I am so worried about delivering this baby I can't even
put it into words. Have you ever watched a birthing video?"

"No."

"Don't," she says. "I don't know why I did. I knew it would
make it worse. I think sometimes I do things to torture myself.
Do you know what I mean?"

I exhale. "Yeah."

We look at each other.

She blinks.

"I think you'll be a good mom," I say.

She breathes air out her nose. "Thank you. You're a good sister."

We both turn to look in the mirror. Instead of focusing on
how she is shorter, has smaller features, and no rat tattoos—
I notice that she and I stand similarly. We both have our shoulders back and our heads tilted slightly to the side.

I say, "Should we get back out to your party?"

She tucks her hair behind her ears. "Yes. How do I look?
Can you tell I have a parasite?"

I laugh. "No. Can you see mine?"

She smiles. "Nope."

✳

"What did Gina wear?" my mom asks the second I enter the
house. She's sitting on the couch with no lights on.

I rushed inside after I pulled into the driveway. I think I left
the car door open. I bolted inside the moment I saw the house.

"Are you okay?" I pant.

I regret yelling at her. She seems out of it. She's staring at the wall in front of her. Her voice is off.

"What gifts did Edna get?" she asks.

I sit next to her on the couch. I hold on to one of her hands. I feel like she is a balloon I let go of. I feel like she's floating into space. I hold her hand like it's her balloon string, hoping I can yank her back down to earth.

"Did I fuck you up?" Her voice breaks.

"What? No," I lie.

"I think I fucked you up."

"No." I shake my head. "No, no, you didn't. If I'm fucked-up, it isn't because of you."

She's crying.

"I'm fine, Mom, really," I hush. "Please. It's okay. Come on. I'm fine. You're fine. Everything's fine. I'm sorry I yelled at you earlier. Did you see my text? I said I was sorry. I *am* sorry. Okay? I don't want you to feel bad. It's the last thing I want, really. I'm sorry. Everything's fine. I was just in a bad mood."

She isn't listening.

"I'm sorry," I say.

"Mom? Are you listening to me?"

She isn't.

"Mom, listen to me."

"Hey Mom, did you know moons can have moons?"

"They're called moon moons. Isn't that cute?"

"Did you know everything is stardust, Mom?"

"You and I, even. You knew that, right? Right now, we're in space. Look at us. We're in space, Mom. Isn't that something? Why are you sad?"

She has tears rolling down her cheeks. I feel like she can't hear anything I'm saying.

I think of the time I unlocked her bedroom and found her on the floor. I think of her looking like a wax figure.

"Mom." I shake her. "Gina looked terrible."

Maybe if I talk about Gina and the girls, she'll snap out of it.

"You dress so much better than she does, Mom. Really. She's boring-looking. She looked stupid. I think she *is* stupid, honestly. I think she might be homophobic, too. She was rude to me recently, actually—"

Her eyes open. "What?"

Maybe I shouldn't have told her that.

"What did she do?" she asks. Her voice is her own again.

"Nothing," I lie. "It was nothing. She just sucks. I just think you should know she sucks—"

"What did she do? She was rude to you? Tell me what she did."

Her eyes are dry now. She looks angry.

"She, well," I stammer. "S-she ran into me. I was having coffee with that girl Polly. And she was weird about it. I don't think she knew I was a lesbian, but after it was clear we were on a date, she kept calling us friends. And Polly was kind of rude about it too, to be honest. Or maybe she wasn't. She's sort of blunt. She was just unwilling to pretend she didn't pick up on Gina being off. It wasn't that bad. It was just a little tense. Edna apologized to me about it. She and Kira heard about it and—"

"Did Gina apologize?"

Her face is pink.

"Yeah," I lie. "She said sorry."

She narrows her eyes. "I can tell when you're lying."

✳

My mom went to bed early. We watched an episode of *Dateline*. I told her I'd sleep over, but I'm not tired yet. It's not even dark out. It's dusk. I'm sitting outside. The porch light is burned out. A teenager named Cody is playing basketball across the street in his driveway. He waved at me when he came outside. I remember when he was little, and when his mom was pregnant with him. My mom would babysit for their family sometimes. She makes them cookies.

We moved here when I was about eight. Our house was one of the first built in the neighborhood. Our yard was dirt for months before sod was put in. Now my mom maintains a perennial garden out front. She has hostas and purple coneflowers.

I remember this neighborhood when all the lots were mud. I remember watching new houses being erected all around us. I rode my bike through the construction zone, stopping to climb the piles of bricks, pick weeds, or balance on beams of wood. The streets smelled like churned dirt and sawdust.

My mom was proud to move here. It was hard for her to afford it. I remember hearing her chat with her friends about how she had managed it. Her friend brought over a welcome mat as a housewarming gift. My mom teared up when she placed it by the front door. She painted all the walls yellow, because I asked her to, and we went to thrift stores to buy our furniture.

I would ride my bike around the neighborhood for hours, driving through the stormwater pond in the center of the subdivision. I remember sucking on the ends of purple clover blossoms and jumping into the basements of houses that had no upper floors yet. I would lie on the poured cement foundation and look up at the shell of the house growing above me. I would try to picture what the house would end up looking like when it was fully assembled.

I knew that when the streetlights came on, I had to go home. My mom was always sitting on this porch, waiting for me under the glow of our yellow porch light.

When the houses were all built, their lawns had grass, and all the backhoes and mixer trucks were gone, I would look at the houses and think about how I had lain in their basements. Even now, when I look across the street, I think about how I saw that house before it became what it is. I watch Cody dunk his basketball and feel a sort of intimacy with him and this neighborhood and everyone in it because I was here at the beginning when everything formed. Even though Cody and these houses feel far away now, I still know them in some special way.

✳

I am on a date with Kae, the person who I went to get ice cream with before I started seeing Polly, whose car has a ridiculous *meep* sound. We are driving to the movies, listening to the radio. A Janis Joplin song is playing.

Kae pays for the movie tickets, and I pay for the popcorn and drinks.

We sit in the back row of the theater. Kae puts their arm over my shoulders.

We are watching a horror movie. We both stare up at the expansive screen and shovel popcorn into our mouths while a deranged man covered head to toe in the blood of his children screams shrilly into the camera. The music of the film starts to heighten, suggesting that something bad is about to happen.

The hairs on my arms raise. Kae is gripping my shoulders, terrified. They look away from the screen when the music stops. I can see them in my peripheral vision shield their face while

I watch the screaming man's head get axed off. A man in the theater shrieks.

✳

Kae and I are parked beside a forest in their car.

"I hated that movie," they say. "I can't stand scary shit like that."

I don't reply. I look down at my hands.

"I don't get why anyone would be into that, do you?" they ask. "What do people get out of that? I want to watch something happy. Do you know what I mean?"

I look through the window beside me at the forest. I look at the dark spaces between the pine trees.

"Do you think predators live in there?" I ask.

"You mean like wolves? In there? I hope not."

They click the automatic door lock.

We sit quietly looking at the forest.

"Did you want to hook up?" they ask.

I say, "Sure," and climb over the center console.

Kae undoes their seat belt, and I sit on top of them. I am careful to avoid pressing the horn with my butt. Kae has their hands on my hips.

When our mouths touch, it stings. It feels like kissing the stinger of a bee. It is a sharp, startling pain, but I continue anyways. I feel my lips swell and burn but still press my mouth against Kae's, telling myself it will feel numb soon. The longer we kiss, the more my mouth starts to swell. It starts to feel difficult to breathe. My throat is swelling. I feel dizzy.

I open my eyes and look past Kae's head into the forest. I feel a hollow, sinking sensation in my stomach. My hands feel wet. Why are my hands wet? I look down at them. I can't tell in the dark, but I have this terrible image in my mind of them being covered in blood.

I pull away from Kae. I pretend I see something out the window.

"What?" they say, panicked, looking over their shoulder. "Did you see a fucking wolf?"

I press the light on in the roof of the car. I look down at my hands to see if there's blood on them.

There isn't.

"Turn that off! We won't be able to see outside the car if the light's on!" Kae shouts while they hurry me off them and buckle their seat belt.

They strain their neck to look into the forest.

They shudder. "Let's get out of here."

✳

Kae drops me off at my apartment. I don't tell them that I am not staying here. I decide to let it happen. I get out of the car and thank them for the ride.

The building looks taller than it used to. It's nighttime. There is a white light over the front door. I hold my keys, not in the hammer grip, just loosely.

I march up the front steps and open the metal door. I walk slowly down the hallway, beneath the fluorescent light. I turn the corridor expecting to see a bald man waiting for me, but I don't. I unlock the door to my apartment. I leave it unlocked. I put on my podcast and lie in my bed, sprawled out like a dead butterfly in a display case.

I want Polly to call me and talk to me about bugs. I want

her to come over and lie in a pile of my dirty laundry with me. I want her to be here when I haven't cleaned up or put deodorant on. I want us to be rank and disgusting. I want to rub dirt in each other's faces.

I wish I were born different. I wish I could smile at bald men, or call my mom just to say hi, and not to check if her head's in the oven. I wish I were normal.

I want my door to open. I want a bald man to come inside right now and suffocate me. I want to die and be reborn someone new. I wish I could do that. I wish I could molt and shed the outer layer of myself. I want to become someone fresh. I feel rotten; I feel like my insides are curdled and crawling with parasites.

✳

There is a bang on my door. I jump.

It happens again.

I rush to the peephole. I put an eye to the hole and see that it is my bald neighbor.

I smell burning.

He knocks again. He looks angry.

"Can you please turn your TV down?" he shouts into the crack of the door.

What?

He must think my podcast is the TV.

"You always play it so loud. Please. I can't sleep."

I open the door. He looks tired. He is thin and short; he is definitely shorter than five eleven.

I look into his eyes. I watch the blue in his irises for shadows. I wonder if he has a parasite operating his body from behind his eyes, like I do.

I ask, "Is that why you've been coming here? To ask me to turn the TV down?"

He says, "Yes. It keeps me up at night. I work early."

I blink. I feel insane. I look down at my hands.

Am I insane?

"I'm sorry," I whisper. "I'm insane."

"What?" He steps backward.

"I'm half-deaf," I correct myself quickly.

He raises his eyebrows. "Are you really?"

"Yes. I can't hear at all out of one ear."

"Oh, I'm sorry," he says.

"Don't apologize. It's not your fault I'm deaf. I'll turn the noise down."

"Thank you."

*

I googled hearing aids and fell down a rabbit hole. I'm now reading a forum for people with unilateral deafness. I lost track of my objective while perusing the forum because so many people have written about being deaf in one ear, and it's making me tear up. Not because it's sad, but because it's strange to discover that I've had shared experiences.

One person wrote about how they felt socially awkward in school when trying to position themselves in a classroom so they could hear. They were always jockeying for a seat on their preferred side. I did the same thing; I used to show up to class really early so I could get the seat I could hear best from.

Another post said, "People often think I'm ignoring them. Someone once called me a bitch for not saying hi back to them."

A lot of people are sharing similar stories. We all accidentally seem rude.

Another person wrote about turning their deaf ear to people they don't like listening to, and I laughed really hard. I made an account just to write, "I do the same thing."

After reading hundreds of posts, I decided to write one.

✳

Hi everyone, I'm new. One of my ears is totally deaf. I was born that way. Someone broke into my apartment recently, and I suspected it was my neighbor. He was always banging on my door. I've been ignoring him. This has become such a problem that I've purchased a Ring camera; I've had to have a friend sleep over, I've been staying at my mom's house, and it's spurred me going to therapy. Well, guess what? It turns out I was just listening to a podcast too loudly and my neighbor was knocking on my door to ask me to please turn it down. Does anyone else have stories about misunderstandings that came as a result of your deaf ear that might make me feel better for behaving so ridiculously?

✳

One person replied, "LOL. Don't beat yourself up. I once punched a man who surprised me on my deaf side. He was just asking me for directions and startled me."

Another person wrote, "Welcome to our forum! This is why our community exists. It's nice to have a place where people understand you. I totally get why you behaved that way."

Reading this comment makes me feel strangely upset. I read it over three times. I mouth the words, "I totally get why you

behaved that way." I don't often feel like anyone gets why I behave the way I do.

Another person wrote, "But wait. Someone really broke in,
right? Who did that? Are you sure you're safe there?"

✳

Kae texts me the next morning, asking if I want to go for another drive.

I reply:

Hey, this has nothing to do with you, but I need a little space, so I
am no longer dating. Sorry if this is weird, or coming out of the blue,
I just wanted to let you know. Again, nothing to do with you. I really
like you, and I would love to stay friends if you would.

✳

"Have you been looking at the photos of bald men I gave you?"

I am in Dr. Jeong's office again.

I say, "Yes. I—"

Why am I lying?

"No." I pause. "I stopped."

"Why?"

"Um," I say.

Because I don't want to look at them alone and I don't have
anyone to look at them with anymore.

"It's just difficult for me," I say.

"Okay, would you prefer to look at some together today, or
to watch more of your YouTube channel?"

Wow, would I rather be waterboarded or punched repeatedly in the face?

"YouTube, I guess," I say.

She sets up her laptop. She types my username, which is a humbling moment because it means she remembers it. It also means that perhaps she has been watching on her own.

She pulls up a video of me titled "Responding to My Cyber-bullies."

I grit my molars. What am I doing here? I chose to come here. Am I sick? I feel sick. I don't think I'm going to come back. I don't want to watch my nightmarish YouTube videos with another person. I'd rather keep my phobia. I suspect I'll be keeping it regardless. This is just an expensive way of hurting myself.

"Do you remember filming this?" she asks.

"No," I say.

In the video, I am displaying hate comments I've received. On the screen now, I have pinned one that says, "You're fucking ugly."

Rather than listen to the advice of the teachers and adults in my life, I evidently chose not to ignore the bullying. Instead, I filmed myself saying, "If you think I care that I'm ugly, you're on acid."

I cringe. I had clearly never done acid at this point in my life and had no frame of reference. Furthermore, my face and eyes were red, suggesting I did perhaps care.

She pauses the video. "Do you remember any of this?"

"Vaguely," I say. "I think there were a few times in my You-Tube journey when I was targeted by cyberbullies."

"Really? Okay."

She exits the video and scrolls through my channel. She finds one when I was older, around seventeen. This video is titled "I Love Hate Comments." In it, I don't discuss the comments. I just apply makeup.

Dr. Jeong scrolls down beneath the video. There are comments that say, "Ew" and "You're disgusting."

She clicks on the next video I filmed. In it, my face is cold. I don't look like I care.

∗

I am sleeping at my mom's house again. The wall separating the bathroom and this bedroom is not very thick. I can hear my mom brushing her teeth.

When I was a kid, my mom often had a bath right after saying goodnight to me. She would say *sweet dreams*, turn off my light, and go into the bathroom. She would then run the water into the bathtub and sob. I remember trying to sleep while I heard her. I think she thought the sound of the running water muffled her crying, but it didn't.

I remember pulling my blankets up over my head, hoping the fabric would smother the sound. I would hum to myself whenever her crying was especially hard to ignore.

I regularly fell asleep listening to her talk to herself out loud in the tub. She often spoke as if my dad were in the bathroom with her. It was as if she were practicing what she would say to him, given the chance. She would cry, "How could you do this?" and "I forgive you; of course I forgive you."

∗

One morning, when I was still very little, I woke up on my own and went into the kitchen. My mom normally made me breakfast, but I didn't want to wake her up. I knew she had spent her evening crying and role-playing her delusional reunion with my dad. I took one of the kitchen chairs and pushed it in front of the cabinet. I stood on it to reach for a box of Corn Pops.

I poured a bowl for myself, spilling some on the floor, then went to the fridge. I took out the milk. It was a full jug of milk. It was heavy. I tried to balance while pouring it into my bowl, but accidentally spilled it. Milk glugged from the jug, splatting a white puddle on the floor.

I was trying to mop it up when my mom came into the kitchen. Her hair was disheveled, and her eyes were pink and puffy. She looked at the puddle of milk surrounding me, and her eyes welled. She leaned her back against the cabinets behind her and lowered herself to the floor, where she sat cross-legged, extended her body forward, and cried, her veins bulging in her neck.

I said, "I'll clean it up, Mom, don't worry."

She put her hands to her face, and I noticed her arms were cut.

"What happened?" I asked.

"It's just spilled milk, honey, don't worry," she cried.

"No, I mean to your arms, Mom. What happened to your arms?"

She sobbed and repeated, "Don't worry," and I understood that she was out of sorts, so I didn't ask again.

✳

"I spoke to Gina," my mom says.

I'm sitting at her kitchen table eating buttered raisin toast.

"What?" I say with toast in my mouth.

"I called Gina to discuss her mistreatment of you."

"Oh my God." I spit my half-chewed mouthful of bread onto my plate. "Are you serious? What did you say? Jesus Christ. How could you do that—"

"It was fine." She crosses her arms. "I'm sorry, but I had to say something. She listened to me and told me her daughters had a similar discussion with her, and she feels just terrible. She wants to apologize in person to you. So she and the girls are going to come over Sunday after next, if that's okay with you."

My eyes involuntarily roll into the back of my head. I'm gritting my teeth. I'm holding my parasite back like he's a drunk little angry man at a bar, and I'm an underqualified bouncer.

"I also spoke to Edna," she says. "Gina handed the phone to her after she and I spoke. Edna wanted to talk to me too. We talked about the issue, and she apologized on behalf of her mother. She's a nice girl, isn't she? She also mentioned she's having car trouble again. I gave her some tips and told her to feel free to call me again about it. Maybe I should suggest she bring her car here when they come for their visit. What do you think?"

Rather than tell my mom she's overstepped, and that I feel enraged, I say nothing. I stand up and throw my raisin bread into the garbage. I place my plate on the counter, walk upstairs, and listen to an episode of my murder podcast.

*

I wanted to skip my appointment with Dr. Jeong today; however, I did not feel brave enough to cancel. I worried she would ask for an explanation and that I would embarrass myself trying to provide one. I thought of just not showing up, but I don't know what would happen if I did that. I thought maybe she might call the police, as if I had gone missing. Or as if she were concerned because I naively exposed my childhood desire to kill myself.

She and I are now watching a YouTube video of my twelve-year-old self cry. That's right, I filmed myself crying. I provide no clarification in the video explaining why I am upset.

"Can you report this video?" I squirm.

"What?"

"Can you please report this?" I say.

"For what?" she asks.

"An attack on a person."

She laughs. "Do you wish these weren't on the internet?"

I look at her. "Yes."

Obviously I wish these weren't on the internet.

She says, "There's a silver lining to them being there, at least. They're helping us here."

"Are they?"

"I think so," she says. "Don't you?"

I don't want to be rude and say no, but I don't feel helped by these videos. I feel the opposite.

She scans through more of my channel. She reads the comments beneath my videos. Almost all the comments have fire symbols in them.

One commenter asks, "Why do you guys put fire symbols on her videos?"

She clicks "view more" to read the replies.

"She killed someone."

She glances at me. "That's a strange comment, isn't it?"

My chest tightens as if I just saw a bald man.

She reads the next comment.

"Look at her last video. She posted herself lighting a match before her high school was lit on fire. Someone died in the fire. She killed someone."

I hear an alarm going off. I think a fire exit was just opened.

She plays the video of me lighting a match. I watch my fingers drag the match and it spark.

"Do you remember what all this is about?" she asks.

I don't reply. I hear ringing.

She looks at me.

"Are you okay?" she asks.

I smell burning.

I stand up. "I need to use the bathroom."

She looks up at me. "Okay, sure. It's just down the hall, to the right."

I leave the room. I rush down the hall. I cough while I run.

I find the bathroom. I put my hand on the doorknob but quickly pull it away. The knob is hot. It feels like gripping a welding rod.

I touch the door with both my hands. It feels warm.

You're not supposed to open doors when they're hot. There might be a fire behind them.

Maybe I should leave. Maybe I could sneak out the exit and go home.

"Are you looking for the bathroom?" a stranger passing me in the hallway asks.

I look at them.

"It's right there." They gesture at the door. "Is it locked?"

They reach ahead of me and swing the door open before I can warn them not to.

"Stop—" I start to say, but it's too late. The door is open.

I look inside. There is no fire. The person standing next to me gestures at me to enter. I walk inside and lock the door behind me.

I left my phone in the doctor's office. I wish there was music playing in here. I wish I could play my podcast. I wish the room wasn't so silent. I wish I could drown out my thoughts.

I know what I've been ignoring. I feel like the door in my mind has been swung open. I feel like I am looking at the charred remains of what I did.

I started a fire. It was at my high school. I don't know why I did it. I used to play with matches. A kid died.

My parasite is standing next to his charred skeleton like Vanna White. He is smiling like he would next to a new car. "Look!" he tells me. "This is it!"

I am throwing up beside the toilet bowl. I can't position my face in the bowl. I am heaving too much. I'm barfing onto the tile. My hands are touching the dirty floor.

"That's right!" my parasite jeers. "Why'd you do that? You're a monster!"

I put my hands over my ears, but I can still hear him.

He was in the twelfth grade. He was tall. His name was Yusuf. I didn't go to the wake, but everyone at school did. He wasn't burned to death; he died of smoke inhalation. Ben told me it was an open casket. He went. It was the day before we broke up. He said the heat from the fire singed his eyebrows and eyelashes off. They put a wig on him for the wake, but he said you could tell that underneath he was bald.

There's a knock on the bathroom door.

"Enid?"

"Enid? Can I come in?"

It's Dr. Jeong.

"No," I shout. "Don't come in, please."

"I think you're having a panic attack," she says through the door.

I ignore her.

"You're safe, it's okay."

I'm not safe. I'm not okay.

"It's a panic attack. You're okay."

I'm crying and barfing on the bathroom floor. Why did I do this? Why did I come here? Why did I make myself realize this? I already knew I did this. I knew I did this. I just don't let myself think about it. I tuck it into a room in my head where I don't visit. I know it's there. Why did I come here? Why would I let myself come here?

I inhale. I close my eyes.

I keep breathing until the air starts to feel less thick.

The room is quiet except for me panting.

After an extended moment of silence, Dr. Jeong says, "Please let me know when you feel able to talk."

✳

I have returned to the couch. I have a small, cone-shaped paper cup of water in my hands.

"I think our time is way over." I gesture at her clock.

"I canceled my next meeting," she says.

"To call the police?"

"What?"

I sip my water. "Don't you think you should probably call the police?"

"Why?"

"I killed someone."

She tilts her head. "Wouldn't they already know that?"

"No, I don't know. I don't remember what they know."

I don't let myself think about what happened, and so the details have all faded. I can't remember it clearly.

"What do you remember?" she asks.

"I remember my dad calling my house. I guess the police didn't know how to contact me. They connected me to my dad through our last name."

I inhale. Remembering this feels like walking through an abandoned old house that I used to live in. Everything is where I left it, but covered in dust.

"The police told him that his daughter posted a suspicious video on the internet of her lighting a match before the school was set on fire. I assume they said that, of course. I don't know."

I wonder if he thought they were calling about Edna or Kira, or if he knew right away it couldn't be about them. I wonder if the police had to say my name. I wonder if he said, "Who?" or "That's not my daughter."

"He called my mom. I heard them on the phone. I came into the kitchen and saw my mom with the phone pressed to her ear. She looked like she had seen a ghost. It was so bizarre that they were speaking. I could tell that she was freaking out. Her eyes were wide, and her hands were shaking. I could only hear bits of what he said. 'She's fucking killed a kid.' I remember that, especially. He said that exactly. That's how I know I did it."

She squints. "Do you remember being at the school? Do you remember the fire? Were you in the fire?"

I try to remember. I run through the old house in my mind, searching the rooms.

"I don't remember. But it was Chelsea who found the video I posted. She had discovered my YouTube channel in the aftermath of her breakup with Ben. She monitored it while I was his girlfriend. I knew she watched it because she sometimes commented. She wrote things like, 'You're disgusting' and 'You look awful.' Some of those comments were her. I think she called the police."

I remember when I filmed myself, I thought of her. I curated content to upset her. I did things like paint my nails and comment, while I filed my cuticles, "My boyfriend likes this color on me."

I have a video that pans over a teddy bear. It zooms in on the bear's black marble eyes. "Isn't he cute?" I asked my audience. "My boyfriend got me him."

"Were you arrested?" Dr. Jeong asks.

I search my mind.

"I don't think so, no."

"Were you convicted of anything? You work for the National Space Agency, right?"

"Yeah, that's where I work."

"They do background checks, Enid. If this were in your history, I don't think you could work there. How are you reasoning that?"

"I'm not sure. Maybe they missed something."

"This isn't adding up. It doesn't make sense. Can you ask your mom about what happened?"

I rub my face. "I can try to, yeah."

"Okay, are you able to do that before our next session?"

I repeat, "I can try to, yeah."

"Okay," she says. "This is good. You're doing well."

❋

I exit the therapy office. It's dusk. I was in there for four hours. It feels like it is five a.m. and like I have just completed a bender. I have a headache and I feel queasy.

I climb into my car and lock the doors. I pull down the sun visor and look at myself in the mirror. My eyes are red. I rub my cheeks, inhale, and look down at my phone.

I call my mom.

"Hi honey."

"Hi Mom," I say. "I have a question for you."

"You do? Well, you aren't the first person today. Edna rang me earlier to ask some car questions."

I close my eyes. "Did she? How did that go?"

"I think it went well. We actually got to chatting for quite some time."

I bite the insides of my cheeks.

"I know you're nervous I seem crazy, but she called me. She had so much to say. At first it was about her car, but then she asked questions about you and your dad. It felt like she was calling because she wanted to hear about all that from me. I think the car thing was an excuse. She asked about you growing up. She really wants to see pictures. You know, it wasn't all sunshine and daisies over at their place. Have the girls spoken to you about that? She told me stories about your dad. She's been struggling since he died because they actually had quite a strained relationship. Did you know that? I guess he had some anger problems. I knew that, of course, but I thought he was just like that with me. She told me she's in therapy. Did you know she's in therapy, honey?"

"I didn't," I say.

"Well, now you do. It was a good chat, really. I know you're nervous I might seem strange to them, but I don't think I did. I think we had a good chat, really. Tell me if she mentions it was weird, okay? I won't be upset. I really think it was fine, though. Honestly. I think talking to her, and Kira, and their mom more is going to be good for us. I think it will help me."

I inhale.

We sit quietly on the phone for a moment.

"What was your question, honey?" she asks. "You called to ask me a question?"

I look out the window in my car. The trees are changing

colors. There is one tree across the street that is bright red, another that is orange, and a third that is already bare, with its leaves on the ground surrounding it.

I think of my mom when my dad called. I think of her startled face. I feel terrible for doing that to her.

I don't want to bring this up. I don't want to open any old wounds. I don't want to put her through an unpleasant conversation, let alone one where I ask her to confirm that her only child is a bad person.

"Did you know there are planets that orbit dead stars?" I ask.

"Are there really?"

"Yes. There is at least one in the Milky Way. A star's death is spectacularly violent. They expand, become giants, and explode. The explosion is called a supernova, and the light one makes is comparable to an entire galaxy."

"Wow, that's amazing."

"Yeah. When a planet orbits a dead star, that means that it survived the burst. When stars die, they consume the planets near them. They are incinerated and pulled apart. A planet that survives intact would move closer. It would huddle in toward the burned-out star core. When stars die, they become white dwarfs, which is synonymous with a star's collapsed core. A white dwarf is a remnant of what it once was. It is like the corpse of a star."

"A corpse of a star," she repeats. "That is so interesting."

✳

My earliest memory is of sitting at my mother's feet. She was standing with her shoes on either side of me. I think I must have been a baby. I don't think I could walk yet. She was wearing a long skirt. It was windy and her skirt draped over me, then blew away, then draped over me again. She was standing above me, and above her was the sky. I felt how I might inside a cathedral. Her legs were like stone pillars. Her skirt like an altar veil. I felt guarded by her. I thought of her as the sun.

✷

I will never understand how my dad could stand in the glow of my mom, as if an inch from a star, and be unmoved by her formidable light. It has been devastating to watch her fade in response to him. Even when dead, the mention of Gina or his daughters dims her. I don't know how to make her dress up every morning or clean her house. It feels like every time I visit, more of her lights are burned out.

✷

When stars fall into black holes, they seem to do it slowly. Because of gravitational time dilation, they look as if they are paused. If a person were to fall into a black hole, they would be spaghettified; however, to anyone watching, they would look as if they didn't fall.

✷

I don't want to talk to my mom about what I did. I wish she and I both fell into a black hole at eight p.m. on a school night. I want to be paused under our orange blanket, forever watching *Dateline*.

CHAPTER TEN

I went to Vin's house uninvited. I just showed up at his door.

"Are you okay?" he asked as he led me in.

I said yes, but he could tell I wasn't.

He forced me to have a bath. He lit candles and put Epsom salts in his tub. I told him I was uncomfortable having a bath at someone else's house, and he said that was too bad and handed me two towels.

I lie in a soup of myself, wishing I could rocket into space. I want to float alone in the dark, silent void. I want to be the type of frozen asteroid that is burned up by a star, and never creates craters in the moon or kills off dinosaurs.

*

Kira texted me asking what they should bring when they visit on Sunday.

"Hi Mom," I say from the tub. I called her. "Did you know the explosion made by the asteroid that killed the dinosaurs was one billion times more powerful than the Hiroshima bomb?"

"Was it really? Wow. A billion?"

"Yeah, and the impact brought molten lava into the atmosphere that flew so high some of it touched the moon."

"It reached the moon?"

"Yes, and when the lava dropped back to earth, it fell like glass bullets, killing almost every creature that was not already incinerated."

"Wow. I don't know if this is the kind of interesting fact I want to hear, honey. I'd prefer the ones about how sunsets on Mars are blue, or how it rains diamonds on Jupiter."

"Okay, sorry," I say.

"It's okay. Are you all right?"

"I'm fine. Kira texted me to ask what to bring on Sunday."

"Did she? Oh, that's sweet. They don't need to bring anything. I think I'll make a lemon cake, or something."

✳

I have wrapped myself in Vin's robe on his couch. He has poured me a mug of black tea.

I ask him, "Do you know how much of life on earth was killed by the meteor that killed the dinosaurs?"

He says, "I think it's seventy percent. Is it seventy-five?"

"I don't remember."

"It was most of it." He sips his tea.

"Yeah." I nod.

"Not all of it though," he adds.

✳

I am getting a tattoo on my chest of the sun setting. I had to take my shirt off to get it, and the tattoo artist requested I put electrical tape on my nipples, for modesty. I am lying on a bench in the middle of this shop with my shirt off, with black taped Xs over my nipples, feeling my chest rattle.

"Does it hurt?" the artist asks.

"No," I say, but it does.

"You sure? You have a very serious expression on your face," he says.

"I'm thinking," I tell him.

I am thinking about how everyone's behavior is motivated by many secret things. I know there are reasons why people do things that I am not in on. I know I am not the center of the universe. The sun does not revolve around me. There are lots of questions I will never know the answers to. I don't know if wormholes exist, or why my dad didn't like me, or why I started a fire. Maybe there are good reasons. Maybe everything I think is wrong.

✳

My mom and I are sitting on the hood of my car. It is rare to see the northern lights where we are, but the weather network suggested we might be able to tonight.

"Do you remember when I saw that ghost?" I ask.

She looks at me.

"Do you remember that?" I ask again.

"You didn't see a ghost, honey," she says.

"No, I know I imagined it. I just meant remember when I thought I saw a ghost—"

"No, I mean. That was your dad."

"What?"

"Your dad came by to see you after you'd gone to bed. I told him he could go look at you, but he accidentally woke you up."

My stomach drops. "What?"

"I didn't want to upset you. I told him he could only come when you'd gone to bed, but he was so clumsy he knocked over your whole nightstand—"

"Wait." I interrupt her while processing that information. I thought I had seen a ghost. I thought I imagined a vivid ghost in my room. I have been doubting my senses ever since that happened.

"What the fuck?" I say, angry. "I wish you didn't lie to me about that. I've been thinking I'm capable of hallucinating—"

"I'm sorry. He had been so absent. I just didn't want him coming in and out. He wanted to see you, so we thought if he just came at night—"

"Did he do it other times?"

"He did it a handful of times."

Something cracks in my ribs. "Why would he do that? I don't understand why he would do that."

"Well, he loved you, honey; he was just a bad father."

I feel like I just learned that I am actually fifty years old and have been living my life as if I am decades younger than I really am.

How dare he do that?

When I was a kid, I rarely told my mom when I was upset.

Occasionally I'd snap at her, but mostly I would shut myself in my room. I'd film YouTube videos or read books about ghosts. Today, when I feel upset, I try to distract myself. I listen to a podcast. I think about space.

I look at the sky.

"You thought you were capable of hallucinating?" she asks.

I look for the northern lights.

"Yes. I thought something was wrong with me."

"Nothing is wrong with you—"

"No, something *is* wrong with me. I've actually been going to a doctor. She said I am different neurodevelopmentally and that I have mental health conditions—"

"That doesn't mean something is wrong with you."

I look at her.

After some silence, she says, "I'm really sorry for not telling you about your dad's visits. Would you have preferred I tell you? Or maybe I shouldn't have mentioned them at all. Would you have preferred never knowing? What should I have done?"

I often don't want to know the truth because I'm worried that it will reveal something I won't be able to handle. I think that I would rather be ignorant, but maybe that's wrong. When I'm ignorant, I start thinking I'm crazy. I repress that I start fires and I become neurotic. I am so worried that I am a bad person. I am afraid of facing that possibility. But I think, if I were a good person, I would face it. Good people want to know what they did wrong.

"I would rather know," I say.

She nods.

"Mom," I say.

"Yes?"

"Do you remember the fire?"

"The fire?" she repeats.

"At my high school. Do you remember the fire?"

She looks at me. "Are you okay? Your voice is funny."

I'm about to cry.

"Yeah, I'm okay. Do you remember that fire though? The one the kid died in?"

"Yes, that was awful. Of course I remember," she says.

"Was I arrested for that?"

"What?"

"I've been seeing that doctor because I have this weird fear. It's a phobia. I'm afraid of bald men—"

She laughs. "What? Bald men?"

"Yeah. I've been trying to work on it in therapy, and the doctor told me I have PTSD."

"PTSD? What?"

"I have PTSD, yeah. And I guess part of that is avoidance. I have avoided the traumatic incident. I can't remember it very well. But I remember there was a fire. I remember Dad calling you and telling you that I started the fire. I remember hearing about the wake and knowing that the kid who died in the fire was wearing a wig. I think that's where the phobia is coming from."

"Oh honey," she says.

I'm now crying.

"My therapist," I continue, "told me to ask you about it because I don't remember it well enough. I told her about it. I told her that I started the fire, and I killed a kid. She is confused about some of the details. Can you help me fill them in?"

"You're remembering it wrong," she says. "I wish you had asked me about this earlier. I could tell you. You posted a video. Do you remember that? On your YouTube channel."

"Yeah." I nod. "I've seen that. Of me lighting a match."

"Yeah," she says. "You posted that the night of the fire. But honey, that was just an unfortunate coincidence. It was an electrical fire. That girl you were having trouble with. What was her name? Molloy?"

"Chelsea," I say.

"Chelsea, yes. She'd been cyberstalking you and called your dad. Don't you remember? She called everyone with your last name in the phone book until she got him. She told him you started the fire. She got him all confused and worked up. I knew you didn't do it. The police never thought you did. No one ever thought you did that except your dad for a blip, in a panic. There was never any doubt in my mind that you had anything to do with that. You have always been a good girl."

"Are you telling me the truth?" I ask. "Or are you trying to rework the record?"

"This is the truth. I was with you the night of the fire. We were watching *Dateline*. You didn't do it. There were cameras at the school. I remember this all very well, honey. You were terribly upset after your dad called. It was notable because you rarely expressed when you were upset to me. You seldom told me about the difficulties you had at school, but the night your dad called, you told me all about the Molloy girl. You told me you'd been dating her ex-boyfriend out of spite. Remember? You were just sick about it. You said you thought you were a bad person. You had a bit of a breakdown. Maybe you're not remembering because you were so upset? You really don't remember?"

"Are you making this up?"

"No, I remember this all very well. You and I talked a lot about how sometimes good people make mistakes. Remember? You slept in my bed that night. We talked into the night.

We decided you should break up with that boy. What was his name?"

"Ben."

"Yes, Ben. You felt terrible about Ben. But you were just a teenager, honey. You'd been really mistreated by that girl. Everyone makes mistakes. That's what teenagers do. You learned from it, didn't you? I did worse things in high school than try to make mean girls jealous or dump a boy who liked me. Don't you remember talking about this?"

"I couldn't remember," I say. "I just remembered that phone call Dad made to you. He said I killed a kid. He said that—"

"Yeah, well, he said a lot of things," she says. "He was an idiot."

I breathe air out my nose. "You think he was an idiot?"

She nods.

"I always thought you were in love with him."

"I was," she says. "But I've been reflecting a lot lately, since chatting with your sister, and Gina. I think I'm starting to understand who he was better now."

We both lean back on the windshield. I look at the sky. I think about my dad and feel my throat spasm. I think of myself in my earliest YouTube videos. A weird little girl with a chubby face, saying, "I have a dad, he just doesn't like me." I think of myself at seventeen, undoing a belt I once considered killing myself with, while clinging to a boy I didn't like. I think of myself happy being cruel to people I felt rejected by. I realize as I look up at the green lights in the sky that I wasn't traumatized by the fire. I was traumatized by my dad believing the first horrible thing he ever heard about me.

*

I squeeze a lemon. Edna and Kira are coming over tomorrow. My mom is making a cake. She blends entire lemons for it—even the peels. She uses extra lemon zest for the icing, and sometimes she candies slices of citrus fruits to go on top. Usually, she uses limes and oranges for their color.

Someone shoves my shoulder. I drop the lemon I was holding and look up. A disgruntled bearded man is yelling at me.

"How many times do I have to say excuse me before you get out of my god damn way? I've asked you to move at least four times now! What the hell is wrong with you?"

I feel myself instinctively begin to shrink out of his way.

He's yelling, "You're rude! I shouldn't have to say excuse me multiple times!"

I wish Polly were here. If she were here, I bet she would tell this man off. She would probably remind him that we're living in a society. She might even tell him I've recently discovered I have psychological issues partially because I can't hear well, and it's made me anxious. I feel socially weird and on edge partly because of people like him. If Polly were here, this man would probably end up apologizing to me.

His face is flushed and angry. People are looking at us.

He shouts, "What do you have to say for yourself!"

I think of the forum for unilateral deaf people I joined. I imagine myself writing a post about this later. I think of myself typing that I got screamed at by an angry man and bruised a lemon today for no good reason. I'll write that people stared at us and I shrunk until the man finally left me alone.

I frown. I don't want to write that.

"I didn't hear you," I say.

He scoffs, "Oh, you didn't hear me? Is that so? What? Are you deaf?"

"Yes. I am deaf in one ear."

His face drops. "Oh. Are you really? W-well, it's reasonable for a-a-a person to assume that—"

I straighten my posture. "I don't think it is reasonable for you to berate me for not hearing you actually. I can't hear at all in one ear. I'm half-deaf. I don't think I should be yelled at for that. It's a disability."

He opens his mouth. "Yes. I, uh, I couldn't tell. I-I'm not sure what to say."

People are still watching us.

I inhale. It smells like lemons. "I think you should say I'm sorry."

He raises his eyebrows. "Oh? Okay. Yes, you're right. I-I'm sorry."

"What?" I pretend I didn't hear him.

"I'm sorry," he repeats, louder.

I glance over his shoulder and spot Polly. She's walking through the crates of gourds and asparagus away from me. I don't know if she saw me. She's headed toward the door.

My heart starts racing.

My instinct is to run in the opposite direction. To get to the back of the store, to the corner where the milk fridges are. I feel compelled to hide from her, and to never return to this store again.

"Excuse me," I say to the man. I abandon my cart and walk toward her.

"Polly!" I shout.

She keeps walking. I don't know if she heard me.

"Polly!"

I start running. I almost run into someone's cart.

I reach out and grab her shoulder before she can exit the automatic door.

She stops and turns to me.

"Hi," I say.

She looks surprised to see me.

I still want to run away, but I'm not. I'm standing right in front of her.

The automatic door next to us keeps opening and shutting.

After her surprise subsides, she frowns. "You sent me and Joan the exact same breakup text. You couldn't even write me my own text? I would have appreciated a personalized text."

People shove past us to leave the store.

I don't know why I'm startled by this immediate confrontation. I don't know what I expected her to say. I should have known she would address the situation right away.

"What's wrong with you? You could at least talk to me. Why would you behave like that?" she says.

I look down at my hands. "Maybe we should get out of the entrance," I say. People are pushing their carts around us.

"I would like an explanation," she says.

"I'm sorry," I say.

"That isn't an explanation. Is it that you just don't like me?"

"No, I like you," I say.

"You couldn't possibly like me if you would treat me like that."

She examines my face. Her eyes dart from my eyes to my mouth and back.

"I like you," I say again.

She crosses her arms. "Then what's your problem?"

✳

Polly's couch has a new blanket on it. She asked me to come over. She is pouring us drinks in the kitchen.

She hands me a tall mason jar with ice water in it. The ice clinks against the glass.

We are quiet until Polly sighs. I look at the prints my fingers make in the condensation on the glass.

Maybe she needs to know that I am a bad person. Maybe she would understand more if I explained that.

"I went to a horror movie with someone," I say.

She says, "Oh? On a date?"

"Yeah. They said they didn't understand why people like scary things."

She examines my face. "They sound stupid."

I breathe air out my nose.

She looks at me.

"So, what's going on here?" she asks. "Why did you send me that text? What were you thinking?"

I look at my hands. "Um. Well, my therapist told me I have PTSD—"

"PTSD? Are we blaming our mental health problems for bad behavior now? I've got some mental health problems of my own, you know."

I say, "I'm not blaming it, I'm just explaining. I apparently have PTSD. I'm working on it. I might be autistic. She told me that growing up with one deaf ear has probably impacted me socially. I had a bit of a breakthrough recently—"

"You had a breakthrough? Do you mean about your bald-man phobia?"

I nod. "Yeah, I'm getting to the bottom of that."

"Good," she says. "I'm glad to hear that."

We look at each other.

"I'm sorry," I say. "I shouldn't have texted you that message.

I should have called you and explained or met up with you. That was shitty of me. I'm really sorry."

She inhales. "Thank you. Are you sorry about the delivery of the message, but not about the content? Do you stand by the content? You don't want to see me anymore?"

"It's not that I didn't want to see you—"

"What is it, then? Can you explain what it is?"

I look at her. "I can try. It's um."

She leans forward.

"I might not word this right," I say. "Uh. But I have this problem where I worry that I'm a bad person, and that I might hurt people. When I was younger, I was vindictive, and I used people in relationships. I didn't have a lot of friends when I was a kid and I don't know if I missed something other people learn, or if I was born with a defect, or if I caught some sort of bug, but I think something is wrong with me. My mom was depressed when I was a kid, and I always sort of attributed it to my dad leaving. I saw with her what people can do to each other, and have always sort of thought it wasn't worth it. I don't know if this makes sense, but I'm worried I have a parasite. Like there is something bad in me that is liable to take over. I feel like I am a shell for some weird little bug. I wanted to spare you the risk of exposure to that. Do you get what I mean?"

She looks at me for longer than is normal.

"Yeah, I get what you mean," she says.

"I really am sorry," I say.

"I forgive you," she says. "In fact, I'd be open to taking you back, if you grovel a little."

I exhale. "Really?"

"Yes." She smiles. "I love weird little bugs, remember?"

✳

Vin is helping me pack my apartment. I haven't found a new place yet, so I am going to stay with my mom until I do. We have the door propped open with a box.

The woman who lives in the hall across from me peers her head in. "Moving out?" she asks.

"Yes," I say.

She looks at Vin. "Oh, hello again." She smiles.

He waves hesitantly.

"You two have met?" I ask. Why does Vin know the woman who lives across from me?

"Yes, he's the young man I mentioned to you. I've seen him come and go from here a few times." She looks at Vin. "I told her you'd stopped by a few times, when you two missed each other."

Vin's face flushes. He says, "Oh, did you? Thank you."

What?

"Good luck with your move," she says before leaving.

I look at Vin.

"I'm sorry," he says quickly. "I just check that you're okay."

"What?"

"I check that you're okay."

I stare at him. "Are you the one who broke into my house? You come in my house?"

"I had your spare key. Sometimes I get worried. I'm sorry."

I think of him telling me I was paranoid and overreacting. I think of him trying to convince me not to move. I feel angry. I say, "What the fuck, Vin?"

His voice races. "I'm so sorry! I didn't want you to move because I did this weird thing. That's why I was telling you not to. I'm so sorry for making you feel crazy. I just didn't want you to know that *I'm* crazy. This has been eating me up inside. I feel terrible. I haven't been able to sleep. I've been a wreck. I should have told you. I was just checking on you. You don't always reply to your texts. You didn't reply all weekend the time I came and messed it up. I was in here frantic. I'm sorry. I should have told you, but I know it's fucking weird. I just feel like I'm constantly trying to get in with you. Do you know what I mean? You never let me in, but I know I shouldn't have just forced myself in. I thought you were dead. I really thought that. Sometimes, I think something is wrong with you—"

"You mean like a parasite?"

He blinks.

"No, I don't get what you mean when you say that. I meant like you might kill yourself." He has tears in his eyes. "I'm sorry. I realize this is so weird of me, but I want to check on you. You understand, right? I have to check on you sometimes, like our moms. You get it, right? I'm sorry—"

"You think I might kill myself?" I ask.

"Sometimes," he says. He's crying. "You know, you don't wear lipstick at all. It's very hard to tell what's going on."

I stare at him.

"Are you angry?" He has his hands on both sides of his eyes.

"No, I'm not angry," I say.

I'm surprised. It never occurred to me that Vin might be that worried. While I do feel like he's trespassed into my space, stepped over a boundary and behaved inappropriately, I also feel consoled by his concern.

"Are you sure you aren't angry?" he asks.

"Yeah, I'm not angry. I'm sorry," I say.

"I'm genuinely sorry," he says. "It was fucked-up of me to do that."

He wipes his face off on his sleeve and we resume packing. We work in silence until the kitchen is finished, then we sit on top of boxes and sip Gatorade.

I look at him. "Hey. Do you want to meet Polly later?"

He nods. "Yes. How did you know?"

I smile. "I had an inkling."

We look into each other's eyes for a beat. We exchange a look that I know means, *I love you.*

I blink and say, out loud, "I love you."

He smiles. "I love you too."

✳

My phone is ringing. It's two a.m. I am sleeping at my mom's house.

"Hello?"

"Enid?"

"Yes?"

"Hi! It's Kira. Edna's having her baby!"

"Oh," I say. I rub my eyes.

I didn't think they would call me when she was having the baby.

She says, "Do you want to come to the hospital? Come quick!"

"Oh? Does she want me there?"

"Of course!"

"Oh. Okay."

✳

I rush to put my shoes on. The light in the hall upstairs turns on.

"Enid?" my mom calls.

"Sorry if I woke you up," I say from the foot of the stairs.

I look up at her. She is standing on the landing. The light above her head is flickering. It must need a new bulb.

"Where are you going?" she asks.

"To the hospital. Edna's having her baby. They invited me to come—"

"Oh, that's wonderful." She starts descending the stairs. "I guess their visit tomorrow will have to be postponed! Maybe they'll come later with the baby."

"Yes, I'm sure they'll come later with the baby." I put one arm through my jacket.

"Wait just a sec," she says.

She rummages around in the front closet.

"Mom, I told them I'd be right there—"

"Just wait one minute! I have something for them. I was going to give it to Edna tomorrow."

She rushes toward me with a gift bag.

"What is it?" I ask.

"It's a present for Edna and the baby."

She got them a present?

"What is it?" I ask again.

"Oh, it's nothing. It's just something I knitted."

I open the bag and the light stops flickering when I pull out a large orange blankct.

*

"What did they name the baby?" Vin asks.

He is sitting at my desk.

"Amelia Di."

"Isn't that a Victorian murderer's name?" George asks.

He is helping us fix the search tool. Every time he speaks or moves, I jump, but I'm trying to hide it.

"Hopefully she can rebrand it," I say while I query "white dwarf" in the search tool. The three of us just rebuilt part of the backend. I press enter to test if it works.

I close my eyes, hoping it is fixed.

It isn't.

"Fuck," Vin says.

"Wait," I say. "We forgot to restart the crawl."

I restart it, we wait, and then I click refresh.

It's working now. Thousands of results are returned.

George cheers and I recoil, afraid of him.

He doesn't notice. He smiles. "Good work, Enid."

I manage to force a smile back at him.

Vin grins. "Yeah, way to go, Enid. You're a star."

ACKNOWLEDGMENTS

Thank you to all my family and friends, including Corrina, Brock, Mallory, Ainsley, Aaron, Mitch, Chad, Joel, Torren, Bridget, Matthew, Christina, Liz, and the rest of you.

Thank you, Heather Carr. I'm so lucky to have found such a supportive stage mom for my books. I couldn't dream up a better agent. Thank you also to Jade Hui and Loan Le for your editorial work on this book. It's significantly better because of you. I am very appreciative of all your effort.

Thank you to everyone who has supported any of my writing, including Daniella Wexler, Gena Lanzi, Isabel DaSilva, Jillian Levick, Aimee Oliver-Powell, Kirsty Doole, Bobby Mostyn-Owen, Kate Straker, Sophie Walker, Kelli McAdams, Cayley Pimentel, Sarah St Pierre, Janie Yoon, Kristina Moore,

Stacey Sakal, everyone at the Friedrich Agency, Ariel Baker-Gibbs, and many others.

Thanks to the librarians, booksellers, reviewers, and to all the people who have connected me to books. Thank you also to the people on Bookstagram and BookTok.

Thank you to the band Boygenuis for the song "Souvenir." I based Enid partly on the lyric about cutting a hole in your skull and hating what you see. Other songs that inspired this book include: "I'm Enough" by Oscar Scheller and Katie Gavin, "Drunk on Aluminium" by Wintersleep, and "Happy Girl" by Jensen McRae.

Since my last novel, I've received a large number of messages from readers who felt seen in *Everyone in This Room Will Someday Be Dead*. It seemed like I always received a new message in moments when I felt tempted to delete everything new I'd written. To anyone who identifies with Enid or Gilda, I'm glad we found each other. Thank you so much for reading.

ABOUT THE AUTHOR

Emily Austin was born in St. Thomas, Ontario, Canada. She studied English literature, religious studies, and library science at Western University. She received two writing grants from the Canada Council for the Arts. She currently lives in Ottawa, in the territory of the Anishinaabe Algonquin Nation.